C. S. FORESTER

The Sky
and the Forest

LITTLE, BROWN AND COMPANY · BOSTON

1948

PRINTED IN THE UNITED STATES OF AMERICA BY
KINGSPORT PRESS, INC., KINGSPORT, TENNESSEE

The Sky and the Forest

CHAPTER

I

THERE HAD BEEN much rain during the night, and the morning air was still saturated with moisture, heavy and oppressive, and yet with a suspicion of chill about it, enough to make flies sluggish and men and women slow in their movements. But now the sun was able to look over the tops of the trees into the town, calling out the wreaths of steam from the puddles, and shining down upon Loa's woolly head as he walked out into the west end of the street. Four women, not yet gone to the banana groves, ceased their chattering at his appearance and fell on their knees and elbows, pressing their noses against the muddy soil. Loa ran his eye over them as he walked past them; he was more used to seeing the backs of men and of women than to looking into their faces. A little boy came running round the corner of a house — he was of an age when running was still something of a new experience for him — and stopped at sight of the crouching women and of Loa's passing majesty. His finger went to his mouth, but it had hardly reached it when his mother put out her arm, without lifting her face from the earth, and seized him and flung him down, face downwards as was proper, holding him there despite his struggles, and when he had recovered from his surprise sufficiently to wail in protest she managed to get her hand over his mouth and moderate the noise. That was right.

The distraction was sufficient to turn Loa from continuing his way down the street. He stood and looked idly along to the far end. The crouching women, conscious that he was remaining near them, writhed in troubled ecstasy, the bunched muscles along their backs standing out tensely, while their concern communicated itself to the little boy so that he ceased to struggle and wail, and instead lay limp and submissive. The sun was shining brightly into Loa's eyes, but the sun was Loa's brother and did not need to avert his face and grovel in his presence. Loa raised his left hand — the one that held his leafy fan — to shade his eyes as he gazed down the street. He did not know what he was looking for nor why he was doing this, and the realization did not come to him even when he had made certain that nothing was different from usual; actually it was an unrecognized feeling of unrest which had stirred a faint desire that today something should be different. Loa could not analyze nor recognize his emotions. He was a god and always had been.

His brother the sun had now come tardily to recognize the fact, as he sometimes did, and had drawn a veil of dilatory cloud over his face. The tribute was gratifying, and Loa did not need to shade his eyes any longer.

"Ha!" he said, pleased with his power; and he turned, immense in his dignity, and walked back to his house at the end of the street.

Indeharu and Vira made a half-circle so as to keep behind

him and followed him back, as they had followed him out. Indeharu's back was bent with age, but even if it had not been he would have bent it and walked with a stoop, just as did young Vira; it was right and proper to walk with humility when attending upon the god. Loa was free for the moment of the unrest which had manifested itself earlier. His right hand swung his iron battle-ax, and his iron collars and bracelets jangled as he strode along, his naked toes gripping the thin and drying mud of the street. Lanu was playing in the small open space in front of Loa's house and came running up with a smile; Lanu could face the god, for Lanu was a god too, Loa's child. There were other children, with their mothers in the banana groves or behind the house, but they were not gods. Lanu was the first-born. Although that was not why he was a god it was probably the reason why Loa had been fond of him at his birth, before the birth of children became a commonplace, and had played with him and petted him and treated him with so much condescension and fondness that clearly he could not be a mortal who must abase himself in the god's presence, and consequently he had never been trained into abasement.

Loa dropped his battle-ax and fan, and caught Lanu under the armpits and swung him up into the air kicking and squealing with delight, holding him there for long pleasurable seconds before setting him on his feet again. Loa unclasped his leopardskin from about his throat and put it over the boy's shoulders, to Lanu's immense pleasure. The boy clasped the forelegs round his neck with the brooch, draped the skin over his left shoulder, and strutted off, very pleased with himself, while Loa followed him fondly with his gaze. Even a god could love his son.

Loa picked up his battle-ax and fan, and seated himself on his stool; the latter was made merely of three curving branches, polished, and bound together with cane fiber into a distorted tripod. To sit on it at all called for a careful placing of the fleshy parts; to sit on it for long called for constant shifting of them; but it was more dignified than squatting on one's heels — that was what men and women did — and the stool by raising the body above the ground kept it out of the way of ants and other creeping creatures. Indeharu and Vira squatted before him, and Loa swept the flies from himself with his fan and prepared himself to listen to their morning report.

"Uledi dies," said Vira; as much the younger man it was his place to speak first.

"She dies?" asked Loa.

"She does indeed. Now her head is drawn back. There is foam on her lips. Every hour the poison shakes her. Her arms and legs go stiff as she struggles with it, stiff like tree trunks although she tosses about in her battle with the poison, and she cries out with words that mean nothing. Then once more she ceases to struggle, and lies sleeping again. She has slept since last there was yellow water in the river."

"I know that," said Loa.

"There is no flesh on her bones, and now there are sores on her skin."

[6]

"Yes," said Loa, rubbing his chin.

This trouble was not infrequent in the town. For no apparent reason some individual, man, woman, or child, would suddenly become somnolent, sleeping continuously except when roused to take food. Sometimes they slept themselves straight into death; sometimes, as in Uledi's case, they died more violently, but whichever way it was they died once they began to sleep, sometimes in a short time, sometimes in a long time.

"It is a deadly poison," commented Indeharu.

"Yes," said Loa again.

Life could not end except by human agency. Somebody must be poisoning Uledi, and Loa's heavy face was contorted into a frown as he wrestled with the problem. Face after face flitted across the field of his mental vision, but not one seemed to be connected with the poisoning of Uledi. Soon he abandoned his review of the population of the town. Seven hundred people lived in it; he did not know how many, nor did his language contain words for the numeral, but he knew it would take too long to think about every one of them. The bones, the five slender rib bones which lay in his house, would tell him if he asked them.

"Soli is her mother's brother's son," said Vira.

That was a very special relationship, conferring particular privileges in the matter of inheritance, and might supply a motive. Loa for a moment thought the problem solved, but Vira and Indeharu were not looking at each other, and his instincts, the sensitive instincts of an uneducated man, told him there was something suspicious in the atmosphere. He did not have to follow along the path of deduction and logic, from the fact that Indeharu and Vira were carefully refraining from exchanging glances, to the fact that their expressions were unnaturally composed, and then on to the fact that Vira bore an old grudge against Soli — something to do with a haunch of goat over which they had quarreled — and from that to his knowledge of Indeharu's enmity towards Soli. It had never even occurred to him that this enmity issued from the old man's fear of a possible young rival. Loa's instincts leaped all the gaps, without any painful building of bridges, and warned him that he — he, the god — was being subjected to influence, an indirect influence and therefore one to be suspected.

"Soli is Uledi's mother's brother's son," he said, his voice as expressionless as the others' features. "We know that, then."

The slight discomposure apparent in the faces of his two councillors told him that his instincts had been right; Indeharu and Vira were disappointed. He was confirmed in his decision to take no immediate action against Soli.

"The men are felling more trees," said Indeharu, changing the subject, and pointing into the forest towards the area where the tree-felling was in progress.

"They may do so," said Loa. As far back as his memory could go — Loa had been king and god since he was a little boy younger than Lanu — Indeharu had managed the economic details of the town's life satisfactorily. A forest tract had to be cleared two years in advance of the time when the plantain crop sown in the clearing began to fruit, and it was a prodigious effort to make such plans. Loa never troubled himself with them. Yet thinking about the plantain crop reminded him he was hungry, and he raised his voice.

"Musini!" he called. "Bring me food."

"I hear you," replied Musini from behind the house; she had a shrill voice with an edge to it.

"When the trees are down," went on Indeharu, "Tolo will build a house. His father Linisinu and his father's brothers will help him."

"Where will the house be?" asked Loa, and as Indeharu began to reply Musini came with the wooden bowl of food.

Loa looked at the contents with disappointment.

"Baked plantain!" he said, disgustedly.

"Baked plaintain with oil. Precious oil," said Musini, sharply. There was never enough oil in the town, the oil palms being too sparing of their produce. "I have eaten no oil since the moon was full last. The oil is all for you."

Loa put down his battle-ax and fan, took the bowl, and transferred a handful of the plantain soaked in oil to his mouth.

"Is it not good?" demanded Musini, aggressively. "What better food can I provide for you than baked plantain and oil? Is it the heart of an elephant you would like? Or a savory dish of the tripe of a young goat? When last was an elephant killed? No goat has borne a kid for two months."

"Say no more," said Loa, irritated. He had eaten elephant only three or four times in his twenty-five years of life; goat's tripe was perhaps his favorite dish, and Musini touched him on the raw by mentioning it — which was what she planned to do, being a bad-tempered shrew.

"Say no more!" she quoted at him. "Say no more! Then say no more when I bring you rich red oil upon your baked plantains. Say no more until an antelope is caught and we eat the roast flesh!"

"Be silent, woman!" shouted Loa, beside himself with rage. The thought of roast antelope was almost more than he could bear. He was on his feet now, brandishing the wooden bowl and actually dancing with passion. Musini saw the look in his face and was frightened.

"Your servant is silent," she said hastily, and turned to go. Yet even then before she was out of earshot she was grumbling again.

Musini was Lanu's mother, Loa's first and chief wife, and had been associated with Loa since his childhood. She did not prostrate herself before him except on occasions of high ceremonial, because little by little through the years ceremony between the two of them had lapsed as a matter of practical convenience. But her habit of scolding at Loa, of goading him to exasperation, had another origin. She wanted to assert herself, and she felt as if she did not want to live if she did not. She infuriated Loa as a means of self-expression, as an artist paints or a musician composes. Besides, she was drawn to this course of action by a subtle lure, by the indescribable temptation of danger. She risked her life every time she angered Loa. There was a fearful pleasure in coming as near to destruction as possible and then withdrawing just in time. Shuddering fear tempted her like a drug.

Loa took another mouthful of baked plantain with growing distaste, his mind running on devious tracks. That unrest which had set him gazing down the street, which had brought him to his feet at Musini's gibes, was a symptom — although he did not express it so to himself — of his hunger for meat, rich meat, full of proteins and fats and mineral salts. The African forest was niggardly of its meat supply; of all the animals domesticated by man the goat was the only one able to live there, and even the goat did not thrive; a high mortality among the town's herd made goat's flesh a rarity. The plantain was the stable food, which ironically the forest allowed to be produced in utter abundance with almost no effort. A space had only to be cleared in the forest, the suckers planted, and eighteen months later there was a dense grove of plantain trees, each bearing its huge hand of fruit. The crop was never known to fail and there was no known limit to its production. Manioc was almost as easily grown; the work of clearing had to be rather more thorough, the planting was rather more arduous, but with ample virgin soil for the growth a crop was assured in return for small labor. Manioc and plantains; the forest gave these generously, so that there were always bananas and tapioca, tapioca and bananas, on which a man could live. Tapioca and bananas meant a continuous diet of starch; the oil palm lived only scantily and precariously here on the verge of the inner plateau of Africa, and its rich orange-colored oil, so generous of fat, was almost as great a rarity as goat's flesh.

The forest provided almost no meat. The rare forest antelope sometimes fell into a pitfall or succumbed to a fortu-

nate arrow to provide an ounce or two for each of those entitled to a share; at intervals of years an elephant fell into a
similar trap. That was an occasion always to be remembered,
when every man, woman and child in the town would have
five or ten pounds of meat apiece, to be eaten in a wild orgy
that same day before corruption could set in. Monkeys lived
in the treetops two hundred feet overhead; it was more unusual to hit a monkey with an arrow than an antelope, and
it was just as rare for an arrow to find its way through the
tangled branches and creepers to hit a parrot. The leopard
lived among the treetops and was almost as exclusively
arboreal as the monkeys which were its prey; its meat had
an unpleasant taste even for a meat-starved man, and it was
so ferocious a fighter when wounded that its skin was the
one fit garment for Loa the god. Snakes could be eaten, and
frogs could sometimes be caught in the streams, but never
in sufficient quantity to be taken into consideration in the
problem of meat supply. The best meat the forest afforded
walked on two legs; the African forest was one of the few
places in the world where cannibalism was an economic
necessity, where it was indulged in to appease an irresistible,
an insatiable hunger for meat.

Loa was thinking that his late father, Nasa (whose name,
seeing that he was dead, could be pronounced by Loa alone)
was in need of a new attendant. It was some considerable
time since anyone had been sent to serve Nasa, and it might
be fitting that Musini the mother of Lanu should be dis-
patched on that mission; certainly it would convey honor
to Nasa. Musini could be put in a wooden pen for three

days; inactivity for that length of time was desirable to make sure that the meat would be in good condition. Then she could be sent to attend upon Nasa, either by quiet strangulation or by a more ceremonial beheading with Loa's battle-ax — either way would do for it was not a point of great importance — and then there would be smoking joints to eat, meat in which a man could set his teeth, meat to distend a belly that starved on bananas and tapioca. And the irritation of Musini's constant scolding would cease then, too.

Loa was not thinking about this logically for two very good reasons. He had never been under the necessity of thinking logically, and he was handicapped by his language, which, with its clumsy complexities of construction and its total want of abstract terms, was not an instrument adapted to argument or for the conveyance of more than the simplest ideas. His mind was much more a meeting ground for converging impulses, which were checked just then by what Indeharu had to say.

"Last night the moon was dark," said Indeharu. "The river waits for you."

Loa stuffed the last handful of baked plantain into his mouth and swallowed it down. He put the bowl to his lips and tilted it to allow the last of the rich oil to trickle between them. He set down the bowl and called to Lanu, who came running from behind the house, trailing the leopard-skin behind him.

"Will you come to the river?" asked Loa.

"The river! The river!" said Lanu, delighted.

He was ready to start at once, with all the eager impetu-
osity of childhood, but first there were preparations to be
made. Indeharu and Vira turned to shout down the street,
proclaiming the fact that Loa was about to go to the river.
A few people came out from the houses, women with children dragging at them, Litti the worker in iron, an old man
or two, some marriageable girls. Indeharu counted them on
his fingers. There had to be four hands of people present for
the ceremony to be valid, and it took a few moments to
complete the necessary total as some young men came in
from the outskirts of the town, while Loa coaxed Lanu into
returning the leopardskin cloak and clasped it about his
neck again. Indeharu counted up on his fingers again, and
shot a significant look at Loa.

"We go," said Loa.

Towards the river lay the abandoned clearings of the
past centuries; at the present time the manioc and banana
gardens of the town lay on the side of the town away from
the river. So at first the path lay through a thick belt of
felled trees, only now beginning to crumble into their native earth again. In the forest there was always going on a
silent life-and-death struggle for light and air, even for
rain. Every plant dependent on these three — as was every
one, except the funguses — pushed and aspired and strove
to outtop its neighbors, to gain elbowroom where it could
spread out in the life-giving light and air. In the virgin
forest the victors in the struggle were the trees, the vast
kings of the vegetable kingdom, two hundred feet tall, each
ruling the little area around it so completely that nothing

could grow beneath save the funguses which flourished in the deep bed of rotting vegetable matter out of which it rose. The kings had their hangers-on, their parasites, the creepers and vines which the trees themselves lifted towards the sky. These shamelessly made use of the trees in their dignity; rooted in the earth below they swarmed up the unresisting trunks in long slender ropes, up to the topmost branches, by which they leaped from tree to tree, renewing with each other at this height the same struggle for light and air; the successful ones, hundreds of yards long, intertwining in a wild cat's-cradle of loops and festoons which bound the tallest trees together and repressed the aspirations of the smaller trees striving to push through.

But where there was a clearing the scene changed. If a big tree paid the penalty for its very success by being selected to be struck by lightning, or if it had died of old age, or if a forest fire had killed trees over a larger area — and more especially where man had cut down trees for his own purposes — light and air could penetrate to earth level; and the lowly plants had their opportunity, which they grasped with feverish abandon. The clearing became a battleground of vegetation, a free-for-all wherein every green thing competed for the sunlight; until in a short time, measured in days rather than in weeks, the earth was covered shoulder-high by a tangle of vegetation through which no man could force his way without cutting a path with ax or sword. For months, for years, the lowly plants had their way, dominating the clearing; but steadily the sapling trees forced their way through, to climb above and to pre-empt for themselves the vital light. It would be a long struggle, but as the years passed the trees would assert their mastery more and more forcibly; the undergrowth would die away, the fallen trees would rot to powder, and in the end the clearing would be indistinguishable from the rest of the forest, silent and dark.

The abandoned clearings through which led the path to the river were some years old now in their present existence, and at their densest in consequence. The felled trees lay in a frightful tangle, and over them and about them grew the undergrowth; in the four weeks since last that path had been trodden the feverish growth had covered it completely, so that Vira and the young men had to hack and slash their way through. Sometimes the path lay along fallen tree trunks, slippery with lichens; it wound about between jagged branches whose solidity was disguised by greenery as a trap for an unwary person who might try to push through. Old Indeharu toiled and stumbled along on his stiff legs behind the advanced party, and immediately in front of Loa; his whitening head was on a level with Loa's chin. On the dark bronze of his back the sweat ran in great drops like a small cascade of those incredibly rare and precious glass beads of which the town possessed a dozen or two. The sweat-drops coursed down Indeharu's bony back until they lost themselves in his loin girdle; the latter was of bark cloth and was as wet as if it had been dipped in water, so that what with the sweat and Indeharu's exertions it bade fair to disintegrate. Loa himself, half Indeharu's age and twice his strength, felt the burden of his leopardskin cloak;

in this undergrowth, with the sun blazing down upon it, the heat and the humidity were intensified, and the flies bit and annoyed with unusual vigor, while bare feet, however horny and insensitive, were inevitably scratched and cut as they were dragged through the tangled vegetation.

Loa was conscious of all these irritations — no one could not be — but he endured them without debate, for debate was something he was unused to. This was the world as it had always been and as it always would be. His erring sister was wandering again, and when she wandered she had to be recalled, just as an itch had to be scratched.

Now they were through the overgrown clearing, and into the forest, the undisturbed forest, into the twilight and the silence. Huge tree trunks emerged from the spongy leaf-mold, spaced out with almost mathematical regularity by the relentless laws of nature. They soared upwards without change or relief (save for the leafless stems of the vines) until two hundred feet overhead they burst suddenly into branches and foliage making a thick roof through which no direct light could penetrate. Up there lived the monkeys and the birds, and the sun shone, and the rain fell. To be down here in the darkness — for inevitably here it was too dark for any vegetation to grow — was to be inside the crust of the world, cut off from the exterior. Yet within the forest Loa could relax and feel at home. The forest was his brother, just as the sun was his brother and the moon was his sister, and Loa had a feeling that the forest was a kindly, friendly brother. The forest suited his temperament or his physique, and he lengthened his stride until he trod on the heels of Indeharu hobbling along in front of him. Loa poked him in the ribs with the end of his battle-ax as a further reminder to quicken his step. Indeharu was very old, with stores of knowledge as a representative of an almost obliterated generation, but he was just an old man and Loa had no regard for his feelings.

In the forest here there was no hindrance to travel save for the bogginess underfoot; the broad spaces between the tree trunks allowed of easy walking in any direction. So much so that it was the easiest thing in the world to lose oneself in the forest. Without any landmarks, without any sight of the sun, the moment a man lost his sense of direction in the forest he lost everything. He might wander for days, for weeks and months, seeing nothing but tree trunks around him and the somber green roof overhead. There were one or two people in the town who had actually had this experience, and who had been guided home again after a vast passage of time by blind chance and great good fortune. There had been plenty of others who had gone forth on some trifling expedition and who had never returned. They had been lost in the forest. Or they had been trapped by the little men.

This route to the river was as clearly defined as anything could be in the forest. Through the soggy leafmold there wound a faint depression, which a keen eye could detect as a footpath, and the trees on either side displayed frequent cuts and wounds — Loa made a few new ones himself as he walked along, casual chops with his battle-ax that sliced into the bark of the trees, making a mark that would endure for several months until the insects altered its shape so that it did not reveal the human agency that caused it, and until the moss and lichens grew over it and concealed it again.

The disadvantage about a well-marked path was that the little men would make use of it for their own purposes. They would place poisoned skewers of wood under the leaf-mold, on which a man might tread; if he did, then very probably he would be dead in half an hour for the little men to feast on him. And they would dig pits and place poisoned stakes in them, roofing the pits over with a frail covering disguised by leafmold, which would give way under the foot of either an antelope or a man. Vira and the young men ahead were scanning carefully every yard of the path, and two of them had strung their bows and fitted broad-headed arrows to the strings, ready to draw and loose at a moment's notice should a little man or a little woman, or any other game, expose itself within range.

And now the trees suddenly began to be farther apart, the leafmold underfoot suddenly became firmer, and the path took a sharp upward slope. For a few moments it was a steep climb. The forest ended abruptly here, where the soil changed to naked rock on which even in that lush atmosphere nothing could grow. They were out of the forest and under the sky, and a few more strides took them to the top of the rock, looking over the vast river. Loa did not like this. He was inclined to flinch a little as he emerged from the forest. The sky was his brother, just as was the forest, but an unfriendly brother, a frightening brother. He did not like great spaces; they affected him as some people are affected by great heights. Except here on the riverbank he never looked out over great distances. The town street was less than a hundred yards long, and that was the next widest horizon he knew; in the forest the trees were close on every hand, and that was where he felt at home. Here on this pinnacle of rock the sky was enormous and incredibly distant.

And the river! A full mile it stretched from bank to bank; the pinnacle of rock, constituting the bluff at the outside curve of a shallow beach, commanded views of five and ten miles upstream and down — terrifying distances. Except at this outcrop of rock, the forest came to the water's very edge; indeed so great was the pressure for light and air that on the riverbanks the trees grew out almost horizontally, straining out over the water to escape from the shadow of their mightier neighbors, leading a brief precarious life until flood and erosion cut the soil from their roots and they fell into the water. One could never look at the river for long without seeing some great tree come floating down on the turbulent current, turning and rolling in torment, lifting its arms in mute appeal to the pitiless sky as it rolled.

In the distance the river looked blue and silver, but when one looked down into it from the bank it was muddy and brown, although the time of the real "brown water," when the level rose a foot or two and the river took on a more definite color, was still a month or two off. The surface of the river was never still; a storm would work it up into great rollers, and on a calm day like this, when at first sight the surface seemed almost oily, closer observation would reveal great swirls and motiveless crinklings, sinister, ugly movements as the broad water went sliding along, coming from nowhere, going nowhere, hateful and fearsome in its majesty. Loa watched Lanu pick up a fragment of rock and hurl it into the river with delight in the splash and the ring. Behavior like that made Loa a trifle uncomfortable, for it savored of unconventionality, but it was not quite bad enough for Loa to check Lanu — nothing ever was.

Indeharu was waiting for the ceremony to begin. Loa stood forward.

"Sister," he said, looking down the river to the distant reach whither his erring sister had strayed. "Come back from under the water. Come back into the sky. The — the — "

"The nights are dark," prompted Indeharu, as he always had to do.

"The nights are dark, and your sons and daughters cannot fill the sky. Come back. Grow bigger, for the nights are very dark. Come back, my sister."

Somewhere under the surface of the river his sister was hiding; everyone knew of the liking she had for the big yellow river. A few people who had been caught by darkness away from the town and who had been forced to spend the night beside the river had told him of how she stretched her arms out over the water and how her spirit danced on its surface. Every month she wandered back to it and hid herself in its depths, and had to be recalled by her brother.

A cloud of butterflies was flying along the river in a vast bank, reaching from the surface nearly up to the level of Loa's face, more than a hundred feet; stretching nearly half a mile across the river and a quarter of a mile down it. With the wind behind them they passed rapidly downstream, a lavender-tinted cloudbank. Flaws of wind recoiling from the bank whirled parts of it into little eddies, and the sun shining down caught the millions of wings and was reflected back in a constant succession of rosy highlights. Lanu clapped his hands at the sight of them.

"What are they?" he asked, excitedly.

"They come from the sky," answered Loa, heavily.

No doubt they were beautiful, but Loa was too disturbed mentally by the vast distances to experience more than mixed emotions regarding them. His brother the sky was looking down at him from all directions, and he did not like that; it was like having an enemy at his back. Across the river the forest was dwindled to a mere strip of blue in the steamy atmosphere. It was frightening to see the forest so insignificant, the sky so big. It gave Loa no doubts regarding his own status as a god — the first among equals, among sky and forest and river and sun — but it disturbed him violently by its disruption of the usual state of affairs. It was not respectable, it was not usual, it chafed him and irritated him.

"Look! Look!" said Lanu, pointing.

Far up the river there was a dark speck to be seen. It moved upon the surface, and as it moved reflected sunshine winked from it. A boat, with the sunshine gleaming on the

wet paddles. That was a phenomenon to be regarded with a
dull lack of interest. There were other men in the world,
Loa knew, besides the people of the town and the little men.
Some of them went about on the river in canoes. In the
days of Nasa, Loa's father, there had been another town
near, here by the water's edge; but Nasa and his people had
fallen upon it one night and killed everybody in it and had
feasted lavishly in consequence for days afterwards. The
men of that town had used canoes, so Indeharu said. So
other men existed, and some of them used canoes on the
river. And rain fell from the sky; there was no need to
think farther about either matter. The young women and
the young men were gazing up the river at the canoe, and
talking excitedly about it, their excitement mingled with
some trepidation because they knew so little about other
people. But Loa knew no fear; there was no reason why he
should fear anything in the world.

"I go," he said to Indeharu, for he wanted to free himself
from the irritation of thus being exposed to the sky.

"Loa goes back!" proclaimed Indeharu.

Vira hustled the young men off along the path to make
the way safe, and Indeharu followed them. As Loa left the
high point to descend again to the forest the remainder
flung themselves on their faces, their noses to the ground,
for him to walk past them, but Loa hardly spared a glance
for the row of glistening dark brown backs. He walked on
along the path, and breathed more freely and gratefully as
he left the sky behind him and entered into the steamy twilight of the forest. Before him Lanu capered along, full of

the joy of living. Lanu had devised a new way of walking. Instead of taking strides with alternate feet he was trying to step twice with each foot in turn. He poised on one foot and skipped, and then poised on the other foot and skipped, his arms held high as he balanced. So they went back into the forest, Loa swinging his battle-ax and Lanu skipping in front of him.

SOME YOUNG MEN of the town hunting in the forest had captured a strange woman. They brought her back with them, and everyone assembled to look at her and to listen to her absurd speech. Delli, her ridiculous name was, she said — in itself that was enough to make people laugh and clap their thighs. All her words were comical like that, with *l* where *r* should be, and the strangest turns of speech. Everybody in the town knew there were many ways of addressing people; one spoke differently, with different words, if one were addressing one person, or two persons, or many persons, or if the persons addressed were old or young, male or female, married or single, important or unimportant. But this woman muddled it all up, and spoke (when it was possible to disentangle her curious pronunciation) to the crowd as if it were made up of three little children. Everyone laughed uproariously at that.

They brought her to Loa where he sat on his tripod stool with Indeharu and Vira standing behind him, and they swarmed close round her to hear the quaint things she said.

"Who are you?" asked Loa.

"Delli," she said.

That ridiculous name again! Everyone laughed.

"Where do you come from?"

"I come from the town."

That was just as ridiculous as her name. *This* was the town, and everyone knew it. She rolled her eyes from side to side at the crowd, a very frightened woman. She held her hand over her heart as she looked about her, naked save for a wisp of bark cloth. She was a very puzzled woman as well, quite unable to understand why the simple things she said should occasion so much merriment.

"She was in the forest eating amoma fruits," interposed Ura, one of the young men, explaining with the proper gestures how they came to catch her. "She did not hear us. Maketu went over that way. Huva went over there. We went silently forward through the trees. Then she saw Maketu and ran. Then she saw Huva and ran the other way, towards me. I was behind a tree, and I sprang out and I caught her. She hit me, here, on my shoulder, and she scratched with her nails. But still I held her. She could not escape from Ura."

"She was eating amoma fruits?" asked Loa.

"Yes."

Amoma fruits were not good eating; their watery acid pulp could not deceive a healthy stomach for a moment. Children ate them during their games, but no sensible person ever did. Loa stared harder at the strange woman. The scar-tattooing on her cheeks and upper lip was of an odd pattern. She was terribly thin, like a skeleton, her bones standing out through her skin, and her breasts fallen away to empty bags although she was a young woman, not yet the mother of more than two children or so. And her body and legs and arms were covered with scratches, some of them several days old, some of them fresh, but altogether making a complete network over her. She was calmer now, but Loa's next question threw her into a worse panic than ever.

"Why were you in the forest?" asked Loa.

Her face distorted itself with fear.

"Bang bang," she said, and repeated herself. "Bang bang."

That was almost too funny to bear, to see this amusing woman shaking with fright and to hear her say "bang bang!" She goggled round at the laughing throng and took a grip of herself. When she spoke again the intensity of her emotion made her voice a hoarse whisper, but silence fell on the crowd and every word could be heard.

"Men came," she said. "Many men, at night. We were all asleep. Bang bang. Bang bang. Men were killed, women were killed. My man was sleeping beside me, and he woke up and took his spear. Everyone was shouting. Other men of the town came running into the house. Some were wounded. We stood by the door with spears and we would not come out although they shouted to us to come out. Houses were burning so that we could see out. Bang bang. Bang bang. Fire in the night, like red lightning. My man fell down and he was dead. Still we would not come out. Then our house burned. They were waiting for us outside the door so I would not go out when the men did. I jumped up and caught the roof beams of the house. Not all the thatch was burning so I pulled the thatch aside and climbed

[27]

through the roof. I stood there and all the town was burning. Bang bang. Bang Bang. The thatch was burning beside me and so I jumped. I jumped far, very far. The old clearing was beside our house and I jumped into it, right into the bushes. I tried to run through the bushes, but I could not go far, not in the dark. I lay there and saw the flames and heard them shouting. My baby — I think I heard her cry too."

Delli stopped speaking, her hand to her heart again. A babble of talk rose from the crowd the moment it ceased to be repressed by the dramatic nature of Delli's utterance. The fantastic tale must be discussed. Loa waved his arm for silence.

"What did you do?" he asked.

"I lay there," said Delli, "and daylight came while the flames were still burning. I climbed an old tree trunk and looked into the town. The people were gathered at one end, with the strange men round them. Some of them were pale men."

"Pale men?" demanded Loa.

"They had not faces like ours," said Delli, struggling wildly to explain something beyond all experience.

Her hands went up to her own face in feverish gestures trying to convey an impression of features quite different from the broad nostrils and heavy jaws which characterized the only human faces she knew.

"They wore clothes — so."

Delli flung one arm across her breast and her hands fluttered as she tried to give a mental picture of an ample cloak.

"And they were pale men?" asked Loa. Clothes were something he knew something about, for he wore a leopard-

[28]

skin himself and women often wore bark-cloth gowns, but pale faces were something else. "Were they like the little men?"

"No! Oh no!" said Delli.

The forest pygmies were often of a far lighter shade than the village-dwelling natives, inclining to pale bronze, but they had the same kind of features as the rest of Delli's world and Loa's world.

"They were big men. Tall men," said Delli, "with thin noses; and their faces were — gray."

Loa shook his head in admission that this was more than he could understand.

"What did these men do?" he asked.

"They tied the people together. With poles. They tied one end of a pole to someone's neck, and the other end of the pole to someone else's neck."

Loa had never heard of such a thing being done. The whole story was of something beyond his experience, beyond his scanty traditions.

"What did they do next?" he asked.

"They came to the banana groves to cut fruit. And in the old clearings there were many people hidden besides me, people who had run into the clearings when the town burned. They saw us, and they came after us. They had axes and swords, and I think they caught all the other people."

That was quite probable; a man with a sword to cut a path for himself would easily overtake an unarmed fugitive trying to make his way through the tangled undergrowth of an overgrown clearing.

"And you?"

"I went right through the clearing. A man was chasing me but he did not catch me. I came into the forest and I ran from him and then he did not chase me any more. But still I ran, and when I stopped I did not know where I was."

This was something everyone could understand; there was a murmur of agreement in the listening throng. To lose one's way in the forest was very easy indeed; to be fifty yards from the nearest known landmark was the same as being fifty miles from it if once the sense of direction was lost. Loa knew now the explanation of Delli's network of old scars. Plunging through an abandoned clearing to escape pursuit would tear her skin to ribbons. She must have been streaming with blood by the time she reached the forest. The newer scratches must have been acquired in the ordinary course of life in the forest, searching for food.

"Where was your town?" he asked.

Bewilderment showed itself in Delli's face again.

"Many days. Many days away. I do not know. I looked for it."

There was a puzzled murmur from the crowd. It was hard enough for anyone there to realize even that other towns existed. But everyone in the crowd knew his town so intimately and well. Despite their knowledge of the ease with which one could lose oneself in the forest, it was impossible for them to sympathize with someone who simply could not say where her town was. They could not put themselves in her mental situation; a woman might as well say she did not know where her own body was. Delli's face did not lose its look of bewilderment; her expression was fixed and she was staring at something far away.

"I cannot stand," she said faintly, and with that she abruptly sat down.

Still bewildered in appearance, puzzled by the strange new feelings within her, she swayed for a moment, and then her head came forward to her knees, and next she toppled over on one side and lay limp and unconscious. Musini came forward and knelt over her, and prodded the bony back and the skinny loins. She raised one of the skeleton arms and shook her head over it with distaste.

"Nothing there now," she said, letting the limp arm drop to the ground. "She has long been hungry."

"In a pen she will grow fat," said Loa, looking round at Vira, who nodded. It was Vira who attended to the temporal business of Loa's rule, as Indeharu attended to the spiritual. Loa had to say nothing more about the pen; Vira would attend to that. Loa looked down at the skinny limbs; plenty of food, and some days of idleness in a pen, would fill them out again. Even a healthy well fed human was all the better for three or four days in a pen; idleness improved the quality of the meat. Moreover this stranger with the queer speech and the odd experiences might be a more welcome visitor to his father Nasa than some ordinary man or woman of the town — Musini for instance — as she would bring with her an element of novelty. She might amuse Nasa while she served him.

"See that she has food, plenty of food," said Loa to Musini.

It was hot here in the sun, and Loa had been attending to business for more than an hour, quite long enough for him to feel restless and in need of a change of occupation. He rose to his feet, and the assembled crowd instantly fell forward on their faces; they had been close-packed standing up, and now they carpeted the ground two or more deep. He turned and walked back to the narrow strip of shade cast by the eaves of his house. There he would doze for a while; as the village became aware that he had retired they began to withdraw, in proper humility. Silent at first, and moving with constraint, they soon began to elbow each other and to chatter as they streamed off down the street.

A few idlers dallied to watch Musini and a subordinate wife revive Delli with food and drink, but Vira interrupted that pastime by setting them to work on constructing a pen; cutting stakes, pointing them, and driving them deep into the earth with heavy mauls, and connecting them together with many strands of creeper. Everyone else was all agog with the fantastic story Delli had told; they were busy discussing the gray men who wore clothes and had faces different from ordinary people, who killed people with a noise and a flash, and who tied their captives together with poles. Loa's lethargic brain was idly turning over the same matters as he lay in the shade — later Indeharu and Vira would tell him what they thought about it all. And even perhaps at some time he would hear about it from Musini or other women.

For the stagnation of a thousand years — of two thousand years, of three thousand years — was coming to an end. Invaders were entering into Central Africa, the first since Loa's forebears had infiltrated into the forest among their pygmy predecessors, all those many centuries ago. Strangely enough, it was not the European, restless and enterprising though he might be, who was penetrating into these forest fastnesses. The European was still confined to the coastal strip, although European culture and influence was slowly percolating inland. It was an Asiatic culture which was at last reaching out to Central Africa, all the way across the huge continent from the east. Mohammedanism had taken no more than a hundred years after Mohammed's death to flood along the Mediterranean coast of North Africa, to engulf Spain, and even to cross the Pyrenees; but it took twelve hundred years of slow advance for it to creep up the Nile valley, to circle around the Sahara Desert, and now to penetrate into the equatorial forest.

In twelve hundred years the original Arab stock had become vastly attenuated; the invaders were often hardly lighter in color, thanks to continual miscegenation, than the black peoples they conquered. But most of them still showed the aquiline profile that distinguished them from the pure Negro, and many of them bore proof of their Arab blood in their swarthy complexions — the "gray" color that Delli had noticed. Yet they were marked out far more plainly in other ways from the people they were attacking. Besides their guns, and their clothes, and their material possessions, they had a religion that demanded converts, a social organization that made movement possible, and a tradition of activity more important than all.

More than one culture contributed to that tradition. In the Eastern Mediterranean, Greek civilization had profoundly influenced Arab thought. The tiny arable plains of Greece and the Greek islands were no more conducive to stagnation than the deserts of Arabia. It was a world where men went — were driven — from one place to another, where it was of the first necessity to inquire, to seek out, to make contact with other peoples who might supply some of life's necessities. The skeptical, the inquiring turn of mind was the natural one, and the geniuses who arose through the centuries found themselves in a civilization ripe for them; they had available to them languages admirably suitable for argument and discussion, and the invention of writing which would perpetuate their thoughts and enable them to influence the thinking of future generations. It may be strange, but it is true that Plato and Aristotle as well as Mohammed had something to do with the raiding of Delli's village by swarthy half-castes bent merely on acquiring slaves and ivory.

Loa and his people were the product of an entirely different set of circumstances. They never knew what famine was, for the plantain and the manioc provided an unfailing source of food in return for very little effort. Sleeping sickness and malaria and cannibalism combined to keep the population small. The forest made migration — even minor movements — almost impossible, restricting the spread of ideas and the diffusion of inventions. The absence of writing made progress difficult, for each generation was dependent on the scanty information conveyed by word of mouth, and even if the forest people had learned to write, their language — the clumsy, complicated, unimproved language of the barbarian — was enough to hamper thought and impede its diffusion. Thought is based on words, and Loa's words were few and simple yet linked together — tangled together would be a better term — by a grammar of unbelievable clumsiness. And Loa lived in a climate where there were no seasons, where the nights were hardly less warm than the days, where it was easy to do nothing — as Loa was doing now; where there was no need to take thought for the morrow — and Loa was taking none.

CHAPTER

I I I

DELLI LIVED in her little pen a full week. She was not actively unhappy in it, not even actively uncomfortable, for they made it six feet long and three feet wide, so that she could lie at full length, and three feet high so that she could sit up in it. They thatched it roughly with big leaves so that the rain hardly came through at all, and Musini herself gave her another couple of armfuls of leaves on which to lie, which was a sensible precaution, as someone as thin as Delli was at the start, and as scratched, might have broken out into sores had she been compelled to lie on the undisguised earth. They interwove the palisades, and the beams of the roof, with tough creeper stems, so that there was hardly a place wide enough to pass through the bowls of food which Musini saw to it were continually being provided for her.

So for some days Delli was content to lie in her pen recovering from the hardships of her wanderings in the forest. To lie still, to sleep, to fill her belly all through the day with good food; that was all Delli wanted at first, and a few days of it made a great difference to her condition. The bones of her skinny limbs were soon less apparent; her ribs disappeared under a layer of fat, and her previously lifeless-looking skin took on a healthy gloss. It was gratifying to Loa, when he walked past her pen, to see how she was responding to treatment. It boded well for the future; his meat hunger was a perfect obsession now, and all his dreams were positive torment, full of tantalizing visions of meat. In his dreams he could even smell the delicious stuff, and he would wake up with the saliva running from his mouth.

It was only natural, then, that he should be moved to wild rage when Vira pointed out to him one morning that Delli had been trying to escape. She had gnawed through a full dozen of the tough dried vines, and in a purposeful manner, too.

"See," said Vira. "These she has bitten through."

He pointed to the chewed ends, all between one pair of palisades. Then he went on:

"Soon she would chew these, where the wall meets the roof. She would bite through this knot, and this one. And then . . ."

Vira made a gesture to show how, then, Delli would have been able to force the two palisades apart a little way, just wide enough, presumably, for her to slip through. And then in the darkness she would make her way out of the village into the forest, where she would be as inaccessible as if she were already serving Nasa. Anger at the thought of losing her made Loa quite frantic.

"She is a wicked woman," raved Loa. "She is a thief, an adultress."

Loa's language contained some twenty synonyms for "adultress," each expressing a different aspect from which

[37]

the act was regarded; each word was liable to be used as a term of opprobrium, and Loa used them all. His heavy features were drawn together in a scowl of rage.

"She is a devil, an ape," said Loa.

Delli was looking up at him as she crouched in her pen; her eyes were unwinking and her face expressionless.

"Bring me that stick!" roared Loa, and someone ran and obsequiously fetched it.

Loa snatched it from him and rushed at the pen. He could not beat her or strike her with any advantage, thanks to the stout palisades which surrounded her. He could only prod her with the stick, but his prods were dangerous and painful, delivered as they were with his full strength. Delli screamed and rolled over, trying to protect her more vulnerable parts; Loa might have killed her then and there had his rage lasted longer. But sanity came back to him, and he let the stick fall, and wiped the sweat from his face with his hands.

"Bring more vines!" he ordered. "Tough ones. Hard ones. Stringy ones. Mend that hole! Put more vines all round the pen and over the roof, and see that the knots are tight."

A fresh idea struck him, a really important one.

"What old women are there?" he asked. "Ah! There is Nari. Come here, Nari. Vira, tie her legs with vines. Tether her to the pen. Nari, you will watch over Delli. You cannot go away. You will stay here all through the day and the night. If ever Delli tries to bite through the vines you will cry out. Loudly. Have you heard me?"

The old woman stood on her feeble legs with the sun in

her eyes. Oppressed at the same time by the majesty of Loa and by the sunlight she blinked and squirmed.

"Have you heard me?" shouted Loa.

"I have heard you," she piped at last.

"See that it is done," said Loa to Vira. "Musini, see that Nari is fed as well."

He glowered round at them all; he was still too moved and excited at the moment to consider relapsing again into torpor, and he strode off aimlessly at first. It was only when he was on the way down the street that he remembered a reason for going this way. From the farthest end of the street came the regular tapping of a drum; Tali, one of the sons of Litti, the worker in iron, was beating out a new rhythm. He was always experimenting with such things, perhaps to the detriment of his real work. But a good drummer made an important contribution to the life of the town, and if his father would buy him a wife or two whether Tali worked in iron or not that was all to the good.

This end of the street was not nearly as quiet or as clean as the other end where Loa's house stood. Here ran the little swampy stream, tributary to the great river two miles away, which supplied the town's drinking water and carried away its trash. The stink of the rotting piles of refuse was perceptible to Loa's nose where he stood, but refuse piles always stank. Where the forest came right to the edge of the town stood Litti's ironworks, in the shade of a group of large trees. On the flat tops of two rocks glowed charcoal fires, blown to a fierce heat by bellows worked by small children.

Litti was squatting beside them with his eldest son; a short distance away Tali was tapping on his drum while round him a little group of idlers made tentative attempts to adapt a dance step to the rhythm. Litti and his family did not prostrate themselves before Loa; when they were actually engaged in the working of iron there was no need.

"What of my son's ax?" asked Loa.

"It will be made," said Litti tranquilly.

He raised his white head to see where the sun stood.

"Now?" asked his son.

"No, not now," answered Litti.

Loa squatted down on his heels to wait; there was a deep fascination about watching the waves of heat play over the surface of the glowing charcoal as the bellows worked. Charcoal burned without a flame; Litti had the secret of preparing it. He would go into the forest and cut a great heap of wood, set fire to it, and bank earth upon it. After a time the wood would lose its fiery spirit, and change itself into a coal-black reproduction of itself, which, when ignited, needed the spirit of the air blown into it by bellows to make it burn well.

Those rhythms Tali was tapping out were quite captivating; time passed unnoticed.

"Now," said Litti at length.

"Hey!" called Litti's eldest son, rising to his feet, and one of his brothers detached himself from the group of dancers and came to help. With a pair of tongs they opened the larger of the fires, revealing in its heart a glowing lump of material, so hot that it was white and brilliant. They swept the little fire from the other rock (it was only there to make that rock hot) and, seizing the glowing lump in the tongs, transferred it to the hot surface. Then they took heavy iron hammers that stood near by, and began to pound it. At every blow a fountain of sparks shot from the incandescent lump, clearly visible in the deep shade. They struck and they struck, turning the lump with the tongs, until its white heat died away and it glowed only sullenly red and it ceased to give off sparks under the blows. Litti got stiffly to his feet and peered down at the red mass.

"It is iron," he decided. "Soon we will make the ax."

His sons lifted the lump back into the fire, piled more charcoal upon it, and the waiting child set to work again with the bellows. The young men's brown skins glistened with sweat.

"It takes many days for an ax to be made," grumbled Loa. "And after that I shall need a collar and bracelets for my son like these."

He fingered his own ornaments, spirals of wrought iron round his neck and arms.

"That will take longer yet," said Litti. "For that I shall need a wife for my son Tali."

"Let him tell me which girl it is he wants," said Loa, "and I will see."

His bare toes were playing gratefully in the thick bed of dead sparks which covered the soil for yards round, the accumulation of a thousand years, of the labor of fifty generations of Litti's predecessors. Out in the forest, beyond the swampy stream, was an outcrop of reddish rock — it had once been an outcrop, but now it was a basin, for so much of it had been dug away. Within this rock lay the spirit of the iron. When a lump of it was heated to a white glow and then pounded with hammers, the devils that enchained the iron flew off as sparks. Three or four such poundings freed the iron completely, so that it lay in a dark hard lump. Under the influence of fire it softened, and with hammers it could be beaten into any shape desired, and given an edge which would cut wood. But with fire and water the iron could be made better yet. It was a tricky thing to do — even old Litti often made mistakes. But an axhead, or a billhook, or a sword, heated in the glowing charcoal and then cooled in water, grew hard and glittering; and, when ground upon a smooth rock, became so sharp that even the hardest woods to be found in the forest could be cut by it.

The economy of the town was built up round the iron axheads made by Litti and his predecessors. They had enabled the forest to be cleared and crops of manioc and banana to be grown, thereby distinguishing Loa's people from the little men and women who wandered in the forest living on what they could catch, and on what they could steal from the cultivated plots. Probably in the first place the town had come to be situated where it was because of its proximity to the outcrop of iron ore. Yet iron was still a valuable and scarce commodity; an axhead represented several weeks of labor on the part of several men, so that the small axhead Loa was having made for Lanu was an extravagant gift; while the set of ornaments for which Loa was now negotiating was worth a wife — was worth a pension for life, in other words. Litti's iron tools represented a prodigious capital investment. The few iron cooking pots in the town were precious heirlooms, and no one ever dreamed of using iron in arrowheads; sharpened points of hard wood were always used for those. In fact these dwellers among the trees naturally made use of wood for as many purposes as possible, and iron was mostly used for the cutting of wood.

Tali had now perfected the rhythm he had been striving for. There was a neat series of beats, and then a hesitation, like a man stumbling, a recovery, and then another stumble. A man could hardly keep from laughing when he heard that rhythm. It was a good joke, something really funny, catching and captivating. The dancers were grinning with pleasure and excitement. They had formed round Tali in a semicircle, and the dance to suit that rhythm rapidly evolved itself. They closed slowly in on him with mock tenseness and dignity. Then a sudden sideways shuffle, half in one direction and half in the other. A quick interchange of places, a backward swirl, and they were ready in the nick of time to begin the cycle again. It was an exciting and stimulating dance, amusing and yet at the same time intensely gratifying artistically. People came swarming from all points to join in, and the semicircle grew wider and wider. Soli, mother's brother's son of the dying Uledi, leaped into the center.

"Hey!" he shouted. "Hey hey hey!"

He was up on his toes, posturing picturesquely. He reeled

[43]

to one side, he reeled to the other side, while behind him the crowd neatly shifted in time with him, interchanging in a geometrical pattern vastly gratifying. Tali thumped and thundered on his drum. His eyes were staring into vacancy over the heads of the dancers. He touched the side of the drum with his elbow to mute it, and its tone changed from loud mirth to subtle mockery.

"Hey!" shouted the crowd.

Tali introduced a new inflection into the rhythm. He made no break in it; perhaps not even a metronome could have measured the subtle variation of time. But now the drumbeat told of high tragedy, of vivid drama. Soli in the center caught the change of mood, and found words for it.

"The tall tree totters!" he intoned. "Run, men, run!"

The drum thundered, the dancers interchanged.

"Run, men, run!" roared the crowd, catching the final beats.

"It hangs upon the creepers," sang Soli in his nasal monotone. "Down it falls!"

Beat — beat — shuffle — shuffle.

"Down it falls!" roared the crowd.

Tali remembered the shrieking monkey which a few months back had been brought down entangled in the vines when a tree had been felled. He muted the drum again, and Soli followed his line of thought.

"Silly little monkey!" wailed Soli. "How he cries!"

The drum fell almost silent, so that the united tread of bare feet could be plainly heard in the dust.

"How he cries!" mocked the crowd.

[44]

Now the drum changed to a savage mood.

"Watch him as he struggles!" sang Soli.

He allowed a whole cycle of the rhythm to go by to allow the tension to build up. The drum roared savagely.

"Watch him as he struggles," sang Soli. "Cut his throat!"

Beat — beat — shuffle — shuffle.

"Cut his throat!" shrieked the crowd.

Practically everybody in the town had come to join in the dancing now. On one wing Indeharu's gray head was conspicuous, bobbing about as he capered on his skinny legs amid a group of excited girls. Loa stood alone behind Tali; he might perhaps have capered with the crowd, for his divinity was such that he need never fear for his dignity, but the habits of a lifetime kept him by himself. Alone behind Tali he leaped and bounded to the intoxicating rhythm. Strange feelings were stirred up within him by it. Inwardly he was seething; he was bursting with inexpressible emotions. He sprang into the air and shook his battle-ax at the sky above the forest, the distant, unfriendly sky, usually so contemptuous. He felt no awe for the sky now. He waved his battle-ax and by his actions he challenged the sky to come down and fight it out with him, and he exulted when the sky shrank away from him in fear.

Still the drum beat on with its maddening rhythm. Soli or some other had introduced a variation into the dancing; after the crossing over step everybody whirled twice round now in wild abandon. The pace had increased slightly, too; the mocking beat of the drum had perceptibly accelerated. Tali was working on his drum as though possessed of a devil, and the people were leaping and whirling and shouting in time to it. Carried away by the wave of excitement Loa came bounding into the semicircle. Every leap took him a yard into the air; he swung the heavy battle-ax round his head in a wide circle. Soli met him in front of the crowd, and pranced to join him. The ax came whistling through the air, and Soli saw it just in time. If he had not, he would have gone to serve Loa's ancestors at that very moment. But Soli had the quickness of thought that made him such a good extempore singer, and the deftness of balance that made him a good dancer. He ducked under the sweep of the glittering edge. The unexpended force of the blow carried Loa right round, and Soli took advantage of that to bolt into the crowd and make himself inconspicuous there.

Loa made no attempt to pursue him; indeed, he was hardly conscious that he had struck at anyone and he could not have named the man who had had such a narrow escape. The blow was the merest gesture. There would have been gratification in the feeling of the ax cleaving flesh and bone, but there was no sense of disappointment in its absence. Loa forgot the incident immediately. He swung his ax, rejoicing in the whistle it made as it parted the air. He whirled faster and faster, carried round by the weight of the blade. Tali at the drum worked up to a climax, writhing in ecstasy as he pounded out the accelerating rhythm. Faster and faster; no living creature could stand that pace for long. Indeharu over at one side fell almost fainting to the ground, and the girls among whom he was dancing stopped, gasping. As one tree brings down another, or as fire spreads from trunk to trunk, so the halt spread through the crowd. Men and women fell, sobbing for breath, and yet laughing with pleasure. Tali gave a final thump to his drum and allowed himself to fall limp on top of it, as exhausted as the others. The cessation of the music found Loa alone on his feet; the sudden ending of it all struck him rigid, so that for a moment he stood like an ebony statue, the ax held above his head. Then his knees sagged and he sank to the ground as well.

It had been a good dance, deriving additional zest from the fact that it had been entirely spontaneous, without any planning at all. Whatever might be Tali's failings as a worker in iron, he certainly made up for them by his merits as a drummer. He deserved a wife, even though that meant withdrawing the labors of a young woman from the communal activities of the town for Tali's personal benefit. Loa felt full of gratitude towards Tali. He might even in a prodigal gesture have given him a wife for nothing, but he remembered how much he wanted those iron ornaments for Lanu. Tali would have to wait until Lanu's little ax was finished and the iron ornaments well on the way towards completion. It was highly convenient that Litti was willing to put in so much labor to buy a wife for his son.

Over at the place where iron was made, the charcoal fires had burned down to a mere heap of white ashes. Lying within the heap presumably was the lump of iron that Litti would fashion into an axhead for Lanu. The dance had delayed its completion — even old Litti and the children at the bellows must have been drawn into the dance — but that was the way things happened. When Loa walked back to his house he saw Delli lying in her pen, deep in conversation with Nari, the old woman who had been left to guard her. They were the only human beings left at this end of the town when the dance had been in progress. They had fallen into talk, the way women will, despite the difficulties of the strange jargon Delli spoke; despite the fact that Delli had not long to live.

CHAPTER

IV

LOA SQUATTED in his house close to the open door. It was
a dark night, and the darkness inside the house was hardly
relieved at all by the glow of the fire which his women had,
at his command, lighted outside the door. Uledi was dead
of the sleeping sickness, and Loa had to determine who it
was had ended her life. For this purpose darkness was necessary, darkness and flickering firelight. Loa had taken
the bones — the half-dozen slender ribs — from their usual
resting place at the base of the grotesquely carved wooden
figure that stood against the far wall. He had set a rough
hewn table, of dark wood and with short legs, in front of
him so that the firelight flickered over it, and he had laid
the bones upon it. All round him there was a hushed silence,
for the women knew what he was doing. They were frightened as well as awed. In one of the huts close by, a child
began to cry in the night, but the wailing was instantly
stilled as the child's mother caught her infant to her breast.

Loa looked up at the dark sky, and at the same time laid
the bones in a bundle across his palm. Without looking
down, he put the ends of the bones on the table and withdrew his hand so that they fell with a clatter on the wood
— some woman within earshot, crouching in her house,

heard that clatter and moaned softly with fear and apprehension. Still without looking down Loa put his forefinger among the bones and stirred them gently, just a little. Then at last he looked down at the pattern the bones had made. In the flickering firelight the bones were faintly visible against the dark wood. The pattern told him nothing at first, not even when he rested his forearms on his knees and his brow on his hands and peered down at them for a long time. Loa remembered Vira's hint that Soli was Uledi's mother's brother's son. Uledi had owned a knob of pure iron which hung on a string round her neck. She was the principal shareholder in an iron cooking pot with tripod legs — a miracle of workmanship and convenience. Such things might well tempt her principal heir, and yet there was no hint of Soli's features in the pattern the bones had assumed. It reminded him more of the gable end of Huva's house, and yet there was no conviction about the likeness. He pressed his brow against his hands unavailingly; the bones lay uncommunicative, nor could he feel any stirrings of his spirit.

Having sat for so long he raised his eyes again to the dark sky, as black as the black treetops that ringed the town so closely. He gathered the bones up into his hand again, laid them on the table with his palm flat upon them, and then spread them by a twist of his hand. He stirred them again with his finger and then slowly transferred his gaze to them. The fire was glowing red, and the white bones reflected the color. Then one of the logs in the fire fell down, and a little flame sprang up, dancing among the embers. Now the bones began to move, shifting on the table, and Loa felt his knowledge and his power surging up within him. That was a serpent undulating in the shadow, a little venomous snake with red eyes. And these were the rocks at the river's edge, and there was the broad river. The lowering sun was reflected in red from its whole surface. There! Someone had thrown an immense stone into the river, breaking the reflection into a thousand concentric rings. First they spread, and then they contracted and were swallowed up in a dark spot in the middle. The dark spot opened. Was that a flower expanding in the center of it? A flower? A flower, perhaps, but that was Uledi herself within the opening petals — Uledi in her convulsions with the foam on her lips. She turned over on her side and reached out frantically to the full extent of her right arm. She was reaching for — what was that? What was that which evaded her grasp? Something which scuttled for concealment among the shadows over there. Was it Soli, running as he had run for the protection of the crowd before Loa's ax? Loa groaned with the anguished effort of trying to see. Somebody looked back at him over his shoulder for a moment from the shadows; white teeth and white eyeballs. That flashing grin was like Lanu's. It could not be Lanu, not his little son. No, it was a devil's face, now that it showed more clearly, a devil's face, frantic with malignant rage. The most frightful passions played over it, the way waves of combustion played over the glowing charcoal of Litti's furnace fire. The bared teeth champed, the eyeballs filled with blood. It was utterly terrifying. Loa swayed as he squatted. The flame died abruptly in the fire, and as darkness leaped at him he was momentarily conscious of the cold chill of the sweat in which he was bathed. Then his head sank onto the table.

It was several minutes before he roused himself, cramped and almost shivering. There was a foul taste in his mouth, and his legs were weak as he stood up. The bones, when he gathered them together, were cold and lifeless to his touch. And yet he had only to close his eyes to see again that frightful face. Somebody inhuman, of supreme malignancy, had poisoned Uledi. Loa's simple theology recognized the possibility of the existence of devils, but there was no profound lore about them. The major catastrophes of nature passed his world by; his people never knew famine, or droughts, or frost, or earthquake. There was no need in consequence to postulate the existence of evil forces in the world, working against the happiness of mankind. The little people in the forest, with their poisoned arrows and their pitfalls, were human enough; no man could attribute supernatural qualities to men and women whom he not infrequently killed and ate. And disease — sleeping sickness, malaria, typhoid, smallpox and all the other plagues that kept the population constant and stagnant — was simply not recognized as such. Loa knew of no dread Four Horsemen, and his complex language with its limited vocabulary effectively restrained him from ever venturing into theological speculations. Besides, he knew himself to be god; it was not a question of belief or conviction, but one of simple knowledge. He called his wayward sister the moon out of the river every month, and she came. The sky and the forest and the river were his brothers. Nasa his father had been a god before him, and still was a god, leading somewhere else the same life he had led here, attended by his wives, regulating when necessary the simple affairs of his people, and possibly — no one could be quite sure — eating meat rather more often than he had down here.

But there were devils in the world, as Loa vaguely knew. He had heard a story of some, a family of three devils, like men but covered with hair like monkeys, who had once come to the town, before even the time of his father Nasa, and who had torn men and women into fragments before succumbing to the rain of poisoned arrows directed at them. It was a devil something like this, judging by what he had seen among the bones, who had been responsible for the poisoning of Uledi. The little that Loa knew about devils chiefly concerned their aimless ferocity, so there was nothing surprising in the fact that one of them should have poisoned Uledi, who had never done him any harm or even set eyes on him as far as Loa knew. The matter was satisfactorily settled, then, and Loa could announce on the morrow how Uledi had come to die. If he had seen anything else among the bones — if the gable end of Huva's house had stood out more clearly and for a longer time, if he had seen Soli's face, or if the bones had arranged themselves in the pattern of somebody's scar-tattooing, it would have been different. There would have been a human miscreant to denounce. The circumstances of the moment would dictate the procedure to follow after that; if the accused were not well liked, or if his (or her) motive were at all obvious, he

would be instantly speared or strangled or clubbed or be-
headed, but if he protested with sufficient vehemence or elo-
quence he might be given a further chance. There were
beans that grew in the forest; Indeharu knew about them.
They would be steeped in water, and the accused would have
to drink the water. Usually he suffered pains and sickness,
and frequently he died. If he lived, it was a proof that he
had not really intended to kill his victim, but on the con-
trary had done it by accident or without the intention of
actually causing death. The ordeal would be considered a
sufficient lesson to him and the case could be dismissed with
a caution.

Loa's strength was coming back to him. His legs could
carry him easily now. He walked into the darkness of his
house, finding his way with the ease of a lifetime's experience, and set the bones back in their proper place beside the
wooden figure which symbolized something a little vague
in Loa's existence. The half-dozen skulls nailed to the wall
— relics of bygone days and of distinguished individuals —
showed up faintly white, just sufficiently to permit him to
see where he stood. The elephants' tusks, treasured memen-
toes of the few occasions when elephants had fallen into the
town's pitfalls, stood in the farther corner, beyond the bed.
A whole precious leopardskin had been consumed to provide the leather strips that crisscrossed the bed's framework,
and another skin lay on it. No other bed like it existed in
the town; it raised the occupant above the earth and the
myriad insect plagues to be found there, it was cool and
springy and comfortable. That was the whole furniture of

the house except for the few other symbols that hung on the walls — even Loa was not quite sure what most of them implied. The dried snakeskins, the bunch of feathers, had something to do with his royal divinity. Because of that, he thought little about them, although they struck terror into mere humans.

Loa came back to the doorway of his house.

"Musini!" he called. "Bring the girl to me."

He had a new wife whom he had only acquired that day: Pinga, daughter of Gumi. Loa heard a low wail of terror, cut short by Musini's urgent whispering. Musini as an old woman of twenty-five had small patience for the whims of a girl of fourteen.

"I bring her, Loa," said Musini, loudly.

Two dark figures appeared in the faint glow of the dying fire; Loa could just distinguish the girl's slight form as Musini pushed her forward with her hand on her shoulder. The girl hung back and wailed again.

"Go on, you little fool," said Musini brusquely, giving her a final shove.

Pinga's timid steps brought her within Loa's reach as he stood in the shadow of the doorway. He reached out and took her wrist, but at his touch she cried out and tried to pull away from him.

"Idiot!" said Musini's disgusted voice from outside by the fire, but after her first startled movement Pinga stood still except for the tremblings that shook her. Loa, his hand still grasping her wrist, could feel her quivering. He displayed remarkable patience.

[55]

"Why not come to me?" he asked.

"I am frightened."

"You are frightened of me?"

"Of you, Lord, of course. But it is not that. I am frightened of this house — of this house."

The terrors of the god's house presented themselves to her more violently as she thought of them, and she began to drag back from his grasp again.

"Do not be frightened," said Loa. "There is nothing here to hurt you."

"And it is what you have been doing, Lord. What you have been doing this short time past."

Loa was at a loss for a moment. It was very hard for him to realize the effect of the abject terror which lay over the town when it was known that he was at work identifying a criminal; it was something he was aware of theoretically, but he had never known terror himself and was no judge in consequence of what it did to other people. And his house, the house with the skulls, and snakeskins, and the bunch of feathers, and the carved idol, was his home as he had always known it. He could have small sympathy for those of his people who would, literally, rather die than cross its awful threshold.

"That should not frighten you," he said.

"But it does, Lord. My belly tells me I am afraid. You have been here with the dead. You have been finding out about things, and — and — I do not want to go in there."

That thoroughly nettled Loa.

"You are a little fool, as Musini said," he declared, testily.

It irritated him that someone should display such marked

antipathy because he had been divining — divination was one of his natural functions. The girl might as well be frightened because he breathed, or because he had two eyes. It made a personal matter of it, and changed his lack of sympathy to more active annoyance; the girl sensed all this, and her teeth chattered with fear. Paralyzed, she ceased to pull away from him, and stood unresisting.

"Enough has been said," said Loa, with decision.

He dragged her roughly over the threshold, into the greater darkness within. Her active terror renewed itself there, as she thought of the idol and the bunch of feathers close beside her, and she screamed. Loa had his hands upon her now, and the touch of her flesh was rousing in him instincts which overmastered any remaining reasonableness surviving his previous irritation.

Musini wished to extinguish the fire. It had not rained all day, and in that wooden village there was danger in leaving a fire unattended during the night. She had assembled some of the other women, and they had filled wooden pitchers with water and brought them to the fire. Pitcher after pitcher was emptied upon the embers, at first with sharp hissing and sputtering, and in the darkness the heavy steam which arose brought its wet smell to their nostrils. By the time Musini's turn came and she emptied her pitcher the embers were sufficiently quenched for there to be almost no reaction, and there was hardly a sound save the splash of the water on the dead fire. And inside the house the screams had ceased.

Musini looked at the dark mass of the house, almost invisible in the darkness, before she took her way back to her own house. It was not the first time by any means, and by no means would it be the last, that she had brought a young new wife over to Loa's house, most of them trembling and frightened. It was beyond her capacity to wish that she did not have to do this; the conception of human love was something she knew almost nothing about, and the idea of a personal love for Loa the god never occurred to her. She may have noticed that these events upset her and disturbed her, made her sharp-tongued and self-assertive, but even if she did she did not make all the possible deductions from the fact. It was so long since she had become the mother of Lanu her son; men had many wives when they could afford to buy them, and Loa of right had all he desired. She did not know that she wished he did not desire them.

CHAPTER

V

DELLI'S FANTASTIC STORY of the strange people with magic weapons and unnecessary clothing, who had raided her town and carried off the inhabitants, was on its way to being forgotten, like Delli. Had the life of the town proceeded undisturbed for another thousand years, as it had done for the last thousand years, some small fragments of the tale might have survived, imbedded in the lore of the town like fossils in a sedimentary stratum, in the same way as there lingered the memory of the family of gorillas which had wandered into the town thirty years back and which had been slain after a bloody battle. There were still occasional allusions to Delli's story in the gossip of the town; it was still a comparatively fresh joke to shout out "Bang bang!" in imitation of her. But nobody thought of making any deductions from her story; still less did it rouse any feeling of apprehension. The only raiders the town knew about from its own experience, the only enemies that existed, were the little people of the forest. They were a pestilential nuisance in the persistence with which they stole plantains and manioc, and the poisoned skewers and pitfalls with which they beset the forest paths made excursions into the forest dangerous, but all that was part of experience and tradition. Nobody else had ever raided the town, and nobody ever would. Such a thing might well happen to outlandish people with outlandish speech like Delli's, but it could not happen to the town, which was really the world — anything outside it was unreal and of quite doubtful existence.

So that at nights the town lay quiet and unapprehensive. No one dreamed of setting a guard; no one ever lay down to sleep with any doubts as to the morrow. Certainly Loa did not. He was secure not merely in the unchanging present, but also in his knowledge of his own divinity. His lack of imagination about guns and slave raiders might well be excused. He did not know — he could not know — of their existence. He was even unaware that there were parts of the world where the trees did not grow so densely as to cut off the light from the surface of the earth. Two warnings like Delli's, the arrival of another refugee, and he might have come to believe in the necessity for taking precautions, even at the vast sacrifice of some of his belief in his divine nature. But a single, isolated instance was not, and could not be, enough to make him realize the danger approaching the town — all this aside from the fact that he and his inexperienced people could probably never have displayed enough imagination to devise efficient military precautions.

In the Central African forest there often comes a chilly hour before dawn, when the temperature drops to that of a hot summer's day in England. The insect pests grow somnolent, evaporation is easier, and a man who has lain naked through the night, and who has spent almost all his life in an atmosphere like that of a Turkish bath, may reach gratefully for a cover and pull it over him, only half awake, and then fall into an hour of the most restful sleep granted him. Loa had done exactly that, and he was more deeply asleep than he had been during the whole night, when the slave raiders launched their attack. They came from the far end of the town, across the marshy stream beside Litti's ironworks, where there were no overgrown clearings to impede their advance, and they were halfway up the street before the alarm was given.

Loa heard the first screams and cries in his sleep, and muttered a protest against them, turning over angrily, but the musket shots woke him fully. He sat up on his bed listening to the turmoil down the street. Another musket shot echoed in the darkness, and there was no mistaking it. Loa remembered Delli's "bang bang," and a torrent of recollections poured into his brain. The gray-faced men with clothes on, the killings and the fighting . . . His ceremonial battle-ax lay as always beside the bed, and he seized it and sprang to his feet; the girl who had shared his bed was whimpering with fear in the darkness. He paid her no attention, but rushed madly out of the house and down the street.

Even outside it was still dark. Loa saw an orange spurt of flame and heard the report of a musket halfway down the street whence the screams were coming. He had no fear, not even of the guns; his rage at this intrusion carried him in furious haste down the street. Women and children were running past him in the opposite direction, most of them screaming; one of them cannoned into his legs and almost brought him down, but he managed to keep his feet and hurried on. The last house in the street was on fire, and by the light thrown by the flames he could see a group of men gathered round the doorway of another house. People were running out of the door, and as they emerged they were struck down. Loa came yelling up to the group before they were aware of their danger. He swung his ax with all the strength of both arms; the edge of the blade came down on a man's shoulder and clove deep into his body, smashing him to the ground. With another yell Loa whirled the ax again. Someone raised his arm in a futile attempt to guard himself; the ax cut through the forearm as though it had not been there and then shattered the skull. But even while he was dealing the blow someone hit him with a club. It was like an explosion inside his head. He staggered, stupefied but not quite unconscious. Before him there was a white-clothed figure at which he struck, but the man guarded himself with his gun barrel and the ax blade glanced off. Somebody struck him a frightful blow with a club on his left side; the breath came out of his body in a groan, and the pain was atrocious. He reeled, and his arms had no strength to raise his ax again. There was another blow on his head. Orange flames and white clothing wheeled in circles round him and his knees could not sustain him. He fell on all fours and yet still strove to rise, but he could not. Strive as he would, he could not even stay on hands and knees, but collapsed limply face downward, with only a trace of consciousness left him. There was stamping and screaming all round him, as he vaguely knew, but the dreadful pain he was suffering occupied most of his attention, while before his closed eyes circled tangled shapes and colors which effectually prevented him from thinking.

Loa was a brave man, though his courage was indistinguishable from stupidity. As soon as he could he roused himself from his lassitude. His head reeled as he sat up, and the pain in it made him sick — pain was something he hardly knew, and this great pain was a total novelty to him, but yet he strove to ignore it, for he had to go on fighting for his people. The fighting round him had ceased, and the noise of the struggle now centered higher up the street towards his own house. There was a gray faint light of dawn now, by which he could see the two dead bodies that lay beside him. The upturned face of one of them — the man he had almost cloven in half when he struck him on the shoulder — was far blacker than Loa's own chocolate complexion, and the tattooing on cheeks and forehead unlike anything Loa had ever seen before. The gaping mouth seemed to grin, and already there were flies gathering round it. All this Loa seemed to see without seeing. What he took note of was his ax lying there; he had to feel towards it before he could grasp it, for it was hard to focus his eyes. There was a knob-headed club, too, and for some reason he took that in his other hand. He got unsteadily on his legs, stepping clumsily over the other dead man, and went staggering up the street to do further battle for his people, ax in one hand, club in the other.

The raid had already achieved its main objectives. The

men who had shown fight had been killed. A good many women and children, and a few men, had been secured as prisoners already, and were being driven in groups down to the far end of the street where they could be conveniently herded together. There were men and women and children hiding in the overgrown clearings round the town, and they could be dealt with next, those of them who could easily be caught.

Here came Pinga and half a dozen half-grown children, driven along by a couple of the black men, whose spears bore long broad heads of iron, and who carried in their left hands oval shields of hide. The guards raised a shout when they saw Loa reeling towards them, coated with blood and dust, and they came to meet him, while Pinga and the children fell into a wailing helpless group. Loa plunged forward on uncertain legs, but his enemies noted his massive frame and the bloody ax in his hand and came cautiously to the encounter, separating so as to attack him front and rear, and holding their shields before them, their spears poised either to thrust or to throw. For some seconds they circled. Loa sprang forward and struck, but the man he struck at evaded his blow, and Loa only just wheeled round in time, swinging his ax, to ward off the attack of the other. It could not have lasted much longer; a few more seconds and one or other of those spears would have been through him.

But down the street came a white-clothed leader, one of the "gray-faced" Arab halfcastes, with at his heels a dozen Negro fighting men. The Arab took in the situation at a glance. He took note of Loa's sturdy bulk, and shouted to the spearmen not to kill him, while a sharp order to his own escort sent them to take him alive. Loa was ringed now by enemies, and he stood there, desperate, but with no thought of yielding entering his mind. The Arab saw his ferocious determination, the scowling brow, the lips crinkling back in a snarl to show the white teeth, and he put his hand to the pistol in his sash. But a noose of rope, dexterously thrown from behind, dropped over Loa's head and pinioned his arms. His frantic strength tore the rope from his captor's hands, but before he could free himself it had been seized again by others. They swung him round; he dropped ax and club, and someone reaching out caught him by the foot and brought him down with a crash. They threw themselves upon him, and they were experienced in securing refractory prisoners. Someone roped one of his wrists. He actually got to his feet, heaving off the half-dozen men who clung to him, but they brought him down again, flung their weight upon him, secured his other wrist, and bound the two together behind his back. Then they got to their feet, and looked down at him still lying in the dust, his wrists tied behind his back and the first rope with which he had been noosed still coiled round him. Loa glared up at them from where he lay. He saw the Arab looking down at him, the white clothes and the gay sash, the lean dark face with the coarse cruel lips — a face unlike any he had ever seen before.

"Get up," said the Arab.

Despite his queer accent the words were intelligible to

Loa, but nobody had ever given Loa orders in his life, and he still had no intention of yielding.

"Get up," said the Arab again.

Loa may have been too dazed, both by the turn of events and by his recent struggles, to obey or to reply. Yet even if he had not been he probably would have acted in the same way, with a stubborn obstinacy.

The Arab took from his sash a small whip. It was made from a single strip of hippopotamus hide, tapering from a convenient thickness for the hand at one end to the fineness of a knitting needle at the other. Flexible, hard, and imperishable, it was ideal for its purpose; a perfect example of mankind's ingenious inhumanity, in that so comparatively rare a material as hippopotamus hide should have been found by experiment to make the best whip for the whipping of men, and women. It was the dreaded kurbash; wherever the Arab culture penetrated in Africa it carried the kurbash with it — fire and sword and the kurbash enforced Arab dominance over the more primitive races.

The Arab swung the kurbash slowly in his hand.

"Get up," he said for the third time, and still Loa disobeyed.

The Arab struck suddenly and sharply, and Loa started with the pain. It was like sudden fire in his shoulder — an instant acute agony and a lingering intense smarting.

"Get up," said the Arab; now he made the thong of the kurbash whistle menacingly in the air.

He knew how to handle these dull-witted pagans who were even ignorant of the virtues of the hippopotamus hide until they were demonstrated. Now he struck again three times; it was like being touched three times with a hot iron, and Loa, in his sitting position with his hands bound behind him, fell over on his side as he started at the pain of it.

"Get up," said the Arab, with another swinging cut delivered with the full force of his arm, and Loa, without knowing what he was doing, scrambled to his feet; the Arab slashed him again so that the startling pain made Loa leap clear off the ground.

"Next time do as I say," said the Arab.

Bewildered, Loa tried to run, but one of the black spearmen caught the trailing rope that encircled his chest and arms and halted him, and the Arab, following him with three quick steps, struck him again and again, each time the pain being so unexpectedly great that Loa jumped into the air.

"Now go along," said the Arab.

Loa stared about him with frantic disbelief. Pinga and the children were huddled together in a terrified group, terrified not merely at what was happening to them but even more at the sight of Loa treated in this way; that was the clearest proof of the end of their world. The faces of the black spearmen wore expressions of dull disinterest; they had so often seen unruly captives reduced to obedience with the kurbash; those who had caught his rope had done so as indifferently as if Loa had been a refractory billy goat. There was no aid in all the world, in all the world which an hour ago had been indisputably his own, in its entirety, where every object, living and dead, had been dedicated to his service. Now he was utterly alone in it, brought down from superhuman to subhuman in a moment of time. There was agony of mind and spirit in the realization, as far as realization went in that unhappy hour.

The spearmen were herding Pinga and the children down the street.

"Go along," said the man who held Loa's rope, and when Loa did not start immediately he reached forward with his spear to prick him with the point.

The gesture sufficed; Loa had learned the lesson of pain, and he started to walk before his captor down the street. At the far end everyone who had been caught was herded together, many men and very many women and children, naked black spearmen standing guard over them under the orders of a few white-clothed Arabs. At the sight of Loa there arose a thin wailing from the crowd, to see their god and king driven along at the end of a rope. Some of the people even fell down, instinctively, in the attitude of prostration as he approached. The Arab guards laughed at the spectacle, and one of them idly swung his whip with a crack upon the salient curves of a prostrate fat old woman so that she sprang up again with a startled cry, fingering herself in bewilderment. Loa looked round at the misery about him, and sorrow overcame him. Sorrow not merely at his own plight, at his own frightful deposition from divinity, but sorrow too at the plight of his people. Tears ran down his cheeks, and he stood there sobbing, his hands bound behind him so that he could not cover his face.

Many of the raiders were at work beating the overgrown clearings for fugitives; once or twice the loud bang of a musket shot could be heard, as the pursuers brought down a group of pursued for a warning to the rest to stop. Every now and then small groups of captives were brought in and added to the herd.

On the edge of the herd was one of the little people of the forest, with a rope round him, the end of it held by a spearman. It must have been he who had guided the raiders, for the wandering forest pygmies knew the paths and derived much of their food from the plantations of the towns-people. He was a bright-eyed little manikin, naked like all his people, watching with rapt curiosity the destruction of the vast town and the gathering together of this enormous mass of people. Seven hundred people, men, women, and children, had lived in Loa's town. A hundred had been killed, three hundred captured. Of those three hundred perhaps thirty would eventually survive the march across Africa for sale in the slave markets of the Nile valley, of Abyssinia, and of Arabia across the Red Sea.

Two Arabs came along herding a dozen young men of the town, who were bearing on their shoulders the ivory tusks that had been stored in Loa's house. They were a prized collection, of no intrinsic value at all — no one in the town had ever thought of carving ivory — but beyond price for sentimental reasons. Every pair was a memento of a notable occasion when an elephant had been taken in a pitfall, when the whole town had gone on a twenty-four hour orgy of meat eating, whose memory, and that of the feeling of triumph, gave pleasure for years afterwards. Every forest village — although Loa did not know it — had similar accumulations of ivory going back for centuries, and it was the existence of these hoards, as much as the chance of capturing slaves, which had lured the Arabs across Africa from Zanzibar and the Nile. But the sight of his lost collection moved Loa almost as much as the plight of his people; the tears ran down his cheeks and dropped upon his dusty chest.

Here came a spearman, limping awkwardly. A barbed arrow was stuck in the calf of his leg, and he was holding the end of it in his hand so that it would not trip him as he walked. He lay stoically still while one of the Arabs freed the barbs from the flesh with a knife and then cut deeply all round the small wound so that the blood ran in streams — these raiders had had long acquaintance with the forest arrows. Loa looked down at the arrow as it lay on the ground. It was one of Soli's, he could see. So Soli had been alive and free at least until lately, and had taken some sort of revenge upon the raiders. The last batch of arrow poison had been of good strength, and probably had not yet grown too old. Definitely not; the wounded man as he sat there was looking round him in a bewildered fashion. He was babbling foolishly, pointing at nothing. Now his eyelids were drooping, and now he was laying himself down to sleep. Loa watched his death with savage enjoyment.

The nearest house suddenly caught fire and was rapidly consumed by the flames that ran up the dry wood; presumably some ember had been smoldering beside it for some time — two other houses had burned earlier in the day, scattering burning brands. The fire spread to the next house, Huva's; the flames roared in the thatch of dry leaves, and the heat was noticeable even where they were.

Now there was a bustle and a stir among the raiders. Another party was arriving. First came a white-robed Arab with a dozen spearmen. And then emerged the head of a short column, and at the sight of the first people in it Loa caught his breath with horror. They were naked men, men like his own people, and they were linked together in pairs by long sticks whose forked ends were clasped about their necks. Loa remembered what Delli had said about those forked sticks. Each man bore a burden upon his head, and at a command from an Arab they all halted and dropped their bundles on the ground. Two of the bundles jangled loudly as they fell, and when they were opened they contained short lengths of iron chain; the first chains that Loa had ever seen, and he could not imagine their purpose. He learned immediately.

Others of the slaves carried between them bundles of forked sticks similar to those about their own necks. A man of authority among the spearmen — he wore a bristling headdress and his face and body were scarred with fantastic tattooing — picked up one of the sticks. They were five feet long and forked at both ends. He pointed to the two nearest young women.

"Come here," he said.

He put a fork on the shoulders of one of them, and another man took a hammer and staples and one of the lengths of chain, and stapled the latter to the forked ends about the girl's neck, tightly so that she could just breathe with comfort. He clapped the other fork on the other girl's shoulders and stapled a chain to that, too. So the two girls were fastened to each other rigidly five feet apart, unable to touch each other, and yet free to move as long as they moved in unison. They could never run away through the forest bound together like that, and yet each was perfectly free to carry a bundle on her head, and any unwieldy package could be slung from the stick between them. Then he tore off the bark-cloth kilts from the girls so that they were naked, and then he turned to another pair.

"Come here," he said.

He worked with the rapidity of long practice, fastening the captives in pairs, indifferent to their sexes, and stripping them all naked. He came to Indeharu, took one glance at his white hair, and rejected him, making him stand aside, to be joined by other old men and women in a separate group. Loa, when his turn came, found himself bound to Nessi, Ura's wife. Nessi was weeping bitterly, hugging her baby to her breast; they struck her to make her raise her head. When they had chained Loa into the fork they freed him from the ropes which bound him; he was helpless now to make any move without dragging Nessi with him, and the chain was close about his throat, threatening to strangle him if he made any move uncoordinated with hers.

The young children able to walk with their mothers they left free, and many of the women, like Nessi, had infants in their arms; Loa, slowly emerging from his stupefaction, had a momentary gleam of pleasure at the realization that neither Musini nor Lanu were among the prisoners. They might still be free — unless they had been killed. Soon all the prisoners were fastened, save for the children and the group of older people.

"Kill those," said the headman with a wave of his arm towards the older people, and the spearmen closed in on the group.

They beat in their skulls with their knobbed clubs, and thrust their spears through them. The old people died amid a diminishing chorus of screams. Indeharu broke away and tried to run on his old legs, but a flung spear stuck in his thigh, and a black demon, leaping after him, shattered his skull with a single blow that made a horrible sound of breaking bones. Indeharu was the last to die; the others had already fallen in a tangled heap, although in the heap an arm or a leg still moved feebly. The headman snatched the child from Nessi's arms and flung it to the ground, and someone else thrust a spear into it. Nessi screamed and plunged forward, cutting the scream short as the chain tightened about her throat, for Loa naturally did not plunge with her. Fallen to her knees, Nessi tried to crawl to where her dead child lay just out of reach, but Loa stood rooted to the earth, and Nessi could not reach it. The chain dragged against Loa's neck.

All the little children, the babies in arms and those who could only just walk, were killed, so that their mothers would be freed of the burden of carrying and attending them. The children who could run beside their mothers were spared;

those among the boys who should survive both the long march across Africa, and the crude surgery to which they would then be submitted, would fetch high prices in the slave markets of Mecca, higher even than the girl children of undoubted virginity. But the little babies were a liability and in no way an asset; long experience had taught the raiders that to allow a woman to keep her baby was almost certainly to lose them both, and that meant the loss of a carrier.

The slaughter was soon over, and the raiders began apportioning loads among their slaves. The biggest tusk in the town's collection was allotted to Loa and Nessi. It was not one of a pair; maybe the other one had not developed in the elephant's jaw, or anyway its fate had long been forgotten. This one was dark brown with age — an Arab scraped the tip of it with his knife and showed his teeth with pleasure at sight of the pleasant fresh material within. The tusk was five feet long, and of such a weight that a man had to put forth his strength to lift it. They slung it on the stick that connected Nessi with Loa, thereby illustrating a further advantage about this method of securing captives; the stick was of great use for supporting loads of a shape or weight unsuitable for carrying on the top of the head.

Now that everything was ready a party of spearmen started ahead down the path across the marshy stream. Behind them, in single file, two by two, the raiders set the slaves on the march. It soon became the turn of Nessi and Loa. As was only natural, the act of moving from the spot unbalanced Nessi again. She uttered a wail, reaching out for her dead baby, tearing at her cheeks with her finger nails. But a slashing cut from the kurbash brought her promptly out of her hysteria, and her wailing terminated abruptly in a startled cry of pain; she began to stumble after the others, with Loa walking behind her. While Nessi had wept Loa had looked back at the town; at the flaming houses, at the piled corpses. It was not the same town to him, not the same world. One world had come to an end for him, and he was in another, new and raw and unspeakably harsh. He might still be Loa the god and king, but he was a king without a kingdom, a god without worshipers, and he had met a power stronger than his own — the whip. He had learned the lesson of the whip even in this short time, even in his dazed and stupid condition.

Nessi stumbled ahead of him down the path. When she checked at an obstruction, Loa caught his throat against the fork; when she took a longer step, the chain jerked against the back of his neck. The tusk in its slings of vine swung between them to their motion. Sometimes the butt end hit him in the stomach, just below his ribs, and sometimes the point prodded Nessi in the small of the back. The weight of it dragged the fork down against Loa's shoulders and the chain against his neck, and the friction resulting from his motion made the rough wood chafe his shoulders. Loa soon found himself hunching forward, and then leaning to one side, to relieve the chafed places. In the neighborhood of the stream the soil was even marshier than usual in the forest, and at each step Loa sank to his ankles, so that the labor of plodding along with his burden was severe. In the stifling atmosphere of the forest the sweat ran down him in streams, and soon his breath was coming jerkily, and his throat was parched.

The bogginess of the soil gave way to actual surface water, a sluggish little rivulet creeping among the trees. Loa stooped with his burden to scoop himself a handful of water to drink, but Nessi ahead of him was staggering along blindly and unthinkingly. The tug of the chain at his neck overbalanced him, and he fell, bringing Nessi down with him, wallowing in the mud below the few inches of water. They scrambled to their feet; the ivory tusk had slipped in its slings and was hanging precariously. Loa grabbed for it, still not allowing for the rigidity of the pole between him and Nessi. He choked himself against the fork, threw Nessi forward off her balance again, and then he saw, as they floundered, the tusk slip from its slings and fall with a splash into the water.

Sudden agony in his shoulder; an Arab had come up to the ford and was slashing with his whip. Nessi screamed, roused from her brutish misery, as the kurbash bit into her.

"Pick up the tusk and bring it here," snarled the Arab. His pronunciation and use of words were as strange as Delli's had been, but they could understand him.

Loa groveled down into the thick brown water, found the tusk, and with an effort heaved it up in his arms.

"Here!" said the Arab.

The rest of the column was halted behind them, and long experience with many columns had taught this Arab the necessity of keeping them well closed up and on the move.

As Nessi and Loa came to the place indicated beside the stream he impatiently motioned the waiting column to go on, and they splashed down across the ford, two by two, naked and sweating and burdened, their eyes cast down, all of them gasping with the heat and the effort.

"Hang up the tusk again," said the Arab.

Loa struggled with the huge mud-daubed thing clasped in his arms.

"Help me, Nessi," he said. "Turn round."

"Hurry yourselves," snapped the Arab.

Within the triangle of fork and chain Nessi's neck was free to revolve, and she turned herself cautiously, so as to face Loa. Between them they were able with difficulty to replace the tusk in its slings of vine, and Nessi turned herself about again. The column had all gone by; two spearmen from the rear guard were waiting, at the Arab's orders, to herd them forward in the track of the column.

"Hurry! Hurry!" said the Arab.

The whip bit like fire in their flanks as they started forward again and re-entered the ford; at the first sign of their pace slackening the whip hissed in the air.

They plunged on blindly through the sultry twilight of the forest. Soon they had proof enough that they were following the path of the column. A corpse sprawled beside the path, the head five feet away from the neck: a middle-aged woman's corpse, the breasts flaccid and empty. The tattooing on it was not that of anyone in Loa's town; one foot was bent strangely outwards and supplied the explanation of why the corpse lay there. When that ankle was broken there was no chance of keeping the woman on the march, and the quickest way of getting her out of the fork was to take off her head. The body already swarmed with ants. One of the spearmen walking behind them laughed and made some unintelligible remark, which probably did not refer to the dead woman. Loa knew already that dead bodies were far too common to excite a jest.

And then, farther along the path, Loa caught sight of something else. So blurred was his vision with sweat and exhaustion that at first he did not believe that what he saw had a concrete existence. It might have been something real but with no place in this world, like what he used to see among the bones in that other life. A tree had fallen near the path, bringing down with it a tangle of vines, amid which glowed gaudy flowers, and at this point a shaft of sunshine reached down from the outer sky nearly to ground level. There was light and shadow and a screen of greenery. And from the edge of the screen a face looked momentarily out at Loa. It was Lanu, little Lanu, son of Loa and grandson of Nasa, once a god and a god to be. It was impossible that Lanu should be out here in the forest. Of course; now the face was gone. Loa had not really seen it. And then it came again, among the light and shade, indisputably Lanu, indisputably. The face split into a grin, with a flash of white teeth, and then it disappeared again. It was Lanu looking out at him from the cover of the vines. Loa was too miserable and too weary to think of all that implied. He had seen Lanu, and he was faintly cheered, but he had to go on plodding through the forest under the burden of the fork.

V I

BEFORE SUNSET they emerged from the forest onto the bank of the big river. The light was still glaringly bright even though the sun was dipping towards the treetops on the other bank, and Loa, utterly worn out though he was, felt the old sensation of shrinking a little in the presence of the sky, the usual slight vertigo on looking out on those immense distances. The sky was his enemy as well as his brother, and he had always known it. It must be the sky that had dealt him this fatal blow, through the agency of the raiders. Here was the proof of it, this vast encampment surrounded by terrifying distances.

They had reached the temporary base of the slave raiders, a central point where they had established themselves so as to be able to strike out in all directions and sweep up every community within thirty or forty miles. Here a long wide rocky beach ran down to the water's edge covered with only sparse vegetation. A town of many houses stood above it; the townspeople were now either slaves or dead and the raiders lived in their houses. On the rocky beach was gathered all the accumulated plunder — the captives and the ivory. More than a thousand human beings were there, moving about with a certain amount of freedom; what freedom there was, when they were chained two by two, neck and neck, in the forked sticks. Loa looked with dull amazement at this immense number of people; drawn up on the beach was a row of canoes, vast things, and he stared with fearful interest at yet another just coming in to the landing place propelled by a dozen glittering paddles.

"This way," said the Arab.

This was the central dump of the ivory captures. More than a hundred tusks lay together on the ground here, unguarded, for in Central Africa ivory had no more than a sentimental value — that mass represented a fortune only when borne on men's shoulders a thousand miles to Zanzibar or twice that distance to Cairo.

"Put it down here," said the Arab.

Loa allowed the tusk to slide out of the slings to the ground. The relief of being free of the weight of it was unbelievable.

"Go over there and get your food."

The Arab turned away without evincing any more interest in them. His final gesture had indicated a thicker nucleus in the mass of people on the beach.

"Let us go there," said Loa to Nessi.

The grammatical construction he used was unusual to him; self-analysis of course was something quite foreign to him and he took no note of what he was saying. He spoke as one equal to another, not with the complex construction of a superior to an inferior. The physical fact of being chained to one end of a pole while Nessi was chained to the other seemed to make this method of speech inevitable. Nessi began to pick her way towards the little crowd, Loa plunging along after her. Because of the rocky irregularities of the beach they jarred each other's necks as they went along; they passed many other people, all similarly confined in forked poles, all of them as naked as Loa and Nessi. Some were wandering aimlessly, some were squatting or lying on the ground, the individuals in each pair rigidly five feet apart from each other. Among the crowd the situation was more complicated, for the people and their poles were liable to entangle themselves by aimless movements. The focus of the crowd was a wooden trough, beside which stood a couple of white-clothed Arabs and two spearmen. Most of the people were standing dumbly eyeing the trough, not speaking, merely looking. Nessi wound her way through the crowd; the pole behind her bumped against people as she did so; Loa was too weary and numb to make more than a slight attempt to keep it clear. Arriving at the edge of the cleared space round the trough Nessi hesitated, but one of the Arabs singled her out immediately as one who had not already had her ration and beckoned her forward. She approached the trough with Loa behind her.

"Fill your hands," said the Arab, making the gesture of getting a double handful.

At the bottom of the trough there was a thin layer of cooked tapioca, and Nessi filled her hands with it. As she did so she realized that she was hungry, and she bent her head to eat, while Loa behind her fumed with sudden hunger — it was twenty-four hours since he had last eaten, and he had fought a battle and made a long march during that time. His restless movements reminded Nessi of his existence at the other end of the pole, and she wheeled aside to allow him to come up to the trough. He scraped himself a double handful of the glutinous starch. The second Arab standing by, a man of more aquiline features, noticed his iron collar and bracelets.

"Here," he called to Loa, beckoning with a gesture of authority.

Loa stared at him stupidly, but the Arab was not a man to tolerate a moment's hesitation in obedience to an order. With a malignant snarl on his face he repeated words and gesture, and Loa went up to him, dragging Nessi behind him. The Arab reached out and struck him on the mouth with his fist; Loa staggered, dropping most of his tapioca. He winced as the Arab reached out his hand again, but this time all that happened was that his head was roughly jerked back so that his collar could be examined. A mere glance was sufficient to reveal it as base metal, and half a glance sufficed for the bracelets. The Arab turned his back and gave Loa no more notice, and almost instinctively Loa turned to refill his hands at the trough. There were some other late-comers already being fed there, and a warning cry from the guardian of the trough checked Loa in his stride. That Arab had a whip in his hand, and Loa knew whips. But he was hungry. There was a little tapioca still in his hands and he licked at it; two swallows and it was gone. He edged forward again, but the whip whistled in the air and he drew back. Another late arrival was scraping up the very last of the tapioca from the trough. Then the Arab guard swung his whip again in a wide gesture, driving the lingering couples away; before his whip they withdrew reluctantly, bumping each other with their poles.

Here came a whole group of the Arab raiders, white-clothed, muskets in their hands, striding down towards the river. They took their places at the water's edge, and spread mats before themselves. They made strange sounds, and strange gestures, dipping their hands in the running water, prostrating themselves with their backs turned to the hidden sun now far behind the trees across the river. Night was beginning to fall; the eastern sky towards which the Arabs were kneeling was already dark.

"I am weary," said Nessi, sitting down; she had had experience enough now with pole and chain to do so cautiously, and with due regard to Loa — a tug at his throat meant a tug at her own.

"I too," said Loa, squatting down as well.

Five feet apart they sat in the gathering darkness. And then Nessi began to weep. She wept out of weariness, she wept for her dead child, for her lost liberty, out of terror for the future and regret for the past. Her wailing rose thin on the heavy evening air, and her example was infectious. Another woman near began to wail, and then another and another so that the sound spread down the riverbank. Some man shouted his sorrows in a raucous dialect, the hard, clipped words punctuating the wailing. Another man echoed the cry in a cruder rhythm. Now the whole encampment throbbed with the misery of Africa. Loa could tell, by the dragging of the pole in the darkness, that Nessi as she sat was swaying her body backwards and forwards in time with her weeping; she was dissolving in an ecstasy of unhappiness, and so were the others, and their misery was dissipating itself in hysteria.

Loa might have been carried away in the flood; he might have joined the shouting wailing chorus, to sob until he fell asleep like a drunken man, had not his own unhappiness been beyond hysteria. But he had lost more than anyone else there, unless, as was possible, some other local god had also been enslaved. In the darkness Loa's face bore an expression of puzzled thought. So hard was he trying to think that he remained uninfected by the rhythm around him. For until today Loa had been a god ever since he could remember. When he was seven years old — eighteen years ago — a strange sickness, a mysterious magic, had descended upon the town. Almost everyone had suffered from it, and nearly everyone who suffered from it had died. Nasa, Loa's father, had died. Pustules had formed to cover his body, and he had shouted words that had no meaning, and then he had died, quickly. His brothers had died, his wives and his children had died. In every house more people had died than lived, and in some houses everyone died. Loa himself had sickened; he bore on his forehead and on other parts of his body the hollow marks, grayish in the chocolate-brown skin, of the ·pustules which had formed there. But Loa had lived through it, lived to find himself the sole survivor of the house of Nasa, a god unquestioned. Upon him had devolved the duty of seeing that Nasa and Nasa's fathers before him were supplied with attendants consonant with their dignity.

It was he who had to recall the errant moon from the arms of the river, it was he who had to ascertain, by virtue of his divine powers, who were the miscreants of the town, and it was he who, by his mere existence, had to ensure the prosperity and happiness of his people. The few surviving old people — Indeharu, whose skull had been beaten in that morning by a knobbed club, was the last of them — had been able to tell Loa about all this when he was a child. And the younger women had borne children, and the immature had reached maturity and become fathers and mothers. The young men who had taken wives lately had been born after the sickness, and their wives long after, and they had never known any other god than Loa; they knew of the dread majesty of Nasa, whose name none but Loa might pronounce, and they saw people sent to serve him and his majestic predecessors, and the knowledge increased their awe. They knew that Loa was brother to the sky and the forest, that the moon was his sister and the sun his brother.

Loa had never had reason to doubt any of this himself. What he wanted was his; he owned the whole world, which meant his town. The forest round it, with its little people and its vague hints of other peoples, was merely a setting for the town, a chaos in which his world hung suspended, and a chaos, moreover, which was his own brother. He knew of the effectiveness of his powers of divination as positively as he knew that hair grew on the top of his head. There had never been in his mind the least doubt about his divinity, and of course there had never been the least threat to it. He had never been aware of any limitations encompassing himself because he had never sought any. A world of a continuous sufficiency of food, of an almost complete absence of danger, a world of no ambitions and no disappointments, was not a world favorable to metaphysical speculation. A red ant could bite him, although he was a god; this was a world in which red ants could bite gods, and it was not a world in which one inquired into the relative natures of red ants and gods.

This was true only up to this morning, and now everything was different. Loa sat with his fellow captives wailing round him, trying to fit his new self into this new world, while his mind, utterly unused to logic, was weighted down in addition by the grave handicap of a clumsy language. His clubbings of the morning had kept him somewhat dazed until now, but their effect was wearing off at the same time as hunger was stimulating his thoughts. Although he did not join in the rhythmic wailings about him, he yet heard them, and they worked upon him.

His genuine sorrow at the destruction of the town moved him inexpressibly, and he knew now that hunger could gnaw at his divinity, and that knobkerries could smite it and hippopotamus-hide whips could cut into it. Yet it was not easy for the habits of thought of a lifetime to be discarded. Having almost come to grips with reality Loa turned a little lightheaded, thanks largely to hunger and the beat of the rhythmic wailing on his brain. It was his brother the sky who had betrayed him; he had always distrusted the sky, and now his distrust was justified and his perspicacity demonstrated. The sky had extended help to his enemies; it was by the aid of the sky, encamped as they were under its protection, that they had been able to enslave him. A little deliriously Loa vowed vengeance on his treacherous brother. He would degrade the sky, he would kill the sky, he would pay back these sufferings of his tenfold. In the midst of these wild thoughts came the memory of his glimpse of Lanu in the forest. Lanu would avenge him if he did not avenge himself. Lanu would continue the line of his divinity. Although Loa kept silent, he was soon as ecstatic and delirious with emotion as Nessi or any other slave about him. When the fit passed he was both drained and weary, like the others, and like the others he sank into an exhausted sleep, lying motionless under the dark sky with a thousand fellow unfortunates. The mosquitoes and the ants — the myriad insects of Africa — could not break into his comatose slumber, nor could the rocky earth beneath him. He lay like a corpse, and so did Nessi, so that neither of them disturbed the other with tugs at the stick that held them together.

That was a strange bond between them, uniting them and yet keeping them apart. They could never be nearer than five feet to each other, and yet never farther, never out of sight, and yet never within reach. When Loa woke in the dark dawn, he inevitably awoke Nessi. She gave a sharp cry.

"Ura," she said, "where are you?"

Ura was the name of her husband, one of the best of the young hunters. Nessi put her hand up to her neck and the touch of the fork and chain recalled to her the events of yesterday which she had thought momentarily a dream.

"Oh," she wailed. "Ah — ee — ai — "

Then she remembered who it was who lay beside her, and she looked round in the gathering light.

"Lord," she said, "is it indeed you?"

"It is indeed I," said Loa.

He was using again the language of a god, and Nessi was addressing him in the language of a remote inferior.

"Lord, what will they do with me?"

"You will bear burdens for them," said Loa, hesitatingly.

It was not an easy question to answer in any event. The conception of slavery had quite died out in Loa's little community. And Loa found it hard to imagine the existence of other communities, or of distances greater than a day's march. But with a prodigious effort of his imagination he was just able to picture the possibility that the slavers, coveting the ivory tusks, had come a long way for them, and needed bearers to carry them back to their town in a far part of the forest. To mere mortals, he knew, wives were desirable property, something to be coveted, but if any slaver intended to take Nessi as a wife he had shown small disposition to do so as yet.

"Will it be far, Lord?" asked Nessi.

"Very far."

"How far, Lord?" persisted Nessi, with a child's need for exactitude.

"Many nights, many days," said Loa, his imagination making a fantastic leap to such a wild idea.

"But you, Lord, you?" said Nessi.

She was only a mortal and such things might happen to

her within the limits of insane possibility, but now she remembered again that Loa was chained in the other fork of her pole, and of course nothing like that could happen to him.

"Doubtless I shall come too."

The equatorial dawn had fully broken by now, and the overcast sky was shining its light down upon them. Nessi looked at Loa, thinking hard. He was as naked as she was, as naked as all the other slaves about her. He had no leopard-skin cloak, and the only reminder of his former greatness was his iron collar and bracelets. And they were talking familiarly together, Nessi with him, and he had just admitted the possibility of being driven like a goat across the country with the others. Her world was a mad place. And people were no longer putting their faces into the dirt for him, and yet were suffering no apparent harm. Ah, that was the point. No apparent harm; but without doubt Loa would summon his secret powers and rend these slave raiders apart when he decided to do so. At the moment he was actuated by motives for delay incomprehensible to mere mortals — a conclusion that satisfied her vague wonderings. Except that she had a lingering wish that Loa's whim for being in temporary subjection had not involved the killing of her baby yesterday.

"Look, Lord," said Nessi. "There is food."

A full wooden trough had been carried down, and already a mob of slaves were milling round it.

"Let us go there," said Loa, suddenly remembering that he was desperately hungry.

A double handful of tapioca; that was what he got for himself at the trough, and this time he saw to it that he dropped none. He was careful that the pole moving from side to side under his nose in response to Nessi's movements did not interfere with his feeding. Pushing round them to get to the trough were many people from his town, mingled with many more whom he had never seen before. It was significant that already the one sort paid him scarcely more attention than the other. They frequently failed to recognize him, chained as he was to Nessi, and when they did it was sometimes with a startled cry and sometimes with nothing more than recognition, so that Loa knew they knew who he was. Chains and nakedness and misery were leveling them all. And Loa's own personal reaction was not too consistent. Sometimes he was sunk in despair, but sometimes his natural curiosity and interest in the world would break through his depression and his bewilderment. Some kind of selection had gone into his breeding. Some ancestor of his must have been markedly different from his fellows to be accepted as king and god, and the qualities had not been bred out in ensuing generations, for from a mass of people of the royal blood only one received deification, and each god in turn had his choice of the women as a vehicle to continue the royal line. So that even on that first day of captivity by the river, Loa's wits were coming back to normal and beginning to exercise themselves on what he saw.

It was clear that the river and the sky had betrayed him; the raiders had a fleet of canoes with which they could cover great distances and strike without warning. The night before they attacked the town they had undoubtedly made use of canoes to drop down the river, presumably as far as the rocks from which he was accustomed to summon his sister the moon. He saw a flotilla come back with a few slaves, but with the canoes crammed to the gunwales with food, the result of some raid on another town, he supposed. It was obvious that the problem of supplying the large mass of people encamped by the river was a serious one, and could only be solved by ceaseless raids upon the surrounding country. Moreover, this source of supply would exhaust itself in time; and when that time came, the only resource would be for the party to move on, either into some fresh area, or homewards. That was a brilliant piece of deduction on the part of Loa, uneducated as he was; but in one respect Loa was well equipped — between childhood and the present day he had had some thorough administrative experience, for in his town when all was said and done he had been ultimately responsible for the economic working of the life of the place, down to the smallest detail. The duties had not been onerous, in the absence of any difficulties regarding food or population, but they had opened up channels of thought in his brain which were available for the passage of these new notions.

"Let us go up there," said Loa, to Nessi, pointing up the steep slope to the village. He did not make use of the greatly superior form of address, but that used by one lofty equal to another — the way Indeharu would have spoken to Vira in the old days; the old days two days ago.

"Let us go," said Nessi obediently and almost deferentially.

She rose to her feet and they began to plod up the slope, picking their way through the yoked pairs dotted about. This bare rocky slope was a continuation and expansion of the main street of the village above, whose houses they could see. Like the houses with which Loa had always been familiar, they were built of thick planks split from tree trunks, but they were unfamiliar to Loa in the details of their design.

"Those men are different," said Nessi, pointing — they were walking at this moment with the pole diagonally across their course, with Nessi on Loa's left front. By this arrangement it was more convenient to talk, and the pole was not such a nuisance as it was if they walked side by side.

"They are indeed different," agreed Loa.

Nessi had pointed to two armed men lounging by the entrance to the village; they were dark brown rather than the deep black of the spearmen, and they carried shields of plaited reeds, and short stout bows with a few arrows whose heads were wrapped in leaves — poisoned arrows, therefore — altogether, in color and weapons, resembling the men of Loa's town rather than the strange barbarians who had captured them. But they were just as hostile.

"Go away!" shouted one of them as they approached, and, when Nessi and Loa still advanced, he put an arrow on his bowstring menacingly.

"Go away!" he repeated, leveling the arrow with every intention of drawing and loosing.

"We must turn aside," said Loa.

From where they stood they could just look up the street. Naked black women were moving about it on domestic duties, carrying wooden jars of water and so on, and they caught a glimpse of a white-robed Arab. Then Loa led Nessi along the top of the slope, high above the river. On their left hand were the old village clearings, the usual wild tangle of stumps and creepers, so dense that even a single agile man would have difficulty in picking his way through; a yoked couple could never do it. Strangulation or a broken neck would be the fate of one or both of them before they had penetrated ten yards — there was no escape in this direction. At the far end of the clearing the rocky slope had narrowed down to a few yards, and there the forest began, with the path by which they had come. Here lounged two more men with shields and bows. There was no word in Loa's limited vocabulary for "sentries." He had to think of them by the elaborate circumlocution of "men who wait to stop other people passing," but at least that exactly described them.

"Turn back," said one of them as Loa and Nessi drew near.

He was as ready to shoot as had been his colleague at the other end of the clearing, and the whole width of the gap, from where the clearing ended to the water's edge, was no more than fifty yards. Moreover, the spaces between the trees, Loa saw, were closed by a double row of pointed stakes, leaving only the path free. There was no way of escape this way, either. They were on the water's edge here, where the river ran, golden-brown, its otherwise smooth surface disturbed here and there by the ripples and eddies of its progress. Far out, a huge tree was being carried rapidly down, now and again turning over and round, raising fresh branches and roots towards the sky as it went. Loa saw the gaunt limbs raised in silent and unavailing appeal to the sky, and he was shaken by fresh emotion. He was as helpless as that tree-trunk.

"May you die!" he suddenly shouted at the sentries.

He shook his fist at them in rage. "May the bowels of your children rot! May — "

"Oh, let us run away," said Nessi, for one of the sentries was coming towards them menacingly. "Come!"

Nessi tried to run, and when the pull of the chain choked her she put her hands up to it to hold it clear of her windpipe and plunged forward, dragging Loa with her.

"Oh, quickly!" said Nessi.

Her panic infected Loa, and they ran back to lose themselves among the crowded couples along the water's edge, the chains of the yoke dragging at their necks when the irregularities of the ground made them diverge or converge a little.

CHAPTER

VII

IT WAS A STRANGE BOND between them, was that yoke. It held Loa and Nessi together and yet it kept them apart. They could not even touch each other with outstretched fingertips, and yet neither of them could move a yard without not merely the consent but the co-operation of the other. They could never be out of each other's sight or hearing; there was nothing the one could do without the other being aware of it. If one should fall, the other suffered equally. It compelled each to walk with due attention to the other's well-being. When they lay down to sleep on the unlevel ground it was necessary for each to see that the other was comfortable; if one should roll over or slip a little down the slope the other had perforce to conform. They had to be brave together, or timorous together. One could not be restless or try to explore if the other were torpid, nor could the torpid one remain torpid — each had to sink or rise to the other's level of activity. Because of the yoke Loa and Nessi experienced all the disadvantages of intimacy and enjoyed none of the advantages. They could easily make each other uncomfortable and unhappy, but it was almost impossible to make each other comfortable or to console each other. They could not even speak to each other privately — at that distance apart they must needs talk loudly enough for others to hear. All their secrets they must share with each other, and yet they could have no secrets unshared with the world.

For husband and wife, for two people who had long been intimate, the yoke would have caused difficulties enough; but Loa and Nessi had hardly known each other. Loa had been the god, immense and unapproachable, before whom Nessi had to prostrate herself; Nessi had been a pretty wench that chance had never before thrown his way. He knew much more about her now — he knew just how her head was set on her shoulders and how her arms swung as she walked. Looking round the pole he learned all about her back and thighs; as the day lengthened he watched the gradual fading of the weals left by the kurbash. She was a fine figure of a woman, of the slender type which Loa favored (unlike most of his fellows), with good muscles that showed to advantage under her skin when she set herself to climb a slope. Yet she was eternally out of his reach.

It was obvious to Loa by the end of the day that no ordinary attempt at escape would succeed; the simple precautions taken by the raiders, and their centuries of experience in the handling of newly captured slaves, made it quite impossible to get away. The yoke was as important an invention as the kurbash in the Arab subjugation of Central Africa; it was by means of these two instruments that a handful of spearmen and bowmen were able to keep a thousand captives under control.

Keeping everyone stark naked was another simple means

of maintaining dominance. A naked man or woman cannot conceal a weapon, or a tool to assist in escape, or a food reserve to be used in the event of escape. It reduced to some extent, too, the chances of infectious disease and of skin parasites being spread through the camp; but, more than anything else, the mere fact of nakedness was a repressive factor; in the simple communities from which the slaves had been taken nakedness was nothing to excite comment in itself. Nakedness implied poverty or helplessness, for clothing was a matter of ornament and hardly one of protection and had nothing to do with modesty. The naked man or woman felt more useless and helpless and was therefore more easily kept in slavery.

Perhaps the meagerness of the rations doled out helped — no spirit could remain high when only sustained by two double handfuls of tapioca a day. Already Loa was hungry, and he grew hungrier as the days passed. Nessi at the other end of the pole wept with hunger. Never in her life had her belly gone unfilled — usually it had been unsatisfied on a diet exclusively of starch, but never unfilled — until now. She wanted to joint the wistful groups hanging hopelessly round the feeding troughs, and she was inclined to sulk when Loa objected. Loa would rather sit on a lofty point of the encampment and survey the scene around him. He could force himself now to endure the unwinking gaze of the sky, to stare across the mysterious river at the distant shore on the other side, and he was interested in observing the behavior of his guards. The mumbo-jumbo of the Moslems, their ablutions and their prostrations, interested him. He was sharp enough to guess that these formalities were in honor of some god, but he could not guess which god it was. It was more than could be expected of his uneducated mind that it should develop a good working theory regarding comparative religion, but having been a god himself made him something of a practical theologian. Stirring in the dark recesses of Loa's mind there were some curious thoughts, and there was a stern conflict going on. When a man who has always thought of himself as a god begins to have atheistical doubts the conflict is bound to be severe. Loa might well have gone insane if his interest had not been caught by his surroundings — if, for instance, Nessi's whims and moods had not kept him busy, and if he had not been wondering about escaping.

The majority of his fellow captives were apathetic in their misery, content to hang round the feeding troughs or merely sit staring at vacancy. There were a few active spirits, but not many, and the kurbash kept them in check. And if the kurbash did not achieve its end there was another punishment possible. Loa never knew what was the crime of the two of his fellow slaves who suffered the death penalty. They may have tried to escape, or they may have gone insane and struck a Moslem. No one really knew, but everyone knew how they died, for they were perched upon stakes of impalement in the center of the encampment, and there they stayed, screaming throughout one long day, screaming at first so loudly that they could be heard from one end of the camp to the other. Later the screams died down to delirious moans. Loa knew about inflicting death; he had killed people in cold blood himself. And he knew about casual cruelty, the result of carelessness or indifference. But deliberate cruelty of this frightful kind was something new to him. He sat and watched under lowering eyebrows the writhings of the tortured men. It was all part of his education. He had never had to keep men in subjugation — allegiance to him had been voluntary, so ingrained by habit and tradition as to be classed as instinctive — but now he knew how it was done.

There was no attempt at organized sanitation in the camp, and the stench and the flies were consequently appalling; the deluges of tropical rain that fell were welcome in one way, as washing away the filth that lay everywhere, but they added to everyone's discomfort all the same. The naked peoples of Central Africa, like naked people in most parts of the world, detest the impact of rain upon their skin. The slaves tried to huddle together during the storms; Nessi would sit in close embrace with a dozen men and women whose yokemates similarly tried to huddle together at the other end of their poles, all whimpering in chorus, each trying to shelter himself from the pitiless downpour at the expense of the others. But Loa the god sat apart and indifferent (except when Nessi's writhings, communicated through the pole, jerked him off his balance) while the thunder of his brother the sky raved overhead, and the thick clouds obscured the face of his brother the sun so that for a time it was as dark as twilight. He bore the unpleasant nagging of the heavy raindrops on his skin with some kind of stoicism; stripped of his divine dignities he was clinging to his per-

[99]

sonal dignity — about which he had hardly thought before.

There came a day when the whole camp moved off, when the kurbash bit into dark flesh as the raiders herded the slaves into order, when shouts and cries and blows drove the slaves first here and then there in obedience to their masters. Loa and Nessi found themselves loaded again with an elephant's tusk — not likely to be the one they had borne on their first day, but one as heavy and as bulky. It was slung to their pole in loops of cane, and then they were directed, in the footsteps of those who had preceded them, up the slope to the village, along the main street, and out at the other end to a forest path well trodden already.

"Where are we going, Lord?" asked Nessi. She still called him "Lord" and used the honorific mode of address when she asked him questions.

"To their town, without doubt," said Loa with a bland assumption of certitude. He wished he knew.

"And when we arrive there, Lord?"

"Some man will make you his wife."

Loa really thought it more likely that Nessi would eventually be eaten, for that was the fate of wanderers in the world he knew — a few days of rest, and then the ax or the cord and the roasting spit. But he did not reveal his thoughts to her.

"Will a black man make me his wife, Lord?"

"Yes. You will dwell in his home, and for him you will cook the plantains and prepare the manioc. By him you will have children."

"Ah!" said Nessi. Such a prospect, after recent experiences, reconciled her to her fate, which was what Loa was aiming at. He had had enough of her misery.

The forest, the dark silent friendly forest, had already enfolded them. The tusk that swung from their pole was heavy and hard to manage, and already the yoke and chain were galling their shoulders. Ahead of them and behind them serpentined the long line of yoked couples, each bearing burdens, sometimes slung from the poles, sometimes carried on the head. At intervals along the line walked the guards, and at rarer intervals still were the Arabs, the few representatives of an alien culture who by virtue of that culture dominated this vast assembly of human beings. The African spearmen and bowmen who were the Arabs' paid mercenaries could be trusted to see that the slaves did not attempt to escape, but could be trusted very little farther, for they, too, had led the carefree life of the forest and knew not tomorrow. They could never be impressed with the necessity for keeping the line closed up, for hurrying the march, for planning each day's journey from one source of food supply to the next. In consequence the Arab leaders were busy all the time, hastening up and down the line, upbraiding their mercenaries, flogging the slaves forward with their whips, and stationing themselves at different points, where the march was necessarily checked, in order to minimize delays and hurry everyone forward again as soon as possible.

Soon Loa and Nessi were running with sweat; soon weariness began to creep over them as they plodded on through the forest, up and down its scarcely perceptible undulations, over its dry leafmold, across its boggy valleys. From far, far overhead the subdued green light filtered down, from where the creepers tangled together, where the monkeys played and the parrots shrieked. Nessi's step was shortening; a gap was opening between her and the yoked pair next ahead. Very soon an Arab appeared beside them.

"Go faster!" he said, and he caught Nessi a cut with his whip that drew a yelp from her and quickened her pace.

"Faster!" he repeated, with another cut. Then the whip burned across Loa's shoulders so that he lunged forward pushing Nessi ahead. Nessi half ran, half walked until she was up to the pair in front of her, but she had hardly reached them before her step began to shorten again. Almost at once the Arab — he was a man of a strange mixture of races, with a straggling black mustache and rings in his ears — was beside them again.

"Did I not say go faster?" he demanded, pointing to the gap that had opened ahead of Nessi. "Faster! Faster!"

At each word the whip fell, first upon Nessi and then upon Loa. Loa felt the sudden pain, and sprang forwards so that Nessi stumbled and the end of the tusk struck him in the stomach.

"Hurry!" snarled the Arab, making his kurbash sing in the air. On this, the first day of the march of the united column, the Arabs were determined to instill into the minds of their captives the dire necessity for keeping closed up.

Loa learned the lesson at once, linked as it was with the lesson that the hippopotamus-hide whip could inflict pain upon the person of his divine majesty. He kept watch now beyond Nessi to see that the gap did not open again, and when it showed signs of doing so he pressed forward with his neck against the yoke to compel Nessi to maintain her pace; by tensing his throat muscles he had found that he could bear the pressure against his windpipe for some seconds.

"You go too slowly, Nessi," he said.

"Oh Lord! Oh Lord!" wailed Nessi.

Later in the day came a blessed respite, when some delay ahead jammed the column. Nessi found herself stumbling against the couple ahead, who had halted — they were two burly young women, each with a bundle on her head and each with her lips distorted by scarring. They scowled round at Nessi, but Nessi fell incontinently to the ground oblivious to everything except the fact that at the moment she did not have to walk any more. The young women lowered themselves into a sitting position without taking the loads from their heads — it was less trouble to sit with stiff necks and poised heads than to lay the heavy weights on the ground and subsequently have to hoist them up again. Loa squatted too so that the tusk lay along the ground. Far too soon they heard movement ahead of them in the forest, shouts and cries and bustle. The couples ahead of them were getting to their feet in succession and moving on as the Arab came down the line. The two women with the scarred lips rose carefully to their feet, swaying gracefully as they kept their bundles balanced, but Nessi still lay face downward, sobbing. The women moved on, on the heels of the couple ahead of them, at the same moment as the Arab arrived. Loa had seen him coming, and was as much on his feet as he could be — with Nessi lying on the ground and the tusk so precariously in its slings between them. He wanted to look ready to march, for he had learned the lesson that the kurbash hurts. The Arab took in the situation at a glance, and once again his whip drew a scream from Nessi. Even then it took a second cut to get her on her feet, although once up she hurried instantly forward. Loa debated within himself the argument that Nessi had lain on the ground for an extra period of about two breaths, at the expense of two cuts with the kurbash. It was much too big a price to pay, he decided. Yet it was like a woman to pay too much for the satisfaction of having her own way — it was the sort of thing Musini did in the old days.

Musini! Loa had hardly thought about her since the raiding of the village. He knew she was not a prisoner, and he had no reason to believe she was dead. He knew, or he almost knew, in his half-delirious state, that Lanu his son was free, and the obvious assumption was that Musini was free too. Musini had had some narrow escapes. She would have been sent to serve his ancestors if it had not been for the opportune arrival of the woman Delli, to whose tales of the raiders they should have paid more attention, instead of promptly sacrificing her as they did. Musini; his first wife, the mother of his son, aging now, yet full of fire and personality surprising in a woman well past twenty years of age. Perhaps he never would have sent her to serve his ancestors, even if Delli had not come, even if she had always continued her disturbing behavior. Nessi was saying something to him as she plodded on in front of him, but he paid little attention, so preoccupied was he with his thoughts of Musini. There was Musini over there, just visible through the trees, and a boy by her side — Lanu. It was all so matter-of-course that for a moment Loa did not realize the startling implications of what he saw. Musini stepped out from behind a tree and waved an arm. Musini without a doubt — Loa stared at her so hard that he did not pay attention to his footing; he stumbled over a root and with difficulty saved himself from falling.

"I am choked," said Nessi, peevishly, when she recovered from the jerk of the chain against her throat. "Cannot you walk with more care?"

It sounded as she were addressing her husband rather than the god Loa, but Loa had no ears for her. Already the few steps he had taken had changed all the lines of visibility between the trees of the forest; he was already doubtful about just where he had seen Musini, and he could see nothing now either of her or of Lanu. Loa's heart, working hard because of the heat and the exertions of his body, was now pumping harder than ever, seeming to fill his breast so that he could not inflate his lungs. He stumbled again.

"What is the matter with you?" snapped Nessi. "That is the second time you have choked me."

The complaining voice pierced through Loa's preoccupation.

"May hairy devils pull off your arms and legs," he said.

The god Loa had never used or contemplated using curses; in the old days he had ridden as serenely above such earthly things as his sister the moon had ridden serenely above the clouds — the expression he had just used he had overheard at some time or other and stored in his subconscious memory, and now it had come from his lips like the words used by a gently nurtured woman of our day under an anesthetic.

"And may red ants burrow into your belly," retorted Nessi.

Presumably all the way along the line of slaves there were violent quarrels — no couple could spend days tied at opposite ends of a stick without quarreling, unless they were utterly sunk in apathy. Loa did not continue this unseemly exchange of ill wishes; even if he had known any more curses he was too busy trying to look over his right shoulder for Lanu and Musini again. But the path he was following wound about with nothing to call attention to its windings, and the fact that he had first seen them over his right shoulder did not mean at all that they were in that relative direction now.

"Oh, walk more steadily," nagged Nessi. "I am so weary. The pole chafes my shoulders."

Loa paid no attention, and the exasperated Nessi reached up with her hands and took hold of the ends of the fork and gave them a maddening tug, so that the chain at Loa's end rasped violently against the nape of his neck.

"Do not do that!" he said, roused once more to awareness of his surroundings.

"I will do it! I want to do it!" said Nessi. "You make my way hard for me, and I shall make yours hard for you."

And with that she tugged at the yoke again, exasperating

Loa so that he in his turn took hold of the pole and shook it, battering Nessi's fork against the back of her head.

"You hurt me!" shrieked Nessi, but that was just what Loa wanted to do. He thought darkly for a moment of twisting the pole and strangling Nessi as she stood, until he realized that he could not do that without strangling himself. So he made his neck muscles rigid and contented himself with poking Nessi in the back of the neck with the fork. A frightful pain across his shoulders made him stop; the Arab had come up beside them and was cutting at them with his whip.

"Not that!" snarled the Arab.

He gave Loa two more cuts for good measure and then transferred his attentions to Nessi. She screamed as the kurbash bit into her thighs — her back was screened by the tusk slung from the pole. Loa heard the screams and saw the angry welts appear on her thighs, with intense satisfaction.

"Now go on in peace," said the Arab, with a stupid misuse of a forest idiom, but his meaning was clear enough. They went on, with Nessi weeping and wailing over her sorrows, and Loa more and more irritated by her.

In the late afternoon the march came to an end, in the main street of a deserted village. Here there was none of the ample space which had been available at the original encampment. Instead the slaves were herded into the street and packed tight, filling the whole area between the two rows of houses. Loa found himself jostled and surrounded by strange men and women, some of the latter with footsore children running at their sides. A babel of sound went up around him, accompanied by the stench of sweating bodies.

"Is this their town?" asked Nessi, bewildered, through the din.

"I do not know," said Loa, but Nessi had not waited for a reply. She cast herself upon the ground completely exhausted, and so did the other slaves — poles, arms, legs, and bundles all jumbled together.

An hour later, with evening at hand, there was an eddy in the crowd. Two slaves were walking through the press with a feeding trough on their shoulders; they were escorted by a group of Arabs and mercenaries who slashed right and left with sticks and whips to restrain the eager mob. A double handful of cooked plantain each; it called for many troughs to supply even that moderate ration, but they were correspondingly quickly emptied, and brought round again filled with water. The slaves drank from them like animals; and then, hunger and thirst to some extent allayed, they could lie down again, in their own and in each others' filth, to sleep, higgledy-piggledy, like animals, with heads pillowed on bosoms or thighs; and when it rained, as it did twice during the night, trying (as well as poles and chains and loads permitted) to huddle together closer. Around them, during the hours of darkness, a few of the raiders kept guard.

C H A P T E R

V I I I

I<small>T WAS STILL DARK</small> when the slaves on the fringe of the crowd were roused next day; it was hardly after dawn when it was Nessi's and Loa's turn to move off after them. There was a running stream at which they could kneel to drink, at the end of the village, and there were troughs of food prepared from which they could each take their double handful to eat as they walked along — Loa had to rest his hands on the pole so as to eat out of them. The same endless march, the same heat and weariness and misery. The torment of flies and mosquitoes; the hurried mouthfuls of water snatched as they forded the streams. The whip of the Arabs, the sticks of their mercenaries. The same march, the same torments, the same whips, day following day, until the day of deliverance. No slave counted the days.

The man beside whom Loa had slept had entertained him for a brief while with an account of something he had seen the previous day — he talked freely to Loa, whom he was addressing in ignorance of his status. (It might not have been different had he known.) During the march this man had seen a forest antelope, bewildered at the passage of so many men and women, dashing between the trees and then coming to a startled full stop. An Arab was close beside Loa's informant. He had put his gun to his shoulder — the man's pantomime was vivid — and then *boom!* The antelope had fallen down dead. Dead, quite dead, with the blood running from his side and his mouth. Dead, killed at a distance no arrow could be impelled over, killed by the bang and the puff of strange-smelling smoke. The memory of the story gave Loa something to think about as he plodded along behind Nessi. It was a strange power these gray-faced men had. With the bow and the poisoned arrow Loa had been familiar all his life, of course. And he had killed men with an unseen force — more than once he had told them that he was at enmity with them, and that had been enough to make those men waste away and die. But forest antelopes, like parrots and monkeys and red ants, were not subject to his power. Even a man took long days to die. He did not fall bleeding as that forest antelope had done, according to the narrator — as the men had done that Delli had told about. Loa knew the limitations on his powers; these men could do something he could not do. It was a disturbing thought; if they were only men, then what was he?

Here, at a point where the trail made a sharp bend, was an Arab, standing with the stream of slaves flowing past him as he supervised the march with his kurbash flicking in his hand. At sight of him Loa took care to pick his steps carefully, so as not to stumble and invite a blow — he had learned much during these dreadful days. And as he approached he heard the high-pitched twang of a bowstring. He did not see the flight of the missile, but he was instantly conscious of when it reached its mark. He saw it strike, hitting the Arab just below the jaw, where face and neck meet; Loa was within a few yards of the Arab when it happened. The Arab did not stagger; he put up his hand with surprise and took hold of the barbed arrow as it hung down on his shoulder from his face. Some red blood — only a few drops — dripped from the wound. The Arab swung round to see who had attacked him, reaching at the same time for the gun which hung by a strap over his shoulder. But he was unsteady on his feet now; his knees bent under him, and although he braced himself up for a moment they gave way again, and he fell on his face moving only feebly as Nessi and Loa reached him. Arrow poison works fast, when injected into the trunk of the body rather than in a limb, and fastest of all in the blood vessels of the neck. Two people came leaping across the glade to where Nessi and Loa stood by the body. One was little Lanu, his left hand grasping his three-foot bow and an arrow; his right hand held yet another arrow with the bowstring in the notch, ready to draw and loose. And with him ran Musini, naked, with her long breasts swinging in front of her; in her hand she bore Lanu's ceremonial battle-ax, the little ax which Litti the smith had made for him at Loa's special request. The bright edge gleamed in the twilight of the forest. Musini's eyes met Loa's. She momentarily clapped her hand to her forehead in salutation, but she allowed no ceremonial to delay her in the course of action she had planned. She hacked with her ax at the creepers which suspended the load from the pole; they were tough and did not part easily, but Musini slashed away with all the considerable strength of her skinny arms until the elephant's tusk fell to the ground, relieving Loa and Nessi of its considerable weight. No word had yet been spoken. Musini now turned the edge of the ax against the pole which connected the two prisoners. Twice she hacked at it, but it was of a tough elastic wood with a hard surface; it bent under her blows and the ax rebounded from it having made hardly a dent.

"Enough, Mother!" squealed Lanu. He was standing with his arrow half drawn, looking sharply to left and to right beside the dying Arab. "We must not wait."

"Come, Lord, come, you," said Musini.

As Nessi still stood bewildered Musini reached out her hand and took Nessi's, and turned to run through the forest, with Loa lumbering after her. Some of the other slaves made a move to follow them, but Lanu checked them.

"Back!" he shouted in his high voice, threatening them with his arrow. "Back!"

He drew away from the surging knot of slaves and then turned and ran at top speed after the others; Loa running over the spongy unequal ground with the yoke pounding on his shoulders, looked down to find Lanu running beside him. Lanu extended a hand to him, as Musini had done to Nessi, as if to drag his big bulk along after him. Somebody — either Nessi or Loa — tripped and stumbled, and the pair of them fell crashing to the ground, the yokes and chains lacerating their necks, the breath driven from their bodies.

"Come on, come on," shrieked Lanu, dancing beside them.

They scrambled to their feet and Musini seized the bewildered Nessi's hand again and dragged her forward. They heard a shout far behind them — muffled as it reached their ears through the trees — and knew that pursuit had commenced.

"Run, oh, run!" pleaded Musini.

And so they ran through the forest, through the twilight, between the great friendly trunks of the trees. They came to a little brook flowing between wide marshy banks; the mud was halfway up their thighs as they made their way through. It slowed them, but it did not stop them, and, once across, they resumed their heartbreaking pace and kept it up until Nessi began to wail, little short sounds which were all her breathless condition allowed. Her pace slackened until they were obliged to stop and allow her to fall gasping on the ground. Loa fell too, his breath coming heavily, and his legs aching. Musini was content to squat beside him, while Lanu was still sufficiently fresh to make his way back, bow and arrow in hand, to peer through the trees so as to be able to give warning in case of pursuit.

After a few seconds Loa was able to raise his head, and his eyes met those of Musini beside him.

"Is it well with you, Lord?" she asked. She used the honorific mode of address — which she had not used in the days when Loa was god and king — and her wrinkled face bore a fond smile. She put out a hand and caressed Loa's sweating shoulder.

"It is well with me," said Loa.

To Loa's credit Musini's affection took him by surprise.

His fall from divinity had left him with little belief in himself. People had served him when he was a god presumably because that was what he was. Now that he was a naked worthless slave he was surprised and touched that anyone, even skinny wrinkled Musini, should serve him and love him for himself alone.

"My face is bright at seeing you again, Lord," said Musini, and there was some literal truth in the trite metaphor, as a glance at her showed.

A faint cry from the end of the glade forestalled Loa's reply; Lanu was running back to them and his gestures warned them of pursuit.

"We must run," said Musini, getting to her feet. "Rise up, you."

The last words were addressed to the gasping Nessi, and when the latter made no further response than a groan Musini kicked her in the ribs with her tough bare foot.

"Stand up!" shrieked Musini, and took Nessi by the hair to drag her to her feet. The ax swung in Musini's other hand, and she shot a glance at Loa. "Shall I cut off her head? Then we would not have to take her with us, Lord."

"No, she bears one end of the pole," said Loa — a perfectly sound argument, although it is just possible that Loa was actuated by other motives than immediate expediency.

Lanu had reached them by now.

"Come on!" he squeaked.

Nessi had risen to her feet, perhaps as a result of Musini's grim suggestion, and Lanu took one of her hands, and Musini the other, and they began to run again, with weary legs moving stiffly at first, running and running, with a weariness that grew until it seemed impossible even once again to put one foot in front of the other, and when they could not run they walked, with steps that grew slower and shorter as the day went on, as the twilight of the forest deepened with the coming of night.

"Now we can rest at last," said Musini in the end, when it was growing too dark to see even the ground under their feet.

They stopped, and Nessi settled what Loa was going to do by dropping flat to the ground where she stood, so that Loa was dragged down too. With the coming of darkness, there was no chance of the Arabs continuing their pursuit. He was safe and he was free.

"Tomorrow, with the first light, we shall release you from this chain and yoke, Lord," said Musini.

She put out her hands in the darkness and felt for Loa's chafed neck. The touch was marvelously soothing; Loa found himself stroking Musini's skinny arms.

"I am hungry," said Nessi, suddenly. "Oh, I am very hungry. I wish I could eat."

"Shut that howling mouth," said Musini. She was utterly scandalized, as her tone showed, by the familiarity of Nessi's manner of address.

"But I am hungry," protested Nessi.

"Hungry you are and hungry you will remain," was all the sympathy Musini had to offer. "There is nothing to eat now. There have been many days when Lanu and I have eaten nothing."

"There is nothing to eat?" asked Loa. With this turn of the conversation he was now sleepily conscious of the hunger that possessed him.

"For you, Lord, there is this," said Musini.

She fumbled in the darkness, presumably in the little bag which hung from her neck between her breasts, and then she found Loa's hand and pressed something into it.

"What is this?" he asked.

"White ants, Lord, all we have. I gathered them this morning."

White ants lived in little tunnels in dead trees, harmless creatures enough, quite unlike their ferocious red and black brothers. Their bodies were succulent, and could be eaten by hungry people; but these ants had been long dead, crushed into a paste by Musini's fingers and carried all day in her little bag. There was only a couple of mouthfuls of them anyway; Loa chewed the bitter unsatisfying stuff and swallowed it down with a fleeting regret for the double handful of tapioca which had been served out to him that morning.

"It is hard to gather food in the forest," said Lanu.

"That is so," agreed Musini. "Yet has Lanu been clever. He has been like a man, Lord. It was Lanu who made the bow and the arrows. Lanu is our worthy son."

"It was I who killed the gray-faced man," said Lanu. "Did you see him fall? My arrow was in his throat, where I had aimed it. It was I who made the poison. I used the creeper juice. I made it as I had seen Tiri the son of Minu make it."

"It was well done, son," said Loa. "And how was it you came to escape when first the Arabs came to the town?"

They told him between them, Musini and Lanu, of their adventures on the day of the raid and since then. They had fled into the clearing at the first alarm, together, for Lanu had been sleeping in his mother's house. Lanu had snatched up and borne with him his little ceremonial ax, his latest present from his father, and it had stood them in good stead. Without it they would have been nearly helpless in the forest, but with it they had the power that edged steel conveys. Lanu had shaped and trimmed the bow; Musini had braided the bowstring from the flexible creeper fibers. They had followed the slave caravan from camp to camp, living on what they could gather in the forest. With vigilance and precaution they had escaped the snares of the little people, although twice arrows aimed at them had narrowly missed one or other of them. Every day at some time or other they had seen Loa, far more often than he had seen them, and by continual watching they had made themselves familiar with the Arabs' methods, so that eventually they had planned the rescue and carried it out successfully.

"That was well done indeed, my son," said Loa.

There were the strangest feelings inside him at that moment, the oddest misgivings. Lanu was a clever little boy, but it could not have been Lanu who was responsible for all this. Lanu could not have displayed the singleness of purpose, the resolution and the ingenuity which had resulted in his rescue. Lanu might have loved his father, but — Loa's newfound humility asserted itself — it was incredible that

[117]

he would have gone through all that risk and labor to rescue him except at the instance of his mother. It must have been Musini who did the planning and who showed the resolution. It must have been Musini's devotion which had kept them to the task. An odd state of affairs indeed, when women should thus display initiative and determination; there was something unnatural and disturbing in the thought of it.

And it was disturbing in a different way to think of Musini's devotion. In the time of his divinity, Loa would have thought nothing of someone running risks to help him or even to contribute slightly to his comfort; but since that time Loa had been in contact with a new reality. It was not a god whom Musini had rescued — Loa faced the fact squarely — but a slave, a slave in bonds, a worthless chattel. It could not have been from religious conviction that Musini had exerted herself thus. It was Loa the man and not Loa the god whom she had rescued. There must be a personal tie. All this was terribly difficult to work out in Loa's untrained brain and with his limited vocabulary Loa, the man with forty wives, knew almost nothing of love until now. He was facing something nearly as new as what he faced when he first felt doubts about being a god. It called for a fresh orientation of himself. Thanks to his recent experiences, Loa found difficulty in swallowing the undoubted fact that Musini must love him for himself alone. He could not take it sublimely for granted. His exhausted brain grappled feebly with all these astonishing developments, with the new phenomenon of love, with the concept of women

[118]

being capable of decisive action, and then it shrank back exhausted from the encounter.

"I am thirsty as well as hungry," said Nessi.

She was voicing everyone's sentiments, but that did not help her.

"Did I not say shut that mouth?" snapped Musini. "Let us sleep, for we are weary."

The blackest possible night was round them, the darkness of night in the forest, when the hand could not be seen before the face. Beneath them the leafmold was soggy and damp; around them the stifling hot moist air was not stirred by the slightest breeze. Nessi had petulantly flung herself prone at Musini's rebuke, with a jerk at the pole which had forced Loa to change his position. He tried to settle himself again; Musini's arms found him and pillowed his head upon her shoulder regardless of the discomfort the yoke and chain brought her. They slept in a huddled group, bitten by insects, with the sweat running irritatingly over their naked skins until the chill of dawn crept through the trees, momentarily bringing a coolness that was pleasant until it broke through their sleep to set them shivering and huddling even closer together.

CHAPTER

I X

IN THE GRAY TWILIGHT it was Musini who proposed the first move of the day.

"Now let us take off this yoke from your neck, Lord," she said. "Lanu, come and see what must be done."

The yoke was of tough elastic wood; the few links of chain were stoutly attached by staples driven deep into the ends. Lanu tugged at them, as Loa had often done, and equally unavailingly.

"You must cut through the wood, son," suggested Loa.

It was not so easy to do with an ax, although with a knife it would have been comparatively simple. Loa could be of no help; all he could do was to sit as still as he could on the ground while Lanu chipped away at the end of the yoke, with Musini holding it steady in desperate anxiety that expressed itself in fierce curses at Nessi at the other end of the yoke lest she should move. Lanu removed chip after chip; the edge of the ax found a crack in the end of the pole and enabled him to lever off a larger chip still. Eventually both limbs of one of the staples were exposed over most of their length.

"Try to pull that out now," said Lanu, speaking as one man speaks to another.

Loa put one hand to the chain and one to the yoke, tugging with all the strength the awkward position allowed. The veins stood out on his forehead; he tugged and he tugged, and suddenly the staple flew out. Loa dropped chain and yoke, and stepped out, free of his bonds. It was a strange sensation. He could look at Nessi, still held at her end; he could look at her from different angles, and at different distances, and he could step hither and thither without any thought for her. The feel of his free neck and shoulders was almost unnatural. He danced in his sense of freedom and Lanu danced with him. A great wave of paternal affection surged up in Loa. Lanu was no little boy now; recent events had made a man of him, child though he was, but Loa loved him. Nessi was watching them, waiting her turn to be set free.

"Now we can go," said Musini.

She must have forgotten the fact that Nessi was still fastened in her end of the pole; it was only a momentary incident, but it seemed as if Musini intended that she and Loa and Lanu should strike off now through the forest, leaving Nessi to trail the yoke after her until overtaken by inevitable death from starvation or at the hands of the little people. But Loa and Lanu had turned and addressed themselves to the task of freeing Nessi at the moment Musini spoke, so that the implications of the words passed unnoticed. They chipped away at the yoke until a long pull by Loa tore out the staple, and yoke and chain fell to the ground.

"It is gone!" said Nessi, breathing relief.

She knelt and embraced Loa's knees in thankfulness; it was an immediate change in her demeanor. Yesterday they were fellow slaves, sharing the utter equality of the yoke. Today the memories of Loa's divinity came flooding back, and Nessi groveled before him as different as could be imagined from the peevish wench whom he had to placate in the slavers' camp.

"That is well," said Musini grimly. She had picked up the little ax and was swinging it idly in her hand. "And now?"

They all four looked at each other.

"And now?" said Musini again.

Four human beings — setting aside for the moment Loa's fictitious divinity — in the immensity of the twilit forest; naked, their sole possessions the little ax and the bow which it had helped to shape. Their world of security with its solid past of tradition and seemingly changeless future had been destroyed, and this was the moment of their rebirth into a new world, as if they were babies without parents. Rain in thick heavy drops was falling about them from the dense screen of foliage overhead, monotonous and depressing. They were community dwellers, accustomed all their lives to living in the bustle of a town surrounded by their fellows; bred, moreover, for a hundred generations as community dwellers. The little people wandered in the forest migrating eternally in little groups each no larger than a family, but Loa and the others were not little people. In each person's mind, even in little Lanu's, there was the longing for a permanent settlement, for houses, and plantain groves. Their minds went back miserably to the past and returned empty and longing. All waited for someone else to speak, but Lanu and Musini and Nessi turned their eyes upon Loa. It was not inspiration that came upon him. He was voicing his own sentiments and those of everyone else when he spoke, the words torn from him by his inward yearnings.

"Let us go home," he said.

"Home!" echoed Nessi in a fervent sigh.

"Home!" said Lanu with a skip of joy.

For a moment it seemed as if the twilight of the forest had lifted, as if the raindrops had ceased to fall about them. The futility of their existence had ended with the suggestion of a purpose, with a plan for the future. As they thought of home they thought of the sunlight blazing into the town's street, the cries of the children and the smoke of the cooking fires; that vision died out when they remembered what had happened to the town, and yet something remained to which their minds could cling. There would at least be the site of the clearing, overgrown by forest. The banana groves would not yet be overgrown. It was a place they knew, the place where they had spent their whole lives. More than that; the suggestion of going home provided them with an objective. Mere futile wandering in the forest had no appeal for them; home was a goal towards which they could struggle.

"So we will go home," said Musini, nodding her head significantly, chewing the cud of internal calculations.

She did not have to say more to bring them all back to reality. They were lost in the forest; and they all knew what that meant. To go a mile into the forest — in certain circumstances, to go a mere hundred yards — without painstaking precautions meant being utterly lost, so that one direction seemed as good as any other. And they were separated from home by a march of many days' duration. In the forest they had no means of knowing north or south or east or west, and if they had, they still did not know whether home lay to north or to south or to east or to west of them. It was deep in the tradition of the town dweller never on any account to go into the forest beyond the well-known landmarks. And to all of them the forest was the world; they had no conception of any limits to it. Their minds could not conceive of any area that was not twilit by the shadow of vast trees, steamy hot, and dripped upon by torrential downpours of rain. So that not one of them had the faintest maddest hope — or fear — of ever breaking out of the forest by traveling long enough in the same direction. The world to them was made up of illimitable unknown forest with concealed in the midst of it a tiny patch of known, and therefore friendly and desirable, forest encircling their home.

A rush of feeling surged up in Loa's breast. Courage, it may have been; obstinacy, perhaps; desperation, possibly. He could think of nothing beyond the two alternatives, on the one hand of determining to make his way home, and on the other of wandering in futile fashion here in the forest to the end of his days. The first might be mad, unattainable, but at least it was preferable to the second.

"Yes, we will go home," he said. "Home! We will find our way there."

He abandoned himself to the utterly absurd: a fanatic preaching, an impossible crusade, sweeping his audience off their feet. He brandished clenched fists at the lowering forest above them and around them.

"Home!" he yelled again.

"Home!" yelled Lanu, waving his bow.

"Home!" said Nessi.

Musini turned upon her.

"And so before we start for home perhaps you will find us food?"

There is food to be found in the forest, enough to support life if one is content to live like a bird, not from day to day but from hour to hour, with almost every waking moment devoted to the search. Funguses grow in the leafmold and on the trunks of decaying trees — from the true mushroom, clean and delicious but rare, to the watery toadstools, foul-smelling but brilliantly colored, a mouthful of which means death. Intermediate between them come other species of varying degrees of nutritive value and toxicity, all to be noted by a sharp eye when wandering in the forest. There are white ants, not formidable like their black and red cousins, but harmless, with pulpy bodies that offer a good deal of nutriment when eaten alive, but it takes many, many white ants to make a meal, and it is usually a matter of pure good fortune to open up one of the tunneled channels along which white ants circulate. If a great number can be caught they can be crushed into a paste which will endure for a couple of days without rotting, making a ration that can be saved for an emergency, but at the price of some of the nutritive qualities being lost with the pressed-out juices. There are snakes and frogs; on rare occasions a good archer can bring down a bird or even, more rarely, a monkey. To secure a forest antelope the forest wanderer must cease for a time to be a wanderer. He must dig a pitfall in a game-track and plant a poisoned stake in it and wait maybe for days before an antelope falls into it — it will never happen at all if he does his work clumsily so that the antelope's instincts are aroused and he leaps aside from the too obvious danger. In the same way, if the wanderer has time to spare he can — as the pygmies do — plant poisoned skewers in the track, or a concealed bent bow in the undergrowth with an arrow on the string and a trigger device that can be tripped by a strand of creeper across the path; the same device can actuate a deadfall — a log armed with a poisoned stake hung up precariously in the branches above.

The fruits of the forest are doled out by nature with a sparing hand; they are infinite in their variety but sparse in their occurrence; the vast trees which fight their way through to light and air and life leave small chance for fruit-bearing trees to live. Yet some of the vines bear fruit, and it is possible to drag the flexible stems down, tearing them from their hold on the trunks, until the fruit is in reach. The amoma bears a watery fruit with a bitter kernel — either is of some use to fill an empty belly. A giant species of acacia bears pods of beans with indigestible skins yet which nevertheless can be bruised and pounded and cooked into food. There are wild plums — tart, leathery things — which can be found where soil conditions do not allow the trees to grow so tall; wild mangoes, woody and untempting; phrynia; even some of the bamboos which grow in the marshy spots bear berries which can be eaten and will support life.

With all these things Loa and the others had some sort of acquaintance, largely acquired when young; wandering as infants on the edge of the clearing the ceaseless appetite of childhood had been gratified between meals by the gleanings of the forest. Loa knew less about them than any of the others, for he had had a pampered childhood as a god almost from birth. One thing he did know, and that was that it was not by standing still that food was to be found in the forest.

"Food?" he said to Musini in reply to her remark to Nessi. "We shall find it as we go along."

He took the little ax from her hand and picked up the pole which had so recently joined him to Nessi. A few blows and a jerk parted one fork from the stem. The links of chain dangled from the other fork and made a clumsy, flail-like weapon, but a weapon, nevertheless. He brandished it with a feeling of satisfaction and gave back the ax to Musini.

"Let us go," he said.

"Which way, Lord?" asked Musini instantly, and Loa stared round down the twilit avenues between the trees with some uncertainty.

"It was this way that we came," said Lanu. "You can see the tracks. That leads to the path you were following with the gray-faced men."

"That is the way we shall go," said Loa. "They will have

gone far onward by the time we reach the path again."

And with that, with so little ceremony, they began their vast and precarious journey. It was as well that Lanu had made his explanation regarding the tracks, for Loa's unskilled eye could see nothing on the monotonous leafmold. Even Lanu's sharp eyes were put to a severe test, as the profuse rains at dawn had gone far to obliterate the heavy traces they had left in their flight from the slavers. Lanu went in front, his bow and arrow ready for instant action; the others spread out behind him, looking about them as they walked, seeking something — anything — that would relieve in small measure the pangs of hunger that afflicted them the moment they admitted to themselves that they were hungry. Musini found a cluster of fine white mushrooms, and she brought the largest to Loa. It was wonderful to set one's teeth in the firm white flesh, to taste the keen pungent flavor of the raw mushroom, to swallow it down into a stomach that complained bitterly of being empty. Other finds of Musini's she shared with Lanu. Nessi plodded along by herself; what she found went into her own stomach.

They came to the boggy stream which they had crossed yesterday in their flight; the leafmold under their feet grew less and less resilient, and water oozed out of it as they trod; soon Lanu turned back towards them in despair.

"I do not know where we went," he said pathetically. "I can see no more."

He had been proud to guide them up to this moment, and now he was pitifully aware of his shortcomings, no longer a pert young man, but a child again. And once more they all looked at Loa, while round them the silent forest waited for his decision.

"I will tell you which way we shall go," said Loa — he said it to comfort Lanu more than for any other reason, for he had no plan in his mind at that moment.

He looked round him at the silent trees, at the glades opening up around him. He could not think while he looked at them, and so he pressed his fists against his eyes as a stimulus to thought, pressed them firmly in as he used to do when he was a god and had a decision to make. The turning lights before his eyes were not disturbing like those silent glades. His mind grappled with the problem, to bear it down by sheer strength like an unpracticed giant overpowering a skilled lightweight wrestler. Seeping through this bog was a little river, a childish version of the big river wherein his sister the moon was wont to hide herself. The superstitions of his lifetime warred with the hard logic inculcated by his recent experiences, for his first tendency was to think of the little stream as being endowed with human likes and dislikes, as being likely to wander here and there in accordance with its own whim, stopping if it saw fit, going on or going back if it saw fit. But he made himself realize that rivers run eternally in the same way, that some unchangeable law made them do so, just as water would always run out of a tilted bowl. A weak mortal — or an unguided god, for Loa was not quite ready to admit his mortality to himself — might wander in the forest in a thousand directions with no definition of route at all. But a stream must flow from somewhere to somewhere. It at least had a unity of purpose a human could not display.

"Where is the water?" he asked of Lanu, taking his hands from his eyes.

"It is here, my father," said Lanu.

"Lord," interposed Musini, correcting him.

"No," said Loa. "We are men together, and I am father of Lanu."

Lanu's delighted grin was ample reward for the condescension the fondness of Loa's heart had evoked. They plodded through the mud to where the little stream lay between its flat banks; the trees met above it, and all about them their black and naked roots twined over the mud. Loa plucked a fragment of bark from a tree trunk and dropped it into the center of the stream while the others breathlessly awaited his decision. The current here was hardly perceptible, but very slowly the bit of bark moved with the water relative to the bank; Loa was watching it as intently as he had ever watched the heaped rib bones in the firelight. He noted the motion, and looked downstream to where the little river lost itself to view amid the trees.

"That is the way we shall go," he said.

He said it with all his natural authority; he made no attempt to analyze the motives that had brought about this decision. Enough confidence in his powers still lingered with him for him to feel that whatever he might be guided to do must be right. And he was sustained in his confidence by the reception given to his decision by the others. They were lost in the forest, uneasy, aimless, and their misgivings had returned with redoubled force when Lanu had lost the track. It was intensely reassuring to them for someone to set them on the move again in accordance with some definite plan, any plan, especially when they could feel that Loa's supernatural powers would ensure that it was a good plan. It raised them from depression to something better than resignation, and started them again upon their vast journey with new strength.

CHAPTER

X

THERE WERE ADVANTAGES and disadvantages about following the course of the sluggish stream through the forest.
The marshy nature of the soil altered the prevailing character of the trees; they were not quite so monstrous, so that
the smaller species had a chance of survival; there were
wood beans and amoma to be found, and the marshes contained numbers of bullfrogs, big creatures, which could be
caught if the four wanderers formed a wide circle, hip-deep
in the ooze. The thighs of a dozen frogs, torn from the
wretched creatures while they were still alive, and eaten
raw, would have constituted a fair meal even for a man of
Loa's vast appetite, but they unfortunately never caught
even a dozen between them. But if the problem of food was
rendered easier, the problem of travel was rendered harder.
Inexplicably here and there the forest would yield altogether to growth of another sort, to belts of small trees and
tangled undergrowth. The change would at first be imperceptible; the undergrowth would close round them insidi-
ously like some wary enemy, and they would recognize the
nature of the country too late to turn back, too late even to

turn aside, for the extent of the belt on either hand could not be guessed at. Then there would be nothing to do save to plunge forward, stooping under, climbing over, hacking a path when necessary, gratefully following a game-track when one presented itself for a few yards, in an atmosphere yet more steamy and still than among the tall trees, and far more noticeable because of the increased physical exertion necessary to make progress. Even where the vegetation was far too thick for the sky to be seen, they plunged along through suffocating twilight until at last the slow disappearance of undergrowth, an increase in the height of the trees, and eventually the welcome feeling of leafmold underfoot, told them that they were through the obstacle. In these struggles Loa, ax in hand, would lead, with Nessi following him and Lanu following her and Musini bringing up the rear.

It was vastly difficult to retain any sense of direction in that kind of jungle, but they learned that it was a help for them all to echo a cry by Loa, who, hearing the shouts behind him, could judge the direction in which the little column was pointing, and that would help him to correct his own new direction. His instincts were sound enough to save him from ever becoming completely reversed as to his orientation while in the undergrowth; on emergence once more into the dark groves a cast to the right (they were following down the left bank of the stream) would eventually — although sometimes only after a long and despairing journey — bring them back to the boggy borders of the river. It was impossible to stay close to the water's edge;

the bogginess, the sharp roots in the mud, even the leeches which lived there in great numbers, prohibited that.

They were lean with their exertions — the once well-rounded Nessi was lean, so that every rib could be counted, and her breasts shrunken and her hipbones clearly apparent; and they were all scratched and cut so that their bodies were covered with healing scars and open wounds. They had purulent sores where ticks had burrowed into their skins or where the bites of black ants had become infected, and yet they went on through the forest from dawn until dark every day, for twelve hours each day, and no question arose among them of ceasing this monstrous labor. They were still faced with the same alternative, that to halt meant to reconcile their minds to permanent settlement here in the forest, while to go on meant still cherishing the hope of eventually reaching "home." And in Loa's mind there were still some residual traces of his confidence in himself as a god. Something within himself told him to push on downstream, and nothing occurred to make him doubt this inward inspiration, which drove him eternally onward and carried his followers with him.

Yet he was by no means the perfect leader, for he was not nearly as skilled in the details of forest life as were the others. He was dependent on them to such an extent that it seems likely that had he been alone he would have starved. He could not recognize sources of food nearly as quickly as the others could; Musini did much to feed him and even Lanu contributed, vaguely amused at this big father of his who was so incompetent in some ways. He could not make

fire — Musini and Lanu were expert at it and could produce a flame in less than fifteen minutes of work if the
materials were not hard to find. They needed a lump of a
softish wood, and a foot-long stick of hard wood, and some
handfuls of the rotting fiber pulled from under the bark of
a fallen tree. They would loop the string of Lanu's bow
round the stick, and then restring the bow. Musini pressed
the end of the stick firmly into the block of wood, while
Lanu moved the bow from side to side, rotating the stick
rapidly against the block, cutting a short shallow groove
into its grain. As the groove grew hot Musini, still pressing
the stick hard against the block, would take a handful of
dry fiber and cram it round the rotating point, pressing it
down into the groove. The fiber grew hot, the sparks were
caught in it, and soon Musini bent to blow into the handful,
coaxing it into a glow that could with skillful management
be transferred to light dry wood kept ready to hand. It was
a series of operations with which Musini had long been
familiar, and which she carried out with the skill of long
practice. With the fire so obtained they could toast into
digestibility the wood beans gathered during the day, and
anything they might have in the nature of meat could be
cooked on long sticks. The smell of the fire, the smoke by
day and the flame by night, would reveal their position to
the little people, but that was a risk they had to take. So far
they had seen nothing of them except their handiwork —
the poisoned skewers in the trails, and the deadfalls over-
hanging them.

In the lighting of fires, in most of the hunting for food,

Loa was of less use than Musini and Lanu, even less than Nessi. He was both inexperienced and ignorant; it was as if in these practical affairs of daily life his wife and child accorded him a good-humored toleration, even a tolerant contempt. He was to be reverently followed implicitly in matters the others knew nothing about, such as the route they should follow, but when it came to digging out white ants, or toasting frogs' legs on a stick before a fire, he was demonstrably less capable than they were. Lanu would sigh with a resignation prematurely adult, but Musini was even capable of shoving Loa aside. Loa was content to let it be so, for it did not lessen his opinion of himself — it did not even change it — that he should be unable to carry out duties always relegated to boys and women. He was content to squat and think his ponderous thoughts while the women might busy themselves, while Lanu might address himself to shaping a new arrow, chipping and whittling with his little ax, rubbing down on a stone, braiding the binding for the head out of creeper-fibers. Loa could squat and meditate, and eat the food they gave him, while Musini harassed Nessi as always with her sharp tongue. And at night he slept in Musini's loving but skinny arms.

It was ironical in consequence that Loa obtained for them one of the best meals they had. He was walking through the forest carrying his flail, the long pole that had once been his yoke, with the links of iron chain dangling from it, when he disturbed the black snake. Seven feet long it was, as thick nearly as a man's thigh, one of the largest specimens of the most deadly inhabitant of the forest. Loa saw the snake just in time and stopped; the snake was coiled, ready to defend itself, not seeking to strike needlessly, its eyes glaring coldly back at him. Loa stood as still as a statue, with every muscle tense, and then at last he stepped aside to circle round the thing. The black snake, coldly confident in its power, turned its flat head to watch him. Yet there was a second when Loa had an opening, and Loa seized the opportunity. He struck like lightning with his flail, muscles and eye co-ordinating with the exactitude of a primitive man's, his prodigious strength swinging his weapon at a speed equal to the snake's. The iron links struck into the snake just behind the head, probably disabling the creature at that single blow, but Loa struck again and again and again at the coils as they straightened and bent, not ceasing until his arms were weary and the sweat was running down him in rivers. Before him the snake still moved, its unco-ordinated segments heaving although its back was broken in a dozen places. Loa raised his voice in a shout of triumph which brought the others running to him, to look down from a safe distance at the dying death. With his flail Loa carefully poked the head free from the coils — the mouth still gaped and shut — and pounded it into an unrecognizable mass, and even then he was not satisfied until he had taken the little ax and severed the shattered head from the body. He did so with another exultant shout, in which the others joined.

Here was food in plenty, pounds and pounds of it, and none of your belly-aching beans at that, but meat — rich, delightful meat. They camped on the spot; they lit a fire, and Lanu went to work with his ax, skinning the creature as well as he could and hacking it into vast collops — disregarding its slight writhing at each blow — which soon were frizzling over the fire and giving out a savor that brought the water into Loa's mouth as he waited. He burned his fingers, callused though they were, as he seized the hot meat when it was given him; he burned his mouth as he bit into it. Juicy meat, fit food for a god; his big white teeth tore the meat from the bones and he swallowed it down with unmatched pleasure. And when that was finished there was another collop ready to be eaten, and after that another, so that the first pleasure of gratifying a fierce appetite blended with the next of eating steadily to fill an empty stomach, and from that he could progress to the next wonderful step of packing tight a stomach already comfortably full. To eat although he felt he could eat no more was a gratification of the mind acutely pleasurable after so long a while with never enough to eat. He ceased to squat, unable to bear longer the pressure of his thighs against his bulging belly. He lay on his side to eat his last collop, and he feebly let fall the last fragments, lying out straight and enjoying the perverse pleasure of the pain of overeating. He groaned in delightful agony.

It was that night that Loa added Nessi to his long list of wives, and presumably it was because that night he was filled with meat. Ura had been Nessi's husband, but Ura was most likely dead, and Nessi's child was dead, and it was likely that Nessi was a piece of property left without any owner at all, and in that case Loa was entitled to inherit, as he always did in similar circumstances. That was the only way in which a widow could come into anyone's hands who was not a relation, but it was perfectly legal and not unprecedented; but Loa had no thoughts about legality or precedents, and neither, it is to be feared, had Nessi, when Loa reached out his big arms to her in the faint light of the dying fire. It was a plain ebullition of animal spirits; for both of them it was a strange contrast, after having been attached to each other for so long by a five-foot pole, that added a fierce savor to their embrace — and for Loa there was the added contrast of Nessi's gentle submission after Musini's more exacting affection.

Next morning Musini was more bitter of tongue and chiding than ever, and Nessi was pert and inclined to be disrespectful to her, tossing her head at some request of Musini's. Musini darted a glance at Loa to see what his reaction would be, but Loa was experienced in the ways of rival wives — he was especially experienced in Musini's behavior in these conditions — and he blandly ignored the whole incident. He had no intention of being involved in any arguments, and he acted as if he had been completely unaware of any friction at all. He took his flail and started off on the day's march; the ants during the night had made a clean sweep of the remaining fragments of the snake, so that only white bones remained round the ashes of the fire, and already he was hungry, perhaps as a result of his exertions in the night. Certainly he was thirsty; he scooped up handfuls of water from the stream when he walked down to it and drank them with eagerness, and then he set his face downstream on the two coincident businesses of the day, to find that day's food and to go on towards home — if indeed home lay in that direction. And Nessi stayed close at his side, all that day and all that night.

The sky, unseen above the tops of the trees, was disturbed. Day after day in the late evening, the thunder would roll deafeningly, the flashes of lightning were bright enough to illuminate the forest so that the tree trunks could momentarily be seen, and the rain came streaming down in an abundance that spared nothing and no one, causing Loa and his followers hideous discomfort. The little people, in their normal life in the forest, used to counter this difficulty by erecting huts of phrynia leaves, temporary encampments which gave them shelter for several days before they were driven to move on by the consumption of the local food supply, but Loa's people had not the trick of it, and in any case never allowed themselves time before nightfall for any such labor. They had to endure their discomfort, changing their positions on the chilly wet leafmold, shifting back hurriedly when some alteration in conditions above them, some gust of wind perhaps, let loose a torrent of water, falling as if squirted from a hose upon naked skin, down through the roaring darkness. It meant sore heads and bad tempers in the morning, accentuating the nagging ill humor of Musini and the stubborn defiance of Nessi. Even Lanu was at times peevish and irritable, despite his perennial pride in doing man's work; and if the rain came on unusually early, making it impossible to light a fire at which to cook the wood beans they had gathered during the day, it meant going to bed supperless, and an early halt next day to enable them to satisfy their consuming hunger.

Yet there were days when there was compensation for their hardship. They were struggling through one of the stretches of forest where the growth grew thick, where above them the roof of greenery grew thin so as at times even to let through shafts of actual sunlight, when Lanu raised his voice in a high-pitched squeal, soaring up, up, up nearly to the pitch of a bat's squeak.

"Plantains! Plantains! Real plantains!" squealed Lanu.

"Never!" said Loa; that was his immediate reaction to the suggestion that plantains might be found growing in the virgin forest, but he checked himself when he remembered that Lanu might still be a child in years but was a man in the forest.

"Plantains!" cried Musini as Loa made his way through the undergrowth towards them.

So they were; desirable hands of fruit, each plantain almost the size of a man's forearm, many of them verging upon ripeness. Loa and Musini and Lanu, and Nessi when she straggled up to them, stood and gazed at them hanging close above their heads, dappled with sunshine.

"People have lived here," decided Musini. "This was a garden."

It seemed the only possible theory. The tangled jungle about them, of saplings and creepers, had until recently been a town clearing, and the trees had not yet grown sufficiently tall, and the parasites not sufficiently numerous, to destroy the plantain trees. The plantain in its Central African form is a product of civilization, which can only live with the help of man, who must fell the trees and root up the creepers to give it breathing space; the moment man's attention lapses, the forest crowds in again to suffocate the plantain. Normally a clearing will provide two or three crops before the exhaustion of the soil makes it desirable to make a fresh clearing and replant the plantain suckers. But this could not be an exhausted clearing, for here were the plantains in full bearing. And that mass of vegetation over there, Loa realized, of tangled vine and gay orchids, must be the stump of a felled tree, buried already under parasites, and yet not felled too long ago. There was no word in Loa's vocabulary for "year" or "month," living as he did on the Equator where there was never any change of season, but he guessed that that tree could not have been felled at most more than two fruitings of the plantain ago. But where were the men who had felled the tree? He wrinkled his forehead momentarily over the puzzle before he put it aside to indulge himself in the pleasurable knowledge that here were plantains ripe for eating.

Lanu and he hacked a clearing in the steamy undergrowth, felling and dragging aside saplings and creepers alike, so that he could look up and see blue sky above him, a hole in the greenery which had roofed him in for so many days, over the edge of which his brother the sun glared down at him brassily. Loa saluted him with fraternal affection. The habits of thought of a life time were not so easily

[142]

cast aside; whatever doubts Loa entertained regarding his being a god, he still could not see the sun without an instinctive family feeling. Here there was plenty of young sappy wood for the gratings before the fire on which plantains could be cooked, and Musini and Nessi prepared the food, not without the usual friction. Nothing Nessi did seemed to satisfy Musini, and nothing Musini said pleased Nessi. But the plantains were delicious. All their lives they had been accustomed to a diet in large part of bananas, and a return to them after all this time was gratifying. Loa, gulping down the starchy things, never spared a thought for the old days when he had complained bitterly about being given bananas for dinner. He ate with contentment, and Lanu, squatting beside him, ate with relish.

It was not merely a meal for today; the bananas would provide a meal for tomorrow and the day after, for, split in two and toasted before the fire, they shrank into leathery morsels that could be pressed together into lumps which could at least sustain life. With the certain prospect of two days' food before them, they were raised infinitely above the status of nomads living from meal to meal, and they were all vaguely conscious of their bettered station in life, temporary though it might be. At the thought of the temporary nature of the change Loa felt a tiny temptation. Here were bananas, the staff of life. It was open to them to stay where they were, forever, to make a fresh clearing, to build themselves houses, to begin a new town. But he put the temptation aside without even considering it and without even knowing he had been tempted. He was going "home," and the difficulties he had encountered so far in the forest made no difference to his resolution.

"We need more plantains," said Musini. "Come, Nessi!"

The two women left Loa and Lanu sitting together. Lanu was preparing a bow for his father out of one of the saplings they had cut; he was shaping the stave with his little ax, fining it down progressively towards the ends, with many a careful look along the length of it to make sure he was keeping it balanced.

"A big bow this will be, my father," he said. "The cord will have to be tough for you to draw it to the full."

"Musini will prepare the cord, and then your father will draw it," said Loa, the contentment arising from a stomach full of plantains making him drowsy. Night was gathering for its final rush upon them, and he was ready to sleep.

"I sent an arrow today," gossiped Lanu, "against a bird beside the stream. Gray and white he was in color. Oh, how he flew back into the trees when my arrow went past him! My arrow plunged into the marsh and I lost it — a good arrow it was, too. When I have finished this bow I must make many more, both for you and for me."

He chipped away delicately with the ax at the bow stave; the fine steel edge took off the shavings as neatly as could be desired. Lanu, squatting with the bow between his knees, was an epitome of mankind. He was using steel and making a bow, two of the greatest inventions which have brought about man's material progress. But more than that; he was making a bow not for instant use, but against a future need, displaying that thought for the morrow which enables man to rise superior to the animals about him. And also he had not invented the bow; he was copying what he had seen other men doing, making use of tradition whereby every generation can rise superior to the preceding one. Tools, forethought, and tradition made the history of man's advance, and the boy with the ax and the bow exemplified all of them.

Musini came quietly back with a hand of bananas on her back, and squatted down to peel them and dry them at the glowing fire; Lanu gave her a moment's attention as he worked on the bow.

"We shall need a long stout cord for this bow, my mother," he said.

"I will make it," she answered quietly. She licked her fingers to keep them from burning, and began to turn the bananas on the wooden grill.

"I could eat more now," said Lanu, and Musini handed him a hot plantain without demur, and brought one to Loa when he held out his hand.

The minutes passed as they ate and worked and gossiped; Loa found himself nodding off in the darkness as sleep crept upon him.

"It is dark now," he said. "Where is Nessi?"

Musini came over to him from out of the faint light of the fire.

"Do you always want Nessi, Lord?" she asked softly.

[145]

"Here am I, the mother of Lanu, and here is your bed which I have prepared of banana leaves. Think no more about Nessi tonight."

Loa was too well-fed and sleepy to question the arrangement.

"Lord," whispered Musini in the darkness, "I — I — am your servant."

That was a declaration of consuming love in the limited vocabulary of Musini and Loa. A leopard snarled frightfully in the treetops not far off, and the monkeys he was stalking chattered and bustled in affright, and the sound of their terrified movements came down to the unhearing ears below. Then simultaneously came the last frantic shriek of a stupefied monkey who had fled along a branch within reach of the waiting leopard, and the triumphant howl of the leopard as his iron claws closed upon it. Then there was silence through the forest.

And in the morning Nessi was not with them, although so assiduously did Musini attend to their wants that her absence was not forcibly called to their attention. Musini found embers in the remains of the fire, and blew them into a glow. She toasted a fresh supply of bananas for their morning meal. She wrapped fresh leaves round the bananas she had dried the night before, and she bound them with creepers to make the bundles easy to carry. Loa heaved himself up a little stiffly in the wet morning air, and only now did he bring thought to bear on the subject of Nessi's absence. It occurred to him that she was perhaps sulking some distance off because he had chosen to lie in the arms of

Musini the night before. Women had curious whims and fads, and took exception to the oddest things.

Well, he was not going to involve himself in any of the women's quarrels. Let them settle them among themselves. He stepped off into the undergrowth, flourishing his flail, his feet leading him along the path they had trodden down towards the banana trees, and there he found Nessi, and knew the reason why she had not come back to them. The quarrel between her and Musini was undoubtedly settled. The ants were swarming over Nessi, into her open eyes, and the gaping mouth from which a blackened tongue protruded, and over the body which was already swollen with corruption after the long hot night. Loa saw all this, and walked quickly back to the others, and Musini raised her eyes from her work to look at him intently.

Lanu's thoughts were progressing along the same lines as had Loa's.

"Where is Nessi?" he asked. "We wait for her."

Loa moodily poked the ashes of the fire with the end of his flail, and at length Musini answered for him.

"We shall wait no longer for Nessi," she said. "She will not come with us today, nor ever."

"But why not?" asked Lanu, yet as he asked the question a glance at his parents' attitudes gave him some hint of the truth.

"We shall go on without her, my son," said Loa, heavily.

"Indeed we shall," said Musini, and with those words Loa caught a vague glimpse of himself in his true role.

God he might still be, but he was a family god now, literally familiar and not to be feared. To be humored, perhaps, placated a little when necessary; something more like a mascot than a tribal deity, to be led and coaxed in the ordinary affairs of life. The powers he had were something unaccountable but not because of them was he to be dreaded. He might know the way through the forest; he might at some future time again make use of supernatural forces when he read the past or divined the future with the heaped-up bones; he might be more than man in some ways, but in others — at least in Musini's eyes and probably in Lanu's — he was less. He could not carve a bow or make a fire, and to that extent he was dependent and parasitic upon his family.

Loa felt all this, although he did not think it out logically. But when they left their camping place and set out on their day's march he purposely did not lead them past Nessi's body. He did not want Lanu to know every detail of the truth, for it seemed to preserve for himself a little of his dignity if Lanu did not know everything. This was a tottering world; to find women not only resenting their husband's polygamy but actually taking such drastic steps about it was almost as great a shock to him as his original deposition from divinity. And during the day Musini strung phrynia leaves on a length of creeper and made for herself a kilt which she girt about her waist. It was a saucy and provocative garment, like those which marriageable girls extemporized before they graduated to the more sober bark cloth of marriage — bark cloth took long to prepare and there was no chance of making any here, so that there was plenty of excuse for Musini's action, and yet the association of ideas was somewhat disturbing. Until now she had been apparently content to go naked.

CHAPTER

X I

THE OLD CLEARING in which they had discovered the banana trees was of great extent; they had to struggle for a
long way through tangled undergrowth in the steaming
heat, climbing over fallen trees, hacking their way through
bushes. There was a wide area of young forest, where the
creeper-wreathed saplings were just beginning to assert
their mastery over the more lowly forms of vegetation. It
was a level area, and in a clairvoyant moment Loa realized
that it was the actual site of a town. Houses had stood here,
and presumably there had been a big central street, and the
surface during the lives of countless generations had been
worn down to the bare earth. Catastrophe — fire, presumably — had come to the town, and had swept it utterly out
of existence, and now the saplings sprouted where once the
houses had stood, and the creepers and mosses covered the
ground. A raid by the gray-faced men may have caused the
fire. No one would ever know.

The little people were present in the forest round here in
their usual numbers, all the same, for the wanderers were
continually seeing their ax marks on the trees, and sometimes their poisoned skewers in the paths. And then one day
they met them face to face — or rather a single one of them,

first, who appeared at one end of a short glade when they entered the other. He vanished in a twinkling behind a tree, from which a second later one of his short arrows came lobbing towards them, so slowly that they could distinctly see the single leaf which feathered it rotating in its flight. Yet slowly as the arrow came it bore death on its point, they knew. They sheltered behind the trunks, Lanu peering round with an arrow on his string ready to shoot back when a target should present itself. But the little man behind the tree had raised his voice in a loud cry to his companions, and they heard answering cries. Their peril was extreme; if they stayed where they were they would soon be surrounded, and if they moved to their right they might be hemmed in against the river and its marshes, and if they retreated they would come, he knew, to a stretch of difficult country. To the left lay their hope of safety.

"Come," said Loa, looking round at the other two, at Lanu grinning boylike with excitement and Musini tense and anxious behind the tree.

Together they leaped across the glade, risking the arrow-flight, to the safety of the trees beyond. Loa's mind was working automatically; with the tail of his eye he was watching the trees, noticing the passages through them, lest there should be too much danger in exposing themselves in their regular progress across successive glades. They paused at last for breath in the lee of a thicket, and Loa could think again about what they should do next. They could withdraw, hoping to get round the tangled country at their backs, or they could continue to circle to their left to pass round the little people altogether, and this was the sensible course to take, for the alternative meant actually a mere postponement of the problem. Loa gesticulated to demand silence and that they should follow him. He rounded the thicket and they began a cautious progress through the forest, flitting from one tree to the next, waiting to peer and to listen, and then flitting on. His own bow was slung across his back, nor would he take it in hand. He had Lanu beside him to shoot when necessary, and he himself carried that which would deal out a quicker death than the poisoned arrow. Loa held the chain of his flail close against the staff, so as to prevent its rattling, and their feet made no noise upon the spongy leafmold, and all round them prevailed the stillness of the forest. Yet through that stillness, they knew, little men were creeping, with arrow on string, seeking for them, little men to whom they were only meat on two legs. At that thought Loa could not prevent himself from glancing down his naked body whose joints might soon be roasting over a fire. And he himself, the Loa who dwelt in this body . . . ?

He was in too great danger to continue such an unprofitable speculation; he shook it off, and flitted on to the next tree, and from there to the next. In their attempt to achieve silence they were more successful than even the little people. As Loa stood behind his tree making ready for his next move he heard a tiny sound, a foreign sound, distinguished from the insect noises of the forest and, his ears told him, not related to the overworld above the treetops; one single brief noise of wood against wood — an arrow against a bowstave?

A bowstave against a tree trunk? He swiveled his eyes round towards Lanu behind his tree and Lanu was looking at him, with a world of meaning in his expression. He, too, had heard the sound. They froze in their attitudes behind the trees, utterly tense, only Loa's eyeballs moving as he stared through the creeper which swathed the tree trunk that sheltered him. So they waited, their straining ears rewarded by no further sound.

And then Loa saw an instant of movement, so brief that his eyes were not quick enough to pick up any details, an instant of something showing and then disappearing, behind a tree. He looked at Lanu, and Lanu had seen it too. His knees were slightly bent so as to give him more purchase for the instant drawing of his bow. Then Loa saw another movement, this time a trifle more prolonged, sufficient for his eyes to register a pale brown figure moving from one tree to the next, and immediately later another flash of movement followed. A little bowman was coming diagonally across their front with all the precaution to be expected of a man who knew that there were enemies in the forest. He was unaware of their immediate presence, all the same, as his movements and his direction proved. It was impossible to guess his future course, whether Lanu would be able to get a clear shot at him or not. Loa knew that Lanu was ready to seize any opportunity; a glance back at Musini showed her standing like a statue. Whether she knew what was going on or not she was sensibly imitating her menfolk in making no movement at all, and as she stood she would remain invisible to the little man for a long time to come.

[153]

The little man came on to another tree; his next advance might expose him to an arrow from Lanu's bow. But it did not, for the pygmy chose instead — by pure chance, obviously — another route which kept a couple of trees in a direct line between him and Lanu. This time, as the little man paused before going forward again, Loa could see part of him quite plainly: the naked shoulder and left arm, the hand holding the bow, and the forearm protected against the bowstring by its bracer of wood. The faint breath of wind that was stealing through the forest was luckily blowing away from him — the little people have keen noses, and Loa was sweating with excitement. Loa waited ready to spring. The distance was too great for him to charge yet, for the little man would hear him in plenty of time to draw his bow and send a poisoned arrow home. And when the little man hurried forward again no opportunity presented itself — Loa would have had to pass round a tree to intercept him, and the delay might be fatal, as Loa decided. Now the little man was no more than twenty-five yards off, out of sight altogether again behind his tree. Loa could only know he was there without seeing him; he could only wait, poised, hardly able to believe that the little man could be ignorant of their proximity. Yet he was. He emerged from his tree to move on to the next, still not offering a clear shot for Lanu, and Loa hurled himself forward in one frightful leap. The little man heard Loa's first movement, and swung round, but he was far too late. A swinging blow from the flail struck the left hand that held the bow forward; the flail circled without losing its momentum and the next blow fell on the little man's head with its sparse peppercorn curls. After that it was like killing the snake, raining blow on blow on a body that writhed feebly at first and then lay quite still.

Lanu was beside Loa, dancing with excitement after his long restraint, but his good sense was displayed in the fact that while he still had an arrow on his bowstring he had not discharged it. He spurned the dead body with his naked foot, capering in triumph, but Loa turned upon him with a warning gesture, and he instantly fell silent again. They had made too much noise as it was, with an unknown number of enemies prowling through the forest in search of them. But if it was a line (as presumably it was) which was beating through the forest they had broken it by killing the little bowman; it was the moment to push boldly through. Loa beckoned his family after him and hurried forward with all the speed precaution allowed. It was Musini who lingered by the dead body to strip it of its poor plunder, the little bow and short arrows, and the small knife stuck in the waistband. Loa frowned at her, for he was afraid of the noise that these things might make carried in Musini's hands, but Musini ignored his disapproval. She stuck the knife into her own waistband, slung the bow on her shoulder, and followed her husband with an arrow in each hand.

They hurried from tree to tree, waiting to look and to listen, and then hastening on. They had just had the best possible lesson in the results of incautious movement, and they took it to heart. Loa saw a footprint in the soft earth beside a tree, and leaped aside instinctively as if it were a snake, but it was only a pygmy's footprint, as the small size

[155]

and the high instep proved — perhaps it had been made by the man he had just killed. At another moment Lanu held up his hand imperatively for them to stop, trying the air with his nostrils. The others imitated his behavior. Faint upon the air was a scent of wood smoke, the tiniest trace of it. There was only the gentle air of wind through the forest, which must be carrying to their nostrils the smoke of the little people's cooking fires. The camp must be upwind in that direction, with the women and the little children and the old men; the line they had broken through was composed of the hunters. Loa swung round and headed off in a fresh direction, for he had no wish to come to the camp — there might still be some hunters there. They crossed a broad lane trampled through the forest by a herd of elephants — the air was redolent with the fresh droppings — and pushed on without pause. They were hungry and thirsty, but there was neither time nor opportunity to gather food when from behind any tree the feathered death might come without warning. Later in the day came a storm, when Loa's brother the sky raved above the treetops, his face dark with rage, until within the forest everything was nearly as black as night, and streams of water poured down upon them, chilling their naked bodies and wetting their braided bowstrings until it would hardly be possible to send an arrow thirty yards.

They camped in misery, huddling together, all three of them, at the foot of a tree where the earth was not quite so damp, but they had hardly lain down when a terrible event brought them to their feet again. The sky had demonstrated his rage in a final access of mania. The roar of the thunder was accompanied by a flash of lightning which played all round them; they were deafened and blinded, and the thunder's roar was accompanied by a rending crash. The tree next to theirs had been smitten by the sky's lightning-ax, and had split from summit to bole. The paralyzed seconds which followed were punctuated by the sounds of wreckage falling. In the pitch-black night a great branch fell with a crash beside them, shaking the earth. Above them the blasted tree slowly tore through the spiderweb of creepers and crashed sideways down, shattering the branches of its neighbors, until it hung at an angle, unseen, over their heads, while the smaller fragments, falling from branch to branch, rained down all round them.

They clung to each other in terror, with Lanu howling loudly in the middle until Musini quieted him. Indeed the sky had been very angry with them, and they were lucky that he had missed his aim. Yet what had they done to rouse his anger thus? He was still very angry, for his ravings could still be heard overhead; at any moment he might return and deal another blow — Loa clung to Musini at the thought of that. What could it be that had infuriated him so? What had they done differently from usual? Loa searched his memory and his conscience. They had killed the little man, but surely the sky would not be angry with his own brother for the killing of a mere forest pygmy, and yet — *was* the sky his brother? The old habit of believing it, rudely shaken when the slavers captured him, had asserted itself again lately, but never with its old force, and now

Loa's doubts returned redoubled. He might be — he probably was — only one more inconsiderable ant creeping about among the trees. He thought of the dead body of the pygmy, lying in the abandon of sudden death, the red blood oozing from its wounds. The little people were malevolent magicians. Perhaps by spells and incantations they had roused the anger of the sky. Maybe his victim, after death, had ascended to the sky and himself clamored for vengeance in a way that had admitted of no denial. Maybe he had returned and was creeping about even now in this utter blackness that surrounded them. Loa thought of the uncounted dead of the forest and the numberless ghosts — why, even Nessi might be among them — that might be stalking between the trees until terror overcame him and he howled as loudly as Lanu had, and he searched urgently for Musini's embrace, shaking with fright.

"Peace, peace, Lord," said Musini soothingly.

Her hands stroked his shoulders and his spine and by their soothing touch moderated his terror. Such a little man that he had killed, a full two feet shorter than Loa's own massive bulk. The low growl of thunder, far distant now, that responded to this thought was in its way reassuring. The sky may have been angry, but his anger was clearly subsiding. He may have struck a mighty blow, but, when all was said and done, the blow had missed. He, Loa, was still alive. He had once been enslaved, but now at least he was free; a homeless wanderer in the forest, but free. The pygmy may have invoked the anger of the sky; but the pygmy was dead, and he was alive, with his flail ready to his hand to kill any other little magicians that might cross his path. He would not only kill them but he would eat them, roasting their bloody joints at a fire and champing them up with his teeth. A magician roasted and eaten and borne within his own belly could do him no harm — the idea of it appealed to Loa's comic sense and set him off in a roar of laughter that startled Musini far more than his howlings had done, for she was a level-headed person and her husband's eccentric hysterias still occasionally took her by surprise.

But the laughter was a more cheerful and reassuring symptom than howlings of terror. All three of them gradually subsided into sleep as the rain ceased, despite their fright and the wet and the hunger, and when daylight came there was something oddly cheering in the sight of the shattered branches all round them, and the huge tree hanging almost directly over their heads — the whole top of it, and a portion of the trunk, while the rest of the trunk was split and rent nearly to the ground. In truth the sky had dealt a mighty blow and had missed. It was even possible that Loa's brother the forest had come to their rescue, for was not the treetop sustained by the creepers and branches of the rest of the forest?

All the same, the forest might not really be their friend, for with their awakening came the realization that they were utterly lost. Today there was no friendly stream at hand to give them the comfort — even perhaps the false comfort — of a sense of direction. Their wide detour of yesterday, forced upon them by their encounter with the little people, had taken them far away from it, and in which direction it now lay was more than any of them could guess. All the glades of the forest looked alike to them, and they could not tell by which one they had arrived the night before in the darkness of the storm, and the deluges of rain had washed away all hope of recognizing their trails.

"Which way, Lord?" asked Musini; her ignorance led her to address him with the honorific, instead of as any wife might speak to any other husband.

"I will tell you," said Loa, heavily.

Really he had no notion at all, but admitting it would be of no help to anyone, and certainly not to himself. He squatted down and pressed his fists into his eyesockets in the old gesture. It helped him to shut out distracting influences; for that matter it helped to stop him from thinking sensibly, so that his instincts and his subconscious memory were allowed full play. In the inner recesses of his mind calculations took place without his knowledge or volition, estimates of how far, and in what directions, they had gone in their circuit round the little people. Something was stirring in his brain when he stood up again and peered round him. So slight was the trend of the ground about them, as far as they could see through the trees, that no cool, thinking mind could have noticed any at all, but all Loa's physical sensitiveness was active. He had not thought at all — he had not even made the simple deduction that downhill would lead to water — but he could tell which was the way, and he could point to the right direction. He wanted to go downhill, and he knew which was downhill.

"Come," he said, and he started off, so that the others had to collect their poor impedimenta and hasten after him.

The thought that was in Loa's mind as he led the way was quite irrelevant; he was thinking that if Nessi were still with them this would be just the moment for her to say that she was hungry, and his recollection of her peevishness went far to reconcile him to losing her. For Musini never complained, bearing hardship and danger without a word — Loa was thinking idly at this moment about how poorly Nessi would have come through the ordeal of yesterday — and Lanu was a hard-bitten veteran. It was Musini and Lanu who contributed the whole sum of their small knowledge of how to live in the forest. It was Lanu who knew how to make a bow, Musini who knew how to braid bowstrings. Loa did not even yet know which creeper it was whose juice made arrow-poison. Musini had the domestic knowledge, which was of great use; Lanu, thanks to his boy's experiences in a childhood spent wandering about and around the town, and his observation of what men did, knew of the other arts. But Lanu's cheerful endurance of hardship, his fatalist carelessness about the future, his manual skill and ingenuity were qualities beyond all price. All that Loa could contribute to the partnership was his physical strength and his mind, which thought quickly after his recent experiences; and, above all, the fact that he was Loa, the born god, accustomed to lead and to be obeyed, with a natural assurance that might command confidence or at least blind faith.

Confidence and faith were put to the test during the next several days, for it was not that day nor the next that they came back to the stream. The forest undulates very slightly; it is to be presumed that Loa led his party on a course far from straight, while the necessity for seeking food naturally made their progress slow. They were hungry all the time — hardly sustained by funguses and white ants — white ants took long to collect and were not at all sustaining. The forest fruits did not even cheat their stomachs, but rather mocked them. They saw traces of the little people here and there, which keyed them up and set them peering fiercely about them, and not only because of the danger. The little people were meat, meat on two legs. Loa's starving stomach yearned for a pygmy, and he longed to meet one alone in the forest — away from his fellows — so that he and Lanu could kill him and make a fire on the spot to cook him. But chance brought no little men their way.

In the end chance — or Loa's instincts — brought them back to the stream again. For some time their course had lain along a minor watercourse, a mere thread of water winding through boggy undergrowth. And then the boggy area grew more extensive, the character of the forest changed perceptibly in a morning's march, and they found themselves beside what they had come to look upon as their own stream — if indeed it was the original one; it may well have been some other. That did not matter, and the thought did not occur to them. Here was a tree round whose base had fallen ripened pods of forest beans; that was what mattered most, while they could hear bullfrogs croaking in the distance. They camped at once, and lit a fire, and Lanu and Loa left Musini beside it to pound and roast beans into digestibility, while they went off to catch frogs. While there were beans and frogs no one need despair.

X I I

FOR FOUR OR FIVE DAYS more they followed the course of the stream. The water surface of it was wider than before; here and there it even widened into marshy pools a hundred feet across, so wide that the trees did not meet over them and they could see the sky overhead, and with reeds and weeds growing thickly in them, wherein lived a myriad birds and a myriad mosquitoes. On one occasion Loa found Lanu crouching intent and anxiously on a bit of firm ground beside one of these pools. Lanu gesticulated for silence and Loa crouched beside him obediently. A big gray parrot came flapping across the lake, and settled on a branch within range, and Lanu trained his arrow round upon it inch by inch, the motion almost imperceptible. At last he released the arrow, and with a sharp hum of the cord it sped true and straight at the parrot, which dropped stunned into the still water of the pool. Lanu gave a cry of triumph, and started towards the bird; his feet were actually in the muddy water at the edge when there was a surge upon the surface. A huge evil head emerged with gaping jaws, the jaws armed with large conical teeth — the most frightening, the most horrible sight they had ever seen. The jaws engulfed the floating parrot, and the head disappeared, to be replaced momentarily by a long tail that swept the water and then vanished in a flurry; the ripples broke against Lanu's legs as he stood petrified in the shallows. He fled back terrified to cling to Loa, and Loa embraced him to comfort him, although he was terrified as well. No transmitted memory of hairy devils could equal that sight, and the unexpectedness of it added to the horror.

"What was it? What was it, Father?" asked Lanu, his frightened hands clutching at Loa's bare skin.

"Some snake or other, without a doubt," said Loa, with all the calm he could muster; he was preventing himself from shuddering at the memory only by the strongest exertion of will. It was his love for Lanu that made him exert this self-control when he had never tried to control himself in his life.

"Let us go away from here, Father," said Lanu. "Let us go quickly."

"We shall go," said Loa, as soothingly as he could; he still made himself retain his calm in the face of the infection of panic. "First pick up your bow and your arrows and your ax. We need not leave those for the snake."

The matter-of-fact words went far towards calming Lanu. He obediently picked up his weapons with one hand while he wiped his beslobbered face with the other. He was in no panic as he led the way from that fatal pool, so that Loa walking in his footsteps felt that they were not walking fast enough, although he refrained from saying so. That water-dwelling devil had turned a cold, horrible eye upon them as he swallowed the parrot; Loa, shuddering, wondered if that glance would cause them to waste away, would cast them into the sleeping sickness, perhaps, or bring them ill fortune in the matter of food or in their next encounter with the little people. It had brought them ill fortune at the moment, for the matter of that, because all they had for supper that night were the beans Musini had bruised and toasted for them.

Musini listened to Lanu's voluble account of the horrible apparition in the pool.

"Big, mother. Big — big — big!"

Words failed Lanu when he tried to tell of the ugliness of the creature, or the frightening effect it had upon him.

"Indeed a big snake," said Musini, looking at Lanu's outspread arms.

She glanced at Loa, who was chewing beans, and the glance told her a good deal about Loa's feelings; she knew him too well to be deceived by that stolidity of manner.

"Such things live in the water," said Musini, indifferently, "as elephants do in the forest."

It was Loa whom she was trying to cheer up; she herself was frightened by Lanu's description, and in other circumstances she might have allowed herself to indulge in her fear, but as it was she cunningly set herself to minimize the occurrence. Her allusion to elephants was apt and effective, for the elephant, huge and terrible though he was, was not the object of utter fright such as this new creature inspired. Elephants were the lords of the forest, roaming where they would; if they chose to enter the town's banana grove and strip it of its crop nothing could deter them, and yet elephants were not supernatural. Once in a great while one would fall into the pits dug for them, and would die upon the poisoned stakes and under the poisoned arrows shot into them by brave men. Loa had eaten roast elephant, and a man could hardly cherish superstitious fears of something he had eaten and whose tusks had for so long adorned his house.

"That is so," agreed Loa, parentally pontifical, and Musini could see that this time it was not all a pose. Being married to a god for a dozen years had given her a curious insight into the supernatural.

They went on down the stream, skirting the marshes that bordered it. The marshes grew wider and wider, compelling them to keep farther and farther from the water, until at last, without almost no warning, they came to the great river. Walking in the twilight of the forest, they could see a growing whiteness beyond, shafts of light penetrating between the tree trunks; they smelled the raw smell of the decaying river vegetation, so unlike the faintly musty smell of the forest, but they were not ready for the full revelation when they reached the river, when they stepped out from the last tree into the immensity of the daylight. The river was huge at this point, gleaming metallically in the sunshine. The farther bank was a mere dark strip on the horizon, and Loa, looking across at it, felt the familiar inward shrinking and vertigo at the brightness and the immense distances. He wanted to cower back, but Lanu was beside him troubled by no misgivings. Overhead Loa's brother the sky, the vastest thing in all their experience, glared down at them; but at their backs was his friendly brother, the forest, ready to afford them shelter and protection. With the moral support of the forest, and with Lanu and Musini beside him, Loa was willing to meet the sky's unyielding stare — the sky that had flung lightning at them, the sky which made them miserable with rain, the sky under which that awful creature had emerged from the lake to swallow the parrot. But Lanu and Musini were paying only scant attention to the sky; it was upon him that they were conferring their blinking respect, for he had led them through the trackless forest through all these endless days and had brought them out here to the river, which they knew and recognized. Neither of them knew how much chance had had to do with it; neither of them had followed the obscure reasoning in Loa's mind — more instinct and superstition, if the truth must be told, than reasoning — regarding the flowing downhill of water, which, combined with his memory of the trend of the country, had determined him on their course.

Neither Loa nor his family knew about the possibility of rivers flowing in great arcs; they had no means of knowing about it. They turned and set their faces downstream along the great river. They had a definite route to follow, and were much the happier in consequence. They knew that it was possible for someone lost in the forest to wander for a lifetime in an area ten miles square, and they could be certain this at least would not be their fate. It was not easy to travel at the water's edge — in fact marshes and the obstructions of the forest made it almost impossible — but it was easy enough to find their way along a short distance from the river, certain that it was on their right hand. Often they were within sight of the water and its marvels. They gazed breathlessly one day at a herd of vast creatures disporting themselves in the shallows, snorting and grunting, swimming with deceptive ease and lumbering through the reeds like elephants in a manioc patch. More than once they saw canoes upon the water, the paddles flashing in the sunshine. That meant men were there, and not the little people of the forest, either. Loa knew much about canoes as a result of his experience in the slavers' camp, so that he could give answers to Lanu's eager questions about them — conveying information that was satisfactory, if not correct.

At the water's edge there was more chance of a fair shot at one of the birds which flew in clouds among the trees, and once Loa himself managed to hit a monkey with an arrow. The little brute fled straight up a tree before the poison began to work in him, and he clung for a long time to a branch, crying pitifully — Loa and Lanu would have laughed at the amusing sight if they had not been so desperately interested in the chance of getting fresh meat — as the paralysis crept over him, and even when he showed no signs of life he still clung on, far out of reach, while Loa and Lanu waited below, almost in despair before the muscles relaxed and the dead monkey came tumbling down through the branches to fall with a satisfactory thump to earth. That night they ate fresh meat and rejoiced; it was fortunate, from the point of view of all forest hunters, that the minute amount of poison introduced into an animal's circulation paralyzed its brain but had no effect on the human stomach, at least after cooking.

Not many days later, one afternoon, Lanu put back his head and tried the air with his sensitive nostrils.

"There is something that I smell," he said.

Loa and Musini tried the air likewise.

"I smell nothing, my son," said Loa, and Musini agreed with him.

"Yet there is something," persisted Lanu.

He said so again that night when they camped, hungry after an unprofitable day, and after an hour's march the next morning Musini, too, turned to Loa with the remark that there was a scent in the air. Loa blew his nostrils clear and tried the air again. Perhaps there was something, the faintest smell of wood smoke, perhaps — a camp of the little people a great way off, presumably. Lanu and Musini disagreed with him. That was not the smell. And an hour later some variation in the wind bore the smell down upon them in greater volume, and Loa knew they were right. He sniffed carefully. Wood smoke undoubtedly was the main constituent, but there was a series of undertones of odor as well. A whole torrent of memories, of stored-up images, flooded into Loa's mind as he sniffed. It was the smell of a town: the smell of wood smoke, of cooking, of decaying vegetable matter, of refuse, of humanity — it was the smell of home.

"That is the smell of a town," said Loa, announcing what Lanu and Musini had long before suspected.

They looked at each other, all three of them, as they wondered what they should do next.

"We shall have to go round it," said Loa.

With difficulty he was forming mental pictures of the situation. He had never seen a map or a plan in his life, so that he could not slip into the easy method of the civilized man of visualizing a map first and then plotting a route upon it. He had to plod along step by step; at least his experiences with the slavers had shown him other towns than his own, but it was home that he knew best. He thought in terms of home; of a town in the forest, with the river running some miles away from it. Surrounding the town would be the old clearings and the new banana groves and manioc gardens. Beyond the clearings there would be the area frequently or habitually traversed by the men of the town, the hunters wandering through the trees with their bows in the hope of a shot at monkeys or birds, digging pitfalls for antelopes — or for elephants on occasions when there was an unusual burst of communal energy — and closer in there would be the fringe where the older children would seek for forest fruits. It would have to be a tremendously wide sweep that would carry Loa and his family right round the town without any possibility of contact with any of the inhabitants. Also, in the neighborhood of the town there was a far greater likelihood of meeting the little people, who were attracted there by the chance of stealing plantains (Loa remembered the depredations of the little people at home) and goats and the coveted weapons of iron; and by the chance of getting for themselves meat on two legs. Loa, exchanging glances with his family, knew that he and they were in greater danger than usual.

Yet round the town they had to go. Loa strove, without arithmetic or maps to help him, to calculate how long a journey it would be to go safely round the town on the side away from the river. A day's march was such a variable quantity. It depended both on the ease with which food was found and upon the obstructions offered by the forest. The occasions when town dwellers camped in the forest were very rare indeed, so that — this was a triumph of Loa's calculating power — half a day's march from the town would mean they were safe from town dwellers, though not from the little people. To circle the town at a distance of half a day's march and to come back to the river again would take — how long? Loa could form no idea. It was far too difficult a problem for him. It meant a prodigious number of days, he could be sure, and the detour into the forest would be dangerous in another way, too. It might take them so deep among the trees as to make it impossible for them to find their way back to the river at all. After all their efforts they might be lost in the forest. It would certainly be quicker, and might well be safer, to push through between the town and the river. Loa put his limited vocabulary to work to explain this to his wife and son, and the suggestion met with their approval. They continued their way as close to the water as they could, proceeding with the utmost caution. If some lucky chance should bring them in contact with an isolated town dweller, the question of meat for their supper might be solved. They were hungry as usual.

The character of the riverbank changed as they went along. The land began to trend upwards, with the water washing at the foot of a low cliff of earth; even the nearly vertical face of the cliff was thickly grown with vegetation, young trees projecting out from it almost horizontally. No tree had a long life there with the cliff being steadily under-cut by the river, for this was the bluff at the far end of a loop. They had to keep to the top of the cliff, for the water lapped at its very foot. Behind them the sun sank slowly across the river, his face almost obscured in a sullen haze.

They came to a point where the cliff face was seamed by a steep gully running down to the water; a weak spot in the face had been deeply undercut and had collapsed, leaving a fairly easy descent with a little beach at the foot of it. It seemed a good place in which to camp, with convenient access to water, while the sides of the gully would conceal their fire at the bottom. As if to make the site completely desirable, at the lip of the gully grew no fewer than three young trees of the species of giant acacia, which gave them the forest beans which constituted the bulkier half of their diet. With one accord they halted there and busied them-selves with preparations for the night, gathering beans and dead wood. It was for Musini and Lanu to light the fire; Loa saw them start work and then with ax and bow climbed back up the gully; a little good fortune might bring them some addition to their meager supper, and in any case it was desirable both to keep guard up here against some sur-prise attack and to reconnoiter the ground round about. At the head of the gully he paused to look back; down by the water Lanu and Musini were bending over their preparations for a fire, while the sun, now buried in a purple cloud, was slowly approaching the almost invisible farther bank of the river. Right underneath it was a vague speck — some canoe, possibly, on some mysterious journey.

Loa wandered off into the twilit forest. Despite the need for silence he had to take the precaution of slicing with his ax a bit of bark from some of the trees he passed, for it was necessary that he should find his way back to the gully; in his left hand he held his bent bow, with the string fitted into the groove of an arrow whose shaft was clasped under his forefinger and thumb. A single motion would enable him to draw and loose, should a monkey or a bird happen into range. Only a few black leathery funguses rewarded his search, and he ate those as not worth the trouble of carrying back; he found nothing else before the increasing darkness of the forest warned him to return to the gully. He turned back, to pick his way from blaze to blaze — even now his vigilance not relaxing, lest some of the little people should be following up his trail, unlikely though that might be with night coming on.

Faintly through the silent forest there came a high-pitched cry, twice repeated. The first sound of it brought him to a halt, looking about him with all the vigilance of a man who within an hour may be hanging on a roasting spit, but the repetition sent him hurrying through the trees with a reckless lack of precaution. It was Lanu's voice, he knew. Lanu was in danger, in fear; Loa broke into a run, his heart pounding with anxiety. He emerged at the top of the gully while it was still full daylight. A wisp of smoke drifted out across the bronze river from a little fire; but there was no human creature in the gully, no one at all. He ran wildly down it, his naked feet sliding in the loose earth, and there, beside the fire, he could read part of the story in the footprints that had torn the ground round about it. Many men had been there, and there had been something of a struggle. A single arrow, one of Lanu's, lay at a distance from the fire, but everything else had disappeared; save for that a clean sweep had been made. A thick chain of footprints — where individual ones could be distinguished they pointed both to and from the fire — led along the beach at the water's edge, and Loa, following the tracks round the little point there, could read the rest of the story in the mud, for there, with the water lapping up to it, was a deep groove, the mark of a canoe grounding, with the muddled footprints all about it.

It was all plain now. A canoe with many men in it, seven or eight at least and perhaps a dozen, had crept into the shore here, concealed by the point from Musini and Lanu in the gully. The men in the canoe had seen the fire from the river and had paddled silently to the shore close beside it. Creeping round the point they had peered round to see the woman and the boy intent on their work at the fire — a pair of deep footprints showed where a single scout had stood still for a long time staring at them unseen to make sure it was not an ambush. Presumably he had turned and beckoned to his fellows. Then had come the sudden rush;

Musini and Lanu had been seized — it was then they had uttered the screams Loa had heard — and carried off to the canoe; and now they were gone, Loa could not tell whither, for a canoe leaves no tracks. The sun plunged into the forest across the river, leaving above it a pile of purple cloud. In a few moments it would be dark, and Loa, distracted with misery though he was, hastened back to the fire to search about it in the last gleam of daylight. He did not find what he feared he might; look as he would, he could see no drop of blood upon the torn-up earth. Whatever else had happened, it was probable that neither Musini nor Lanu had been wounded. No spear had pierced them, certainly. No club had dashed out their brains; even if they had been merely clubbed into insensibility a drop or two of blood would have probably fallen from the battered scalp, and he could be almost sure that none had done so. Night swept down upon him even while he bent to reread the story of the torn earth. He stumbled back again to where the canoe had grooved the beach, the last place where his wife and son had touched the earth, and there, in the darkness, his misery overcame him. He sat down and wept, his forearms on his bent knees, his face upon his forearms, shaken by his sobs, while round him the water lapped and gurgled and chuckled.

In time he grew calmer, with the calmness of something approaching despair. He looked out unseeing in the blackness of the night across the river. Overhead a star or two showed faintly between the clouds; there was no moon. Oddly at that moment of supreme misery he realized that he had not, for a very long time, called the moon from out of her retirement in the river. There had been a time when he and his whole world had sincerely believed that she would not leave it if he did not call her, that the nights would remain dark if he did not summon his wayward sister back to the sky. His sister! Alone there by the pitch-dark river Loa had a moment of self-realization, of self-contempt. The moon was no more a sister of his than she was a sister of the little people's. He was a mere mortal, like anyone else, and the most lonely and miserable of mortals at that, and the most useless. It was his grievous fault that Musini and Lanu had been captured. He remembered with a sneer his precaution in going to reconnoiter the landward side of their camp, without any thought at all for the peril that menaced them from the water. He had even seen the canoe across the river, and in his utter folly he had given it no thought. The dark invisible water lapping at his feet mocked him as he sat with his face in his hands.

It was a terrible night, a night of misery and despair, in which his few moments of sleep were tortured by frightful dreams. He was a gregarious animal suddenly confronted with the possibility of lifelong compulsory solitude, a defenseless animal without a friend in the world, the prey of every living creature in the forest. But that was only part of his emotion. He was stirred as deeply as might be by the loss of his wife and child, Musini and Lanu, who had stood by him when he was a slave, who had chosen to encounter hardship and peril to set him free, whose devotion to him had never faltered. He had a sense not merely of physical

[176]

loss, but of spiritual loss as well. While there was emotion left in him he wept for Musini and Lanu, until at last he was completely exhausted. Even with the dawn he still sat in melancholy apathy. Possibly he might have stayed there and starved if a new stimulus had not aroused him. It beat upon his ear for some time before it penetrated into his consciousness — the steady rhythm of a drum. A drum! There was no doubt about it. Not very far away in the forest a drum was beating out an exciting, triumphant meter, borne clearly through the trees to his ears. He had no doubt that it came from the town whose odors his nostrils could just detect. It called him to action, roused him to do something.

His subconscious may have been at work during the night, underneath his misery. Or the sound of the drum may merely have called forth a prodigy of thinking in his brain. The town was near. Was it not possible that it had been people from the town, incredibly using a canoe, who had captured Musini and Lanu? And in that case was it not likely that Musini and Lanu were still captives in the town? They had been carried off alive — they probably had not been slain yet. It was not so much hope as a ferocious determination that filled him and quickened his sluggish pulse. He picked up ax and bow and arrows. A few forest beans scattered round the remains of the fire caught his notice, and he ate them raw for a scanty breakfast, and he drank deeply of the water of the river. Then he started off towards the town, desperate, the enemy of mankind. The sound of the drum came more and more clearly through the trees, accompanying the scent of humanity. It almost made Loa abandon the caution of movement which had become habitual to him; but he still instinctively scanned the ground before him for pitfalls and poisoned skewers; he still halted at every glade to look ahead and listen for enemies. Along with the sound of the drum he now heard human voices, roaring a chorus to the meter. There must be some kind of rejoicing in the town.

His sense of direction told him that he was keeping closer to the river than he expected, and he had not gone downhill at all — he was walking along the top of the bluff. He had no clear idea of what he was going to do; actually he was so desperate that he may have been courting sudden death. The forest suddenly became dense and overgrown, with shrubs and creepers intermingled, and, with the noise of the town increasing, he guessed he had reached the edge of the belt of old clearings round the town. With his mind suddenly made up, he plunged into the undergrowth, creeping under, climbing over, hacking a way through with his ax, keeping a wary eye open the while for snakes. The sweat poured down his dark skin, for in the undergrowth the heat was intense and the labor heavy. He wriggled on and on cautiously, with the din of the town growing ever greater, until at last he parted a bush in front of him and had a clear view. He could see a circle of houses of a strange type — round houses, thatched differently from what he was accustomed to. They faced onto a central space; between the houses he could see something of it, and the coming and going of many people, first this way and then that way. A dance was certainly in progress. He wanted a better view than this, and he turned to his right and began to crawl along, keeping in the final fringe of dense vegetation through which progress was not too difficult and yet which screened him from possible sight as long as he kept down. A hundred yards of this opened up a wider vista between the huts. He could see fully into the central open space. Cautiously he backed into the undergrowth, and, lying full length, parted the grass stems before his eyes as he looked out. A man lying flat is more likely to escape observation than one standing up, being below the natural eye-level.

There were trees standing in this open space, unlike the main street of his own town, and at the far side the dance was going on; more people than he could count (and yet, he thought, less than had dwelled in his own town) moving from side to side in a great semicircle to the beat of the drum, which was out of his sight. Under a great tree a little group of standing figures centered about a seated one; Loa could just make out the movement of fans which, he guessed, were keeping the flies off the chief. He had no word for "chief"; he had to phrase it to himself that if this were his town that man would be he. He almost thought of the chief as the "Loa" of the town — the clearest proof that Loa had learned much in the last weeks regarding his own relative importance, both present and past. But it was not the chief, it was not the dance, that attracted Loa's attention. He did not spare so much as a glance for the tethered goats which meant milk and meat. What attracted his attention was a little palisade of stakes in the shade of another tree, a good deal nearer. It was more than a palisade; it was a cage, wound about with creepers. Loa's heart nearly came out of his mouth as he saw it and guessed what it might imply. He swallowed painfully and fought down the impulse to crawl farther out of the undergrowth for a nearer view. It was just the sort of pen in which humans destined for food might be fattened; but, look as he would, he could see nothing—so closely woven were the sides of the pen and so deep the shade in which it stood—of what was inside it, if anything.

Everything he could see of it told him that it was in use; it seemed to be complete, and no one would trouble to re-build a pen when the victims had been taken out. But if the inmate, or inmates, were lying down—as was to be expected—he would not be able to see them. Loa looked all round the village and the open space. He was as near to the pen as he could ever get unobserved; there would be no advantage in a further change of position. He set himself to wait, to see what would happen. The sun blazed down into the undergrowth around him so that he was in a steady trickle of sweat; insects plagued him and hunger and thirst assailed him, but he forced himself to lie there waiting; he called to his assistance all the endless patience of the forest.

If there was a victim in the cage it might well be Musini or Lanu—they even might both be there. He had not realized, when they camped the night before, either how near they were to the town nor how near the town was to the river. It was confirmation of his previous theory. Being as near to the river as this the town might easily be populated by the canoe-using people whom he knew to exist, and if it were, it seemed far more likely that it was a canoe from this town which had captured his wife and child than one from any other town. If that were the case it would be Lanu and Musini who would be in that cage. Their captors would certainly fatten them before eating them; Loa remembered realistically how worn and thin they both were. He called forth fresh reserves of patience.

At last the drum ceased to beat and the dance stopped. At first in ones and twos and then in an increasing stream people began to leave the place of the dance and distribute themselves through the town. Loa lay very close to the earth and peered out with only one eye, for there was much more chance of detection now that there were idle eyes to glance round the circle of vegetation that hemmed in the town. People entered the houses near at hand; Loa could hear the voices of the women, sometimes raised stridently as they chided the children. Then an old woman emerged from one of the houses; on her white hair she carried a big wooden jar; in each hand a wooden dish. Loa watched her with tense excitement. Straight to the pen she went, squatted carefully with her head still upright to put down what she held in her hands, and then lifted down the jar. Then she began to unfasten the pen. She passed in the big jar, and received it back again — Loa could not see from whom. Then she passed in one of the wooden platters, and proceeded to open the pen at another point. She passed in the jar, took it back, and passed in the other platter. She went to the first place again, took out the platter, passed in the jar again, and received it back. She fastened up the pen at that point, and then exactly repeated her actions at the second place. Then, with empty jar and platters, she made her way back to the house again. There could be no clearer proof that there were two people in the pen — a child could have made that deduction. Loa was quite certain. And the fact that two people were there made it more likely that they were Lanu and Musini; pairs of victims must be rare.

Loa lay in the undergrowth while the sun mounted over the town and the heat rose to its hideous maximum. It was plain enough that if he intended to rescue his family he must wait until nightfall — a child could have made that deduction, too. But it was not so easy to make detailed plans. Loa had to make his unaccustomed mind think; what was harder still, he had, almost for the first time in his life, to set himself consciously to work observing and learning. He had to study the town and its ways, basing his plans on what he saw and on the deductions to be drawn from his observations. His forehead wrinkled with the effort. And he was very thirsty, and if he had not been so acutely conscious of his thirst he would have been unpleasantly hungry. It called for all Loa's reserves of character to make himself lie there and rivet his whole attention on what was going on before him.

On the far side of the clearing, over on his right, there seemed to be an entrance into the town, by which numerous people came and went. Yet the river must be very close at hand there. Yes, of course. There were women coming and going, and without any doubt they were bearing water jars on their heads; to judge by their gait, empty jars when they went out and full ones when they returned. There was a house concealing the actual pathway from Loa's view; he could only see people as they emerged from it and as they entered into it. Yet there was just a subtle difference in their manner of walking the moment they appeared or disappeared; Loa strained his splendid eyesight to make sure. There could be no doubt about it. At that point there was a steep downslope, and that house must be built on the very lip of the bluff running down to the river, and up that slope the town's drinking water must be carried.

Men used the same entrance frequently. Loa saw a little group come striding in with something of triumph in their manner. One of them bore a string of glittering white things which he displayed for inspection to the passers-by before disappearing into a house. Loa could not imagine what they were, for he had never seen fish before, but he did at least reach the conclusion that the town's canoes must lie at the water's edge at the foot of the path there. He could think of no other reason for men to use the path.

When, during the coming night, he had freed Musini and Lanu, they would have to escape from the town. Over there was one possible exit; so much he knew. At least half of the town was closely ringed in by tangled second-growth forest, such as was sheltering him at the moment. It might offer shelter, but it offered small possibility of escape. No one in darkness could possibly make his way into the undergrowth for more than a yard or two. It might be that the three of them could hide there during the darkness, and

[183]

with the coming of light make their way out through the tangled belt — the way he had come — to the freedom of the forest. That would be very dangerous, all the same, because the moment the escape was discovered there would be a serious search, and they might be tracked and hunted down in the undergrowth. It was a possible scheme, but not a very good one. Loa's utterly untrained mind struggled frantically with these alternatives. It was a terrible effort to deal thus with theories, for he had done hardly any theoretical thinking in his life. To weigh one intangible against another was for Loa an exercise far more unusual and exhausting than the schoolmen had found the theological speculations of the Middle Ages.

On the far side of the town, beyond the point where the dance had taken place, women appeared every now and then carrying hands of bananas on their heads. At that end of the town, as far as Loa could vaguely make out, there was some sort of street running into the open square, and it was from this street that the bananas were being brought in. That must be the way to the cultivated ground, to the banana groves and the manioc gardens, and it was another possible way of escape to the forest. But Loa ruled that out as soon as his mind was able to weigh the pros and cons; it was a long way over there, it involved going down a street, and there was no certainty that the way would not be barred by clearings, or that they could find it in the dark if it were not. Loa began to pay more and more attention to the exit from the town to the river. He was not consciously learning its bearings — his imagination was not lively enough to lead him to do that — but he was learning them subconsciously.

Another old woman was carrying out food and drink to the pen. Loa watched all her actions, which were just similar to those of the old woman who had preceded her. He saw the big jar of water being handed in, and he groaned with desire. His unexercised imagination was quite capable of visualizing the cool water in that jar; his parched tongue moved over his dry lips at the thought of a long drink. As thirst began to consume him, Loa almost came to envy Musini and Lanu in their pen. The temptation began to come to him to withdraw again into the overgrown clearing, to find his way out through it back to the river where he could slake his thirst in the hope of returning to his present hiding place before dark. Loa resisted the temptation; everything about that scheme was too dangerous. It was for the sake of Musini and Lanu that he forbore; peril to him meant peril to them, and in that case he was prepared to endure his thirst.

Thirst at least made him forget his hunger. The appetizing odors that came from the cooking pots excited no emotion in him at all; he analyzed them with curiosity and interest, but they did not make him hungry as he lay there slowly roasting — simmering, rather — in the shade. The strange unknown smell of cooking fish came to his nostrils, and he observed it with distaste, for to him it was unpleasant; it heightened the prejudice, the hatred, he felt towards this town, so that when a stronger whiff of it than usual reached him he unconsciously wrinkled his upper lip in a snarl and his hand went out to the ax that lay beside him.

The great heat of the day was over now for him; it was a grateful moment — a moment almost sharply defined — when the sun ceased to glare down on him and the tops of the trees behind him interposed between him and the sun. The shadows in the open space of the town became longer, and with the movement of the sun he could see the pen more clearly. It was very like any pen that would have been constructed in his own town, except that it had been given little gable ends and ridgepole roof, almost like the houses in his own town and in contrast with the houses in this town. The roof was thatched with leaves, presumably to keep out the rain, for the tree under which it stood gave it shade. Certainly this town gave much attention to its captives. Even as Loa watched he saw a third meal taken out to the pen, and how many had been given before his arrival he did not know. Musini and Lanu were being well fed in preparation for their feeding of others. And as the shadows grew longer still, Loa saw the same old woman who had brought the last meal escorted over to the pen by a couple of men. They took lengths of creeper and tethered her to the pen, by the waist and by the ankle, apparently — it was too far off for the smallest details to be seen — and left her there. That was exactly the way Delli had been guarded after her capture; it ensured that the prisoners would not pick apart during the night the fibers that caged them in. That was all that was in the minds of the townspeople — it was all that had been in Loa's mind when he had given the same orders regarding Delli — but it was a complication when it came to a question of rescue from without. Loa grimly noted on which side of the pen the old woman chose to lie down.

Evening was nearly at hand now. The shadows of the trees were stretching far, far, across the open space. A couple of boys gathered together the half-dozen goats that had been tethered to browse on the edge of the town, and herded them away to some unseen destination where presumably they would be safe from the nocturnal attack of leopards. Everybody in the town, it seemed, chose this time of day to come out to gossip and exchange news, just as they did in Loa's own town. There were passers-by innumerable in the open space — a few of them clustered now and then about the pen to view the curious couple confined there. Loa thought from their movements that they laughed heartily, and this puzzled him a little. Even if he had remembered how everyone had laughed at Delli it would not have helped him to draw the right conclusion. He had not learned yet to be objective enough to think of Musini and Lanu as figures of fun to strangers. He saw the spectators slap their thighs and prance in apparent amusement, and he could not think why. But he did not let that problem bother him; he conscientiously devoted those last few minutes of daylight to a final study of the ground, so that when darkness came he was ready for action.

The first impulse was to move at once, but he resisted it sternly. He had to wait until the town was asleep. The limitations of his vocabulary and the culture in which he lived expressed themselves in his lack of any idea corresponding to the word "hour." He could divide the day from sunrise to noon, from noon to sunset, but he could not express to himself the idea of waiting a couple of hours. "As long as it would take a man to get hungry" would have been one of his ways of expressing the period of time it would be desirable to wait, but Loa was hungry already and any such term would have appeared absurd to him in consequence. In the utter darkness of the night there were a few gleams of light in the town, but only two or three. On the far side there was the glow of a fire, and near it were two small points of light. There could not well be more, not even in this town where fish from the river supplemented an almost purely carbohydrate diet. Oil to supply fat was far too scarce and precious to be wasted in lamps, although even Loa was acquainted with lamps — a wooden saucer of oil in which floated a lighted wick of vegetable fiber. If men wanted to stay awake, they could sit in the dark or by the light of a fire; but few men did. The night was the time for sleep, eleven hours of it at least, and any light at night time attracted so many insects as to make it undesirable to stay near it.

It was not surprising to see the lights soon go out and the fire die away to nothingness, but Loa still waited. Now his brother the sky came to his help — the sky which so often before had malignantly plagued him; furthermore, the help the sky brought was in the form of the rain which usually distressed him. There was a very distant rumble of thunder, so distant that not even a glimmer of lightning was visible in the town, and then came the first heavy drops, falling

like pebbles on his back. Loa blessed the rain. He turned
over and opened his mouth to the sky, and the rain that
fell into it eased his frightful thirst. Soon it was raining
with African violence, deluging down as if the whole atmosphere had been made of water. The roar of it was tremendous; he allowed himself to wriggle out from the undergrowth into the open space, and he instantly found a
puddle from which he could drink his fill. While the rain
fell nothing could be seen or heard; now was the time for
action.

The string of his bow had long been released. He slid his
arm into the loop and slung the bow over his shoulder, and
then with ax in one hand and two arrows in the other he
proceeded to crawl forward towards the pen. The roar of the
rain made elaborate precautions unnecessary, but Loa took
no risks. He inched himself forward through the mud into
which the bare earth of the open space had immediately
been converted. The very houses between which he first
passed were invisible on either side of him. Chance depres-
sions made big pools in which he had to be careful not to
splash, but all the same he went straight through them.
There was the danger that in the night he would not find
the pen; although his sense of direction was acute and although he had studied for so long the line he had to follow
he could not possibly risk making any detour from the
straight. He crawled on and on in the roaring darkness, on
and on, until, inevitably, the doubt began to grow in his
mind as to whether he had taken a wrong direction and had
passed the pen by. For some moments he stopped to consider

that possibility, with the rain deluging upon him, soaking his woolly hair so that the water poured into his eyes and incommoded him. There was nothing for it but to crawl on; if his luck had been bad he would know it when he reached the far side of the open space, and that would be the time to think what he should do next. He put forward his hand to resume crawling, and snatched it back as if it had touched something red-hot. What he had touched was a wet and bony human foot. During that time when he had been considering he had been lying within a yard of the old woman tethered to the pen. As the realization came to him he drew up his knees to spring. The old woman uttered a bad-tempered squawk. She must have been nodding off even in the rain, for she did not appreciate the significance of that slight touch on her foot. Perhaps she had not felt it, perhaps she attributed it to a wind-blown leaf, or perhaps in her stupefied condition she did not react quickly to it although she knew what it implied. That little squawk, almost unheard in the rain, was her instant undoing. The touch of her foot and the sound of her voice told Loa — told his instincts, for he acted quicker than thought — how her body was lying, and his spring carried the weight of his body upon her with a crash, and his hands sought urgently for her throat. His knees in her skinny belly squirted all the wind out of her. His hands found her hair, her face, her throat, and closed upon it. But the struggle was frightful. She was only a skinny old woman, but the pangs of suffocation called out tremendous efforts from her limbs. Her first convulsion threw him off her, but his hands luckily retained their grip on her throat, wet and slippery as it was. It was a lean and skinny throat, and his hands almost encircled it so that their grip was not easily broken, and his thumbs sank deep between the stringy cords on each side. She thrashed about, her legs striking against the pen, but it did not last long. The convulsions died away, and Loa squeezed with his powerful hands until his thumbs almost met round her flattened windpipe. He maintained his grip until he was long certain that she was dead, and then he rose up on his knees, hitching back the bow that still hung from his shoulder.

"Musini!" he whispered.

"Loa!" came the instant reply. "Lord!"

"Father!" said Lanu.

It might not have been they, after all — Loa had no certainty of it — but not then nor at any subsequent time did Loa ever think of that possibility.

"Be quiet," he ordered, and he turned aside in the darkness to feel for the little ax where he had left it; the little ax which Litti the worker in iron had made so long ago at Loa's order as a gift to Lanu, and which had been so immeasurably valuable to them ever since. He approached the pen with it, and felt in the rainy darkness to ascertain what he should do. The pen, as was to be expected, was constructed of stout stakes and crossbars fastened together with vegetable fiber, and he set to work with the ax to sever the fastenings. It was not easy, for those fastenings were of split cane which almost turned the ax's edge. Loa chopped and tugged; he tore the nail loose on his left forefinger almost without noticing it, before he managed to cut through three sets of

[191]

the fastenings. Then he laid hold of the upright and put out all his strength, tugging, with his eyes starting out of his head in the darkness, until a final ounce of effort tore the upright free.

"Let me try to come through," whispered Musini, who sensibly and with remarkable self-control had contrived to stay quiet during Loa's efforts. Loa felt her wriggling in the darkness, her hands touching his knees as she put her arms through. The pen shook with her struggles, and soon Loa knew that she was squeezing through.

"Lord, I am free," whispered Musini, rising to her feet beside him in the darkness. She trod on the dead woman as she spoke, but that did not alter the tone of her voice at all. Her hands patted his shoulders, and she nuzzled her face against his wet chest.

But this was no moment for tenderness. Loa shoved Musini away from him, for his mind was obsessed with the business in hand — had he not, with incredible self-discipline, kept his mind on it for many hours past? It could no more be diverted at present than a charging elephant.

"Lanu," he said, and felt his way to Lanu's end of the pen.

"I am here, Father," whispered Lanu.

Loa felt in the darkness along the top of the pen.

"This is the fastening to cut, Father," said Lanu.

Loa felt his hand touched by Lanu's, which he had put outside the cage, and he was guided to the place. He hacked in the darkness at the tough cane, more than half his blows missing their mark, until, feeling in the darkness, he felt that the fastenings had parted. And he felt, too, Lanu's hand upon him again.

"Cut the one below, Father," said Lanu. "I will finish the unfastening of this one."

Lanu used the mode of address common between children and used by ordinary children towards their parents; obediently Loa addressed himself to the lower fastening. He chopped and chipped away until the fibers parted, and then, crouching low, began on the next one below. When this had given way he put out his strength to tear the upright free from the cage, but it would not yield. He had to cut another fastening, and this time, when he tugged at the upright, it gave way with a splintering crash that could possibly have been heard in the houses despite the noise of the rain.

"I can come through now, Father," said Lanu, and Loa felt him squeeze himself through the gap. Loa was conscious that Musini was embracing their son in the darkness.

"Let us go," he said, and added, "I must take my arrows."

There was no diverting Loa from his purpose; haste could not overcome him in this present mood of his, as this last speech of his proved. He felt for, and found, his arrows in the darkness where he had left them to spring on the old woman, and he gave them and the bow to Lanu, retaining the little ax for himself.

"Come with me," said Loa, setting off into the darkness, so dark still, with the rain falling heavily, that Lanu took his hand and Musini his other arm so as not to part from him.

[193]

There was no need now to crawl along in an effort, expensive in time, to achieve utter silence. The old woman was dead, and no one else in the town would be specifically on guard, so that they could walk, slowly and with caution, through the mud of the open space. The rain beat down on their naked bodies quite remorselessly, with a stupefying effect; it was as well that Loa had a plan in his mind at the start. But Musini still had to ask questions.

"Whither, Lord?" she whispered.

"River," growled Loa.

The single word was all that was necessary. During their confinement in the cage Musini and Lanu had had time enough to familiarize themselves with the topography of the town, and it was by river they had been brought here. But it was Loa who guided them; perhaps because of the numbing effect of the rain his instincts had full play, and his sense of direction could guide him without interference from thought. A sudden sound at Musini's very elbow made them stop dead, all three of them, rigid, until their minds, slower than their physical reactions, told them that what they had heard was the maa-aaing of a nanny goat sheltered somewhere near. There was no further sound, and they moved forward again feeling their way with the utmost caution. The bleating of the goat told them they had reached the ring of the town; invisible to them, houses must be on either side of them. They paused at every stride, testing the ground beneath their advancing feet before transferring their weight. Loa's sense of balance first told him that they were on a downward slope; they were over the lip of the bluff and on the path down to the water. He felt pebbles under his feet, and Musini and Lanu on each side of him were pressing in upon him; the path was deeply worn and intended for the use of people in single file. And as the path steepened before them they could tell that they were among trees again; the noise of the rain on the leaves told them that if nothing else did. Steeper and steeper grew the path, and then through the roar of the rain their ears caught another noise, that of the river, which, sweeping round the bend, came swirling against the foot of the bluff. The next moment Loa, striding forward with less than his usual caution, stumbled over something solid in his path which the touch of his hands told him must be a canoe. They had reached the river.

"Whither now, Lord?" asked Musini as Loa felt round for the ax that he had dropped.

"This way," said Loa, turning to the left — downstream as ever.

Only a few steps took them among the trees, into the odorous forest where they could feel the leafmold under their feet again. It was a nightmare experience. The trees grew thicker and lower here on the water's edge, and many of them were out of the vertical. The slope of the bluff was steep, and although that was a valuable guide for direction in the dark, it made walking difficult with one foot always higher than the other. They bumped into trees, and they slipped and slithered on the wet leafmold. Always present in their minds was the fear of snakes and of pitfalls. Their rate of progress was deplorably slow, but they maintained it for a couple of hours before Loa called a halt. He was weary, although Musini and Lanu, after twenty-four hours of complete rest and good food in the pen, were still fresh. Loa slept, belly down, his face pillowed on Musini's thigh, while the others dozed fitfully as the rain ceased.

It was Lanu who woke Loa, shaking him by the shoulder so that he started up in alarm.

"Father — Lord," said Lanu. "The light comes."

Only the smallest possible grayness was leaking in through the trees around them, but Lanu was as fully aware as Loa of the value of these minutes. At dawn, or not long after, the death of the old woman and the escape of the prisoners would be discovered in the town. Almost for certain there would be pursuit; conceivably, despite last night's rain, their tracks would be picked up. It was vitally necessary that they should make the most of the few minutes' grace which they had gained. Once deep in the forest and they would be safe, save for some unfortunate and unforeseeable chance, from the townspeople.

"Let us go," said Loa, scrambling to his feet.

He ached in every joint, but he made no remark about it. Aching joints were part of the life of the forest — he might as well have remarked on the fact that there were trees round them. He was desperately hungry, too, but that was equally part of the life of the forest.

They could just see the tree trunks about them now, and could pick their way along the slope, while beneath them the river gurgled and chuckled. Very soon full daylight came — for them the greenish twilight of the forest. They hurried along as fast as they could, taking care to make no sound, but not seeking for food, and pausing to listen and look for an ambush by the little people less than they would have done normally. They listened for sounds of pursuit coming from behind them, but they heard nothing; the gentle wind that was blowing in their faces would carry sound away as well as the smell of the town — in their nostrils there was only the scent of the forest, untainted by smoke or humanity.

The slope of the bluff soon became vertical again, so that they found themselves walking on the lip among the tangled trees, with the water some forty feet directly below their right hands. Soon they came to a point where the bank had given way, and Loa emerged momentarily to a view over a long reach of the river, but only momentarily, for he sprang back, his gestures fixing the others motionless. On the broad surface of the river was a canoe, and now a canoe was an object of fear instead of idle curiosity. They peered at it through the leaves, as it passed rapidly downstream with its paddles gleaming wet in the sunlight. Lanu was shaking his fists at it, threatening it with his arrows, and mouthing boyish curses at it — he was far too cautious to say them aloud.

Another canoe was following closely behind, and they could see the men at the paddles plainly enough. It was reassuring that they were not looking at their bank as they passed it. That did not seem as if they were consciously pursuing them, but canoes were such strange unknown things that it was hard to be sure. A moment later Loa had another shock of fear, for the two canoes swung round in the current and lay alongside each other. Loa felt sure that this implied that the paddlers knew they were there and were concerting pursuit of them. But just as he was about to lead a flight deeper into the forest the paddlers bent to their work again, urging the canoes upstream on diverging courses, while a man in the bow of one of them threw overboard armful after armful of some brown material — Loa could not see more exactly what it was, but the proceeding attracted his curiosity and he lingered to watch, against his better judgment. After a while the man ceased to throw the material overboard, and the canoes toiled on upstream parallel to each other, and Loa could see they were connected together at the bows by some sort of rope. It was an odd kind of ceremony; over the water came the song of the paddlers as they worked; the words were indistinguishable but the rhythm was marked.

Loa could not tear himself away from the spectacle, although he well knew that they should be on their way, but Lanu and Musini seemed equally fascinated, and after some time their curiosity was rewarded by the sight of the canoes inching together again, while this time a man in the bow of each canoe hauled out of the river the brown material previously thrown in, which apparently had all the time been suspended in the water from a rope between the canoes. At intervals one man or the other would stoop and pluck something glittering white out of the material, and throw it in the bottom of the boat.

"Fish," said Musini, using a word that Loa had never heard before.

"Very good," said Lanu, with a pat at his stomach.

It was a fishing canoe that had captured them the day before, they explained to him in whispers; they had seen the things and had later eaten them, but this was the first time they had known how they were caught. The word for fish had completely disappeared from Loa's language (if indeed it had ever had a place there) from the time when Nasa his father had gone up against the riverside village and wiped it out. But Loa was impressed by the stress Lanu laid upon the excellence of their eating qualities; one of the old women who had fed them yesterday had told them the name and persuaded them to try the new delicacy, and the townspeople who had gathered round the pen had been vastly amused to hear that the captives did not know what fish was and had never heard the name.

The canoes passed on up the river, casting their net again as they went; the incident was comforting as it tended to show that any pursuit of Loa and his family was not being pressed to the utmost. Yet as the canoes passed out of sight Loa turned his face downstream again.

"Let us go," he said, as he had said a hundred times before.

There was no pursuit from the town that they ever knew about.

CHAPTER

XIII

THEY WENT on along the river as before, and as before they
starved most of the time with an occasional overfull meal to
sustain them. The bluff on which the town stood was succeeded by marshy bottom land as the river wound back in
the opposite loop. Here there was treacherous and difficult
going, where the trees stood waist-deep in slime, so that they
had to pick their way from root to root, and where the mosquitoes ceased to be a pest to become a plague that made life
almost unbearable. Clouds of mosquitoes followed them
closely as they floundered through the marsh, and leeches
clung to them and sucked their blood — they early found
that if they tore the horrid things off without letting them
drink their fill the jaws remained in the flesh to cause a sore
that was hard to heal. Their bare feet, horny though they
were, were bruised and cut by the unseen roots in the mud,
the sky still dripped upon them, and there was more than
one night when it was impossible to light a fire in the general wetness.

It was at a despairing moment in this misery that Loa
decided upon leaving the river. Child of the sky, the river
was betraying them, was taking advantage of a too close
association. Loa turned his back on the water and led his

family directly away from it, intending vaguely to attempt
to use it as a guide without keeping close to it, hard though
that would be in the forest. It was thus he learned to keep
to the higher ground above the river and cut across the
necks of the loops, avoiding the bottoms altogether and saving an enormous amount of distance. It was an almost auto-
matic process. They left the marshes to find themselves on
firm ascending ground; turned to the right to keep parallel
with the river, and shortly afterwards discovered that they
were on the bluff at the head of the next loop, with two
long reaches of the river stretching away before them, with
sky and river their friends and allies again instead of their
irritating enemies.

"That is the way we shall go," said Loa, pointing along
the line of the bluff.

He had learned the lesson of the nature of the river, how
it looped round marshes and ran to meet bluffs, and he spoke
with an assurance that drew a respectful glance even from
Musini.

"It will be good to have easy walking again," said Musini.
"Those marshes were not good for the child."

"The child?" said Loa, off his guard.

The word Musini had used was one that implied a little
baby, and not even as a highly exaggerated endearment
could it be applied to Lanu.

"Yes, the child," said Musini. She bellowed with sudden
laughter. "Ho! Ho! Ho! Lord, can you lie with a woman
all these nights and not expect a child?"

Musini meant the question as pure rhetoric, but it came

very close to the truth. Loa had become a father so often, and with such small after-consequences to himself, and he had had so many other matters to occupy his mind of late, that the possibility had not crossed his mind. Moreover, Musini was an old woman — here was Lanu whose existence proved that — and it was a shock to realize that she was still fruitful. Loa was a little nettled at this revelation of his lack of forethought; he was nettled, too, at Musini's jocular treatment of it and at the way Lanu joined in her laughter. It all stressed the fact which had been brought home to him on other occasions: that he might be a god, he might at least have superhuman powers and qualities, but he could not obtain from those close to him the respect those powers and qualities should ensure for him. It was faintly irritating, especially coming right on the heels of such an important discovery as the practicability of cutting across the necks of the loops of the river. He strode off in something of a huff, only slightly mollified later when Lanu and Musini both brought him mouthfuls of food which they had found for themselves.

Keeping to the high ground close above the river they made considerable progress for some days. There were many things Loa did not realize about this journey of theirs. He knew that they had wasted a great many days by keeping close to the water's edge, but it never dawned upon him that they were within a great arc of the river, along the chord of which he had been conducted by the slavers, so that even allowing for the new saving by cutting off the loops his return journey was at least twice as long as the outward one had been. Moreover, so slowly did they move, thanks to the need for precaution and the need for finding their food, that each day's march was far smaller than he had made on the average when driven by the slavers. Taking all factors into consideration Loa, if ever he were to reach home, would undoubtedly spend twenty days on the return journey for every day that he had spent going out.

There was a further and special reason for the slavers to travel by the chord and not by the arc, leaving untouched the few towns along the riverbank in the curve; Loa never made the correct deduction, although the facts were made plain to him. The great curve of the river lies on one of the upper plateaus of Central Africa; the upper and lower ends of the curve are marked by cataracts and waterfalls; Loa never saw anything of the upper falls, but they were now to reach the lower ones. The tangled forest rose slowly into a low barrier of hills, right across the path of the river, which broke through them here; Loa and the others, close above the water, passed through the same gap without climbing the hills. They knew that the bluffs were growing steeper, and that the loops were not so marked as the river straightened itself, but they were not prepared for what they saw when they came to the lip of the gorge. They had heard, even in the forest, the louder noise the river was making; now they could see why. The river was far narrower, confined between steep banks, and it was angry at the restrictions imposed upon it. It was running with furious speed, roaring with rage. The rocks that impeded its passage were smothered in foam. The swirls upon its surface were not the subtle sleek things that they had been accustomed to see higher up; here they were frantic violent struggles, convulsions like those of the old woman when Loa had his hands on her throat. Anyone could see that the cliffs were trying to strangle the river; and the noise of the cataract was tremendous.

"The river fights with the forest," said Musini at Loa's side, looking down at the deafening turbulence. Matter-of-fact person though Musini was, she nevertheless had an apt word on occasions.

They were destined to see a good deal of the cataract over its twenty miles of length, for its gorge deepened and the cliffs shutting it in grew steeper, compelling them to pick their precarious way at the very brink of the water, where the rocky surface practically prohibited the growth of vegetation, although the cliffs that rose above them bore trees in every ledge, and elsewhere were covered with brilliant lichens and mosses. Shut in between the cliffs, Loa was not as conscious of the vast extent of his brother the sky as he usually was when beside the river; and he even felt a more friendly feeling towards the narrow strip that was visible over his head. The continual roar of the cataract worked on him until he grew lightheaded, and pranced and brandished the ax as he walked along; the lightheadedness might have been partly the result of hunger, because they went with empty stomachs along most of the gorge. It was only when they were near its end that two successive lucky shots brought down parrots for them to eat.

Twice at points where the water lapped the foot of the

cliff they were forced to climb the cliff face, with endless difficulty, until they reached a shelf along which they could make their way until it was possible to descend again. Up there Loa's head swam even worse than when he emerged into open spaces, but he suppressed, as he always had done, any mention of this sensation, for Lanu seemed actually to enjoy being on a height, while Musini hardly spared a glance down the gorge and clearly acted as though, given a firm footing, she did not care whether the drop at her elbow was five feet or five hundred. The god Loa of his previous existence could without qualms have acknowledged feelings of weakness, but the present Loa, who was little use at lighting fires, and who was not as good a marksman as Lanu, and for whom respect was blended with tolerance or even amusement, could not afford to do any such thing. It was only rarely nowadays that Loa would even admit that he was hungry, although it is to be doubted if the appearance of stoical indifference that he cultivated made much impression on Musini.

The gorge gradually flattened out without any abrupt change; the surface of the river gradually became wider and less studded with rocks, and its course became slower. It was not until they found themselves among trees and enjoying the mushrooms and white ants of the forest that they realized the gorge had ended. What really brought it home to them was Loa's noticing of a creeper carelessly lying between two trees — just too carelessly; concealed behind the tree was a bent bow with an arrow on the string, to be loosed at a touch on the creeper. They were back among the little people again; all along the gorge they had seen no sign of them.

This side of the cataract the river seemed to run straighter, without so many turns, and consequently without being so marshy at the banks, so that it was a little surprising when they found themselves entering into an area of bog which seemed to extend a long way inland. It was soon obvious that they could not struggle through it, and so they turned to their left (left-handed away from the river, right-handed towards it, as always) to seek high ground. Keeping to the forest rim, at the fringe of the marsh, they were forced to make two days' detour; it was on the afternoon of the second day that they came out upon a prospect that halted them abruptly. It was only a little bluff upon which they stood, but it commanded a wide view. To their right was the reedy marsh, with occasional trees standing in it, and with water visible here and there among the reeds, and far beyond it they could just see the broad surface of the river. But in front of them, at their feet, lay another river.

It was nothing like the size of the big river, but it was far greater than the numerous little threads of water through which they had splashed in the course of their journey. One might shoot an arrow across it, hardly even drawing the arrow to the head, but there was no leaping across it or splashing through it, that was obvious. There were black depths in that river, here where it made ready to join with the bigger river, wherein devilish creatures might well live. It was an obstacle they could not pass.

"So," said Musini at Loa's side. "Another river."

She looked at him sidelong. There may even have been something of malice — at least of bitter amusement — in her glance, as though to question what the god Loa proposed to do in these new circumstances. As Musini advanced in her pregnancy, in that essentially womanly business, she was inclined to leave men's affairs more to men, and to withdraw into herself. It was plain that she washed her hands of all responsibility for the present situation.

"What next, Father?" asked Lanu, eagerly. He still had faith in his father's superior intellect and experience.

"Wait, my son," said Loa, as ponderously as he could while trying to keep despair out of his voice.

He sat himself down upon the bluff, at the foot of a great tree, and addressed himself again to a study of the landscape — more to keep despair out of his mind than for any other reason. Down to his right spread the marshes of the river junction — actually the delta of the tributary — alive with birds, reedy and marshy and everywhere intersected by water channels. Ahead of him lay the little river, little by comparison but immeasurably wide when their own help-lessness was taken into account. To his left the river wound among the trees of the forest out of sight, and behind him — he knew what was behind him. In his mind fluttered the notion, not very well defined, that all rivers have their sources somewhere, so that by turning to his left he could follow the tributary upstream until it became passable, and then, crossing it and turning to his right, he could follow it back again to this junction. The notion fluttered in his mind and passed out again. He had not yet learned enough about the world; he might have thought of such a scheme had the obstacle before him been smaller, had it been such that he could nearly jump across it, but he could not really believe that such a major stream as this could start from nothing.

In that case the problem was insoluble. Even the old trick of pressing his fists into his eyes was of no help. He pressed until wheels of fire circled in his sight, and he reached no conclusion; he only fell into despair. Musini and Lanu waited by his side for him to announce his decision, and he said nothing, sitting morose and silent against the tree. It was easy enough to fall into apathy, to sit there not thinking at all, with all his thinking processes clogged by despair, while dark shadows played in his mind. So far during all this while, ever since he had assumed command of the party, he had been borne up by faith, by that much of the blind belief in his own powers which had survived his capture by the raiders, or by a mere animal fatalism which had urged him along. Now all this was at an end; everything was in ruins. He sat there conscious of nothing save misery and depression.

In time Lanu and Musini became restless.

"Father," said Lanu.

"Lord," said Musini. "Loa. Husband."

She raised her voice with each word; it was the first time in her life that even she had ventured to address Loa by the familiar expression "husband," but she could not rouse Loa from his apathy. She put her hand on his shoulder and shook him gently.

"Leave me in peace," said Loa, heavily, without raising his eyes to her face. "Peace" was not a fair description of his state of mind, but it would serve in comparison with what he would feel if he were roused and set to thinking again. And he was tired, mortally weary. Lanu and Musini exchanged glances. It was obvious that there was no reasoning with him when he was in this mood.

"Come," said Musini to her son. "Let us gather food."

Loa stayed where he was in his melancholy for all the rest of that day. He did not shake off his mood even when Musini came to him in the evening and told him that food was ready for him. The thought of food roused him sufficiently to get him stiffly to his feet to walk back among the trees where the others had lighted a fire, but he sat and ate his food silently, his brooding depression conveying itself to Musini and Lanu so that they talked, when they talked at all, in whispers. And when he had eaten he lay down and slept with no more words either; he slept heavily, oppressed by formless dreams, so that he awoke in the morning unrefreshed and as deeply sunk in apathy as before. Lanu and Musini looked at him as he sat staring at the ashes of last night's fire without seeing them. They shook their heads and moved silently about him.

Then they heard sounds, sounds which penetrated even in Loa's consciousness and roused him instantly, which keyed them all up and which set Loa grasping for his bow and arrows and then started them all creeping silently back to the riverbank; not breathing a word to each other, creeping like beasts of prey towards the source of the noise. Loa wriggled like a snake for the last yard or two to the point where he could see the river. With his chin buried in the leafmold he peered over a root at the base of the tree, showing no more than his eyes as he gazed down the brief declivity at the water. It was a canoe, not one of the big canoes he had seen casting nets in the river, but a smaller craft altogether, tiny and cranky, hardly larger than was necessary to hold the two men who sat in it, propelling it slowly along with their paddles. They were big men, much scarred and tattooed, and the one in front wore on his head an ornament of gray feathers, and there were bracelets round the arms of the one in the back. Their paddles touched upon the sides of the canoe as they worked; that was one of the noises that had attracted Loa's attention, and now and then they exchanged a word — that was the other noise. One of them laughed, and clearly they felt themselves in no danger.

But they were well out in the middle of the river, and already a little downstream of where Loa lay. It would be a long arrow flight that would reach them, and if they died there in the middle of the river they were as much out of reach as the other side of the river was. Loa turned his head slowly to where Lanu lay in like concealment. Lanu had the same grasp of the situation. He was lying perfectly still merely watching, and when his eyes met Loa's their lack of expression told Loa that he, too, could see no reason for immediate action. They watched the canoe paddle slowly down the river, far out of reach, but not out of sight. It turned into one of the minor channels among the reeds, and

Loa waited long before he rose and cautiously led the way among the trees at the water's edge in pursuit. With the patience of the leopard on the tree branch, with the cunning of man, they crept after the canoe, slipping from tree to tree, wading through marshy patches, standing stock-still behind cover when there was the least chance of being observed.

Loa found it hard to understand what the men in the canoe were doing, especially as frequently they stopped out of sight for long intervals in one of the narrow reedy channels. On the occasions when he could see them one or the other of them leaned perilously over the side of the canoe and drew something out of the water, and sometimes he would toss something white into the bottom of the boat — these mysterious fish, Loa supposed, which Lanu and Musini had talked about. But once they stopped for a long time still, with one man standing in the canoe — all Loa could see was the black dot of the man's head over the level of the reeds. This stop explained itself. Loa saw the man's arm rise in the unmistakable gesture of bending and loosing a bow; the canoe had been waiting for one of the innumerable marsh birds to come within range.

The canoe threaded its way in and out among the reeds, and Loa watched it with his interminable patience; patience the more laudable because he was not waiting for something certain, nor even for any definite possibility. He was just waiting, in case something, he knew not what, should happen. He and Lanu were close to the water's edge here, each behind a tree. Before them ran one of the reedy channels of the delta; about them was marshy land, not impassable, with the roots of the trees growing in it — Musini was farther back, waiting too, with the same patience. About them brooded the sweltering heat and the deep silence of the forest, and the reek of the delta was in their nostrils. The distant cry of birds only served to accentuate the silence about them as they stood like statues, not daring to move because the canoe was out of sight and they did not know where or when it would reappear. Then they heard sounds, coming from not far away — almost the same sounds as had first broken in upon Loa's apathy, the sound of wood against wood, the murmur of voices, even a laugh like the one they had heard before. Loa's muscles tightened; he notched his bowstring into his arrow and half drew it. He could see that Lanu was doing exactly the same. The canoe emerged round the corner of the reedy channel, heading down it straight towards them. Loa waited with his bow bent, as the canoe crawled along towards them, ever so slowly. At long arrow range the canoe stopped, and again one of the men leaned over the side — Loa could see the canoe heel over dangerously — to draw something out of the water and examine it and drop it in again, something that looked like a basket of reeds. Then the canoe resumed its course towards them, rocking a little with the strokes of the paddlers, yawing a little from side to side of the channel. Loa was actually quivering, so tensely expectant was he, but he must wait — wait — wait. But now the moment had come, with the canoe close beside him, not twenty feet from his arrowhead. He stepped out and drew his bow to the full and loosed, seized another arrow and loosed again, and yet a third time. Lanu's bow twanged beside him. At that close range the hard wooden arrowhead, hardened in the fire and sharpened to a needlepoint, could penetrate easily even through something as tough and as elastic as human skin. Loa's first arrow struck the man in the bow of the boat below the armpit and went in deep between the ribs. His second arrow struck lower and farther forward and penetrated as deeply. Even without the poison on the heads those wounds were mortal. Loa used his third arrow on the second man, who had turned an astonished face towards them with Lanu's arrows sticking in his back and his arm. Loa's arrow whizzed in at the opened mouth at the same moment as Lanu's third arrow struck him in the breast. He fell backwards, tipping over the crazy dugout. Both bodies vanished beneath the dark surface of the backwater, and the canoe, filled with water, floated with only a strip of gunwale showing. Beside it floated a collection of debris — the two paddles, a couple of dead birds, half a dozen white-bellied fish, a bow and some arrows, a wooden bailer.

Loa and Lanu stood by the bank waiting for the boatmen to reappear, but the dark water was undisturbed as Musini came up and stood beside them.

"They are dead?" asked Musini.

"They are there," said Loa, pointing into the backwater. With the relief from tension and from his apathy of yesterday his voice sounded cracked and unnatural.

"They are dead!" said Lanu. "We killed them, Loa and I. With our arrows from here we killed them. How surprised they were when we stepped forward with our bows bent. We struck as the snake strikes. We — "

"Peace, son," said Musini, breaking in on his rhapsody. "And now? The men are dead, and the boat is there."

It was like Musini to call attention to the difficulties ahead. The canoe, just showing above the water, floated five yards from the bank, quite beyond their reach, and Loa was a trifle nonplused.

"I can get it," said Lanu, eagerly.

He took the ax and severed a creeper which climbed the tree beside which they stood, and then, dragging at it with all his weight, he tore it down from its anchorage far enough to be able to sever it again, cutting off a piece twenty feet long.

"See," said Lanu, and, standing carefully at the water's edge, he cast the end of the creeper over the canoe. When he dragged the creeper in the canoe undoubtedly moved, and came an inch or two nearer. Another cast just moved it again.

"Ha!" said Musini, her interest and approval caught.

She looked round her and approached a fallen branch and was going to cut a section from it with the ax, but a glance from her brought Loa to her side, for there was something vaguely improper about a woman using cutting tools of steel. Loa cut off the length she indicated and Musini hastened to fasten it to the end of Lanu's creeper. Now a bold cast beyond the canoe, and a careful pulling in, brought the waterlogged boat much nearer, and two or three further attempts brought it so close that it grounded beside the bank where they could just reach it.

"And now?" said Musini again.

For answer Lanu leaned far out from the bank and took hold of the gunwale of the canoe, heaving at it. Water lapped over the side out of it, and Loa came to his help. With a powerful heave they were able to pour a good deal of the water out, so that the canoe floated against the bank with a fair amount of freeboard. Lanu began to climb in.

"No! No!" said Musini in sudden panic.

She had qualms about this enterprise; the water of the backwater was dark and mysterious, and boats were strange things, and she had fears for her son, but Loa put his hand on her shoulder and restrained her. Lanu climbed into the canoe with a laugh which was checked when the crazy craft wobbled violently under him so that he nearly capsized it again. Common sense made him sit down in the water in the bottom and stabilize the boat a little; he laughed again, but a trifle nervously, and the nervousness was the more perceptible when he glanced round and saw that the canoe had left the bank and he was drifting free. But after all, he had been in a canoe before, when he and his mother had been captured; he knew one could float in one and survive the experience, and his father had told him much about them with an inaccuracy Lanu knew nothing about.

His momentum carried him out to the floating material, and he reached out — with a sudden hesitation on account of the lurches of the canoe — and took a paddle. He waved it triumphantly and was about to try to use it when his eye caught sight of the bailer floating beside him; he had seen a bailer used on his short previous voyage. He took the bailer and set the water flying out of the boat, laughing excitedly again now. With the boat nearly empty he tried to pick up the other floating things. He had to use the paddle he had to get to the other one, and his first amateurish digs sent the little boat circling round in a quite unpredictable fashion, and his attempts at managing it made it rock frighteningly again. But soon he had picked up paddle and bow and arrows and fish and all, looking back at his parents with all his teeth flashing in a grin, while they for their part regarded him with parental pride — combined with a little of the consternation of the hen who has mothered ducklings. It was only a few moments before the obvious fact was brought home to Lanu that the canoe turned away from the paddle; by taking a stroke first on one side and then on the other he was able to propel it in some sort of straight line. It was wonderful. He headed the boat towards where his parents stood, and after one or two failures managed to come up beside them. Loa leaned over and took hold of the side and drew it against the bank.

"We have a canoe!" said Lanu in ecstasy.

Perhaps Musini felt that she did not want to be outdone in the matter of innovations.

"And there are fish," she said. "Give me that one, Lanu. I am hungry."

Lanu handed her the fish and Musini took it in her two

hands. Only once before had she eaten fish, and then it had taken some coaxing on the part of the old woman who had guarded her to induce her to do it, but she set about it now with a determined nonchalance designed to impress her menfolk. She took a determined bite out of the fish's belly.

"Good," she said, with her mouth full.

The flesh was full of bones, and somewhat insipid, but for a hungry woman it was excellent food.

"Give me one too," said Loa.

They all three of them devoured the raw fish; it was not until he began his second one that Loa learned something of the trick of stripping the flesh from the backbone with his teeth, and also convinced himself that neither head nor fins were edible. He swallowed a good many bones but even so the fish constituted one of the few satisfactory meals he had lately had. Loa tossed the last backbone into the river. He was revivified, without a thought for the two dead men lying under the black surface of the backwater.

"Now do we cross the water?" asked Lanu, still in ecstasy.

That was a strange question to Loa, and he hesitated before replying. Could he bring himself to entrust his godlike person to the unstable surface of the water, under the glare of the unsympathetic sky? There was the kindly forest at his back, and under his feet was the earth, marshy at the moment but reassuringly solid compared with the unfamiliar element before him. All the conservatism of savagery, the fears of ignorance, raised a turmoil within him as he faced the decision. But there was only one thing to say, and he said it.

"Yes."

The difficulties were obvious; the canoe was far too tiny to carry three people, they were down in the delta of the tributary, and they knew almost nothing about managing a canoe. Musini took charge of the details; gods might have divine inspirations, but it needed her to put them into execution.

"Let us go back to where we saw it first," she said. "Loa, we can walk there, if you, Lanu, can make that thing come along with us."

That was what they did, Loa and Musini walking along the water's edge carrying the impedimenta while Lanu struggled to paddle along beside them. He had untold difficulties with the little craft, more than once turning complete circles as he tried to propel her along, to Musini's acute but unvoiced anxiety, but eventually they reached the point above the delta where the last distributary parted from the river and the channel was well defined. On the other side lay the forest and the way home. Musini offered herself up for sacrifice.

"Take me over," she said to Lanu. "Then you can return for Loa."

She made ready to get into the canoe.

"Take care! Take care!" squeaked Lanu, by now thoroughly familiar with the instability of the dugout. It rocked violently, but Lanu contrived to keep it the right way up as Musini lowered herself into the bottom, clinging desperately to the gunwales. Her additional weight had grounded the boat forward, but Lanu shoved her free and began to paddle gingerly away from the bank, while Loa watched in frantic anxiety mingled with a strange pride. He saw the canoe circle in midstream, and he watched it take its erratic course across the river. At last he saw it reach the other side, and he saw Musini heave her growing bulk out of the boat and climb out onto the bank. There was a pause while Musini received the things which she cannily decided should be handed up to her without being imperiled by another crossing, and then the canoe came back across the water, Lanu grinning in triumph as he paddled. Loa climbed cautiously in, only half-hearing the warnings and advice which Lanu poured out. It was both sickly and frightening to feel the boat rock beneath him. With one hand he gripped the precious ax and with the other he clung like death to the edge of the boat.

"Sit in the middle, Father," said Lanu, tone and grammar both showing a deplorable lack of respect for a parent and elder, let alone for a god.

Loa shifted his position by a terrified half-inch; the violent reaction produced by the least movement reduced him to idiocy. Lanu gave up the hope of attaining perfect balance and started to paddle, and Loa found the forest receding from him, so that he was exposed on the surface of the water to all the glare of the sky above him and on all sides. He felt as insignificant as any insect as he sat frozen with fear, mocked by the gurgling of the water around Lanu's paddle. Certainly the water was jeering at him, if not threatening him. His eyes could hardly focus on the farther shore, where Musini squatted in the shade awaiting him —

he could only see her at intervals, when the swings of the canoe brought her directly before him, for he could not even turn his eyeballs to keep her continuously in sight.

But they drew up to her in the end, and she rose to greet them.

"First give me the ax," she said.

Loa handed it up to her, and then tried to stand to disembark. The rocking of the canoe threw him into an active panic. He was about to plunge for the shore, careless of the results to the canoe and to Lanu, but, to his credit, he restrained himself, sitting down and allowing the canoe to regain its stability while Lanu sighed with relief. Then he rose more calmly, clutched the roots in the bank, and cautiously heaved himself out. Lanu did not follow him; he sat on in the canoe, grasping the paddle with one hand and a root with the other.

"Father," said Lanu, "cannot we keep this canoe?"

"*Keep* it?" exclaimed Loa, utterly astonished.

"Yes," said Lanu.

It was a new toy to him. He had mastered his fears, and it had been a delightful and exciting experience to learn to control the canoe on the alien water. He had the feeling that he wanted to paddle canoes all the rest of his life.

"We cannot do that!" said Loa, uttering the first words that came into his head.

"Oh," said Lanu.

It could hardly be said that he was disappointed. It was something more than life could really offer, to own a canoe. Gone almost beyond memory were the days when he was a privileged little boy who sometimes wore a leopardskin cloak, and who had a real steel ax such as marked him out far above his playmates. But as the vision receded facts came into his mind to support his despairing plea.

"We might get more fish," he said. "You like fish. You could walk along the bank while I paddled down the river. There might be other rivers to cross. We might — we might even cross the big river!"

That was saying far too much, for to Loa the suggestion was so fantastic as to demand instant rejection.

"No!" he said. "Never! Come out of the boat."

Lanu was near tears, and rebellion stirred within him, not so much against his father as against fate; Musini saw it and came to the rescue with a suggestion.

"Perhaps at home," she said, "you will have a canoe. There we are near the big river, and perhaps Loa will give you one. You will be able to make it."

It was some mitigation of Lanu's disappointment; it distracted him from his present desires by setting him thinking about the future.

"I think I could," he said.

He looked down at the crazy craft that was suddenly so dear to him, trying to note in his mind how it was constructed. A tree trunk had been hollowed out — Lanu saw how the bow and stern were shaped — and to give more freeboard a plank had been attached along each gunwale, sewn to the dugout with fiber, in much the same way as the houses which he just remembered had been built by Tolo and Tolo's brothers.

"Come, my son," said Loa, more gently.

Now that the initial shock of Lanu's revolutionary suggestion had died away, he could talk more reasonably, especially as the nervous tension of his first trip in a boat was dying away too. He held out his hand to Lanu and swung him up onto the bank, and the masterless canoe drifted away from the shore.

"I shall keep this," said Lanu, indicating the paddle which he still retained in his hand — in point of fact he actually did keep it by him for two whole days in the forest, as a memento of the canoe.

They turned to enter again into the forest, all of them a little subdued and silent. Somewhere at the back of Loa's mind strange thoughts were stirring, awakened by Lanu's absurd suggestion about the canoe and by Musini's equally absurd suggestion about making one. Could it be? Might it happen? Fish were undoubtedly good to eat. Out on the broad river a man — not Loa, certainly not Loa, but conceivably Lanu — might enjoy a freedom of movement and an ability to carry baggage that the forest could not offer. The slave raiders had made use of the river. The most vaulting ideas, quite shapeless at the moment, were coming to life in Loa's brain, such fantastic ideas, in fact, that Loa was disturbed by them, tried to put them out of his mind in his distrust of novelty.

Musini brought him back to the world of the matter-of-fact.

"We have these birds to eat," she said — she had fastened

to her girdle the birds picked out of the water after the up-
setting of the canoe. "We should eat them soon."

So that same day that he first tasted fish and first went
upon the water Loa had his first taste of duck. It was indeed
a revolutionary day.

CHAPTER

XIV

THEIR WOODCRAFT had inevitably improved immeasurably since first they had been compelled to live in the forest. Once they had been town dwellers, living a definitely urban life on the produce of a cultivated land, and Loa even more than the others had been an ignoramus about the practical details of life among the trees; he had not had Lanu's intense and recent experience on the fringe of the forest with his playmates. But months of education in the hardest school of all had taught them much. They could flit like shadows through the forest. No mushroom half hidden in leafmold could escape their keen observation. They could read the tracks of the little people and detect instantly their buried skewers and their pitfalls. They were not so continuously hungry and they could make their way among the trees without often coming against obstructions, which their newly developed senses enabled them to avoid without actual thought. And all this enabled them to travel with far greater speed than when they had first begun their journey. They kept the great river on their right hand, cutting off the bigger loops by keeping to the high ground without any difficulty at all, and they were only just conscious of their improvement. If they had been asked, they would certainly

have hesitated before agreeing that they had improved —
at the back of their minds was a feeling that behind them,
at the point where Loa had been rescued from the slavers,
was a bad country where life was very difficult, and that
here life was easier.

The river made a wide, shallower curve than usual, but
in the curve the land was marshy as always, and Loa
branched away from the river without hesitation. There
was something almost resembling a track here, a path trodden by the forest antelope and by the little people along the
easiest going, and Loa led the way along it, silent of tread,
quick of eye, alert and ready for instant action. His eye for
ground, naturally good, and cultivated now to a high condition of efficiency, told him that the river was approaching
him again on his right hand, for the slope was increasing —
imperceptibly to anyone save himself — and the character
of the forest was changing, imperceptibly, again, to almost
anyone save himself. Only the minutest differences told him
this, but he was in no way surprised when the light through
the trees on his right front began to increase, when the up-
hill trend of the ground became more steep, and the leafmold under his feet grew thinner so that he could feel rock
beneath it. At the crest the rock broke clean through the
surface into a succession of low pinnacles, and Loa came out
from the trees into an open space at the lip of the bluff, with
the great river beneath him.

He had been ready for something like this, but not exactly this. He shrank down, he almost cowered before what
he saw, yet it was not his usual weakness in the presence of

great distances. When Lanu and Musini came up to him he could not speak; he moved his lips but could make no sound, so overpowering was his emotion. Lanu looked round him, at the rocks, at the curve of the river, at the trees growing densely about them, projecting horizontally from the steep bank in their quest for light and air. He rubbed his eyes like someone in a dream.

"I have seen this before," he said, and Loa nodded, his chest heaving.

Musini had sat down on a lichen-covered block of rock, for her pregnancy was now so far advanced as to make her seize every opportunity to rest. She looked round her too.

"It is our river," she said. "This is where we used to come from our town."

"It is where you used to speak to the moon," said Lanu to Loa, and stopped a little guiltily. They all knew that Loa had not summoned his sister the moon out of the river for months and months now, and yet she still came back to the sky after each absence.

"So it is," said Loa, hoarsely.

"Through there lies the way home. Only a little way," said Musini, pointing through the forest.

"Yes indeed," agreed Lanu excitedly.

He seized a lump of rock in both hands, whirled it round, and flung it out into the stream, where it raised a splash. That was what he used to do when he was brought here in that other life, but now it was a far larger rock that he threw. He was almost a man now.

"Let us go," he said. "What are we waiting for?"

Loa looked round at the two of them. They had not had his experience. They had never known what it was to be a god one day and a slave the next. This was a moment of triumph, to return after all these uncounted months to a familiar place, but Loa had learned to distrust moments of triumph. He felt apprehensive; he did not know exactly why. But his apprehensions goaded him to a convulsive mental effort, as he made himself try to picture what he expected to find if he went home along the forest path. The first feeling was that he would find it as he had always seen it, always save for the one morning when the slave raiders came. The orderly street with the tall wooden houses on each side, the throngs of women going about their domestic business, even Litti the worker in iron busy at his forge. That was the mental picture that memory conjured up; and he knew, with strange clairvoyance, that Musini and Lanu could see similar mirages. But Loa was a realist now, and no dreamer. The last time he had seen the town the houses had been in flames, a third of the people were captives of the slave raiders, children and old men and women had been lying in a tangled mass of corpses. Loa remembered that once at least during his recent travels he had set foot on the site of a town, a mere area in the forest where the saplings contended with the shrubs and only a few half-choked banana trees remained as evidence that man had once cultivated the spot. Certainly this was all that they might find now.

And on the other hand . . . ? Loa remembered the encounters he had had with people from his town while he was a slave. They had hardly known him, and they had not treated him as a god. So preoccupied were they with their own affairs that they had not evinced any of the respect or the terror which his appearance had once demanded. If there were any people in the town they would have been preoccupied with their affairs for many months. How would they treat him? For a moment Loa felt that he did not care. He would not mind being the least considerable of all the men in the town if only he were home again. He would content himself with no other wife than Musini, he would reconcile himself to begging help of other men to build a house, and Lanu would have to work hard to buy himself a wife; he would endure anything just to be home. His homesickness was intense enough at that moment to make any sacrifice agreeable if he could satisfy it.

This was all very well, but Loa, standing woodenly with his wife and son growing more and more excited in front of him, felt yet other doubts and apprehensions. He could not define them at all, but his recent experiences taught him to be doubtful, to take nothing for granted. Fear had been part of the air he breathed for many months now, and he still felt fear. His whole attitude was in the strangest contrast not only with that of Lanu and Musini but also with his own of a few moments ago. His recent life had been a partial education for him. He had acquired a certain amount of logical ability, he had learned something of human nature, and, above all, he knew now that he did not live in a settled world where the unprecedented did not happen. He slid his hand up his bowstave, bent it, and slipped the string into the notch, and then gently twanged the string to make certain the weapon was ready for immediate action. He examined his three arrows to see that the heads were properly secured and that the notches of the barbs still retained their viscid poison. With his bow over his left shoulder he put out his right hand and gently took the little ax from Lanu, who happened to be carrying it at that moment.

The others looked at him in some surprise, their ebullience dying away when they noticed the gravity of his demeanor.

"Lord," said Musini, slipping naturally into the respectful form of address. "What do you fear?"

Loa the god could not say "I do not know," which would have been the truth, nor could he say "Everything," which would have been a close approximation to the truth. He could only turn a terrible eye on his wife, a cold glare that repressed even Musini and reduced her to apologetic mumblings. Lanu caught the infection and strung his bow without further words, waiting for Loa to make the next move. Loa looked back across the broad river, sullen yet metallic under the sun. He even looked up at his brother the sky; he lingered unaccountably as he spun out these last few moments before starting out on what he felt in his bones to be a decisive move which would affect the rest of his life — affect it to the extent, even, of ending it abruptly, maybe. It was strange to be seeking excuses for lingering here under the callous observation of the sky, when almost at a stride he could gain the comforting twilight of the forest; but he could not put off the move for long, not under the eyes of Lanu and Musini, nor under his own eyes. He hitched his bow more comfortably on his shoulder, took a fresh grip of the little ax, and started along the path to the town.

Lanu and Musini walked with him in silence, the former out at one side of him, the latter in the rear, weighed down somewhat by the burden she was carrying. Lanu scanned the forest ahead of them as keenly as ever he had. In the neighborhood of a town there was always added danger from the little people, who were likely to hang round it both to rob the banana and manioc plantations and to put themselves in the way of obtaining live meat. Chips had been taken out of the bark of several trees which they passed; a gesture from Lanu called Loa's attention to chips of different heights and appearance — both the little people and real men had passed this way within the last few weeks, to judge by the fact that lichens had hardly had time to establish themselves on the cut surfaces. And Lanu pointed, too, to footprints at the base of trees, which, to judge by his expression, confirmed that conclusion. Loa glanced at them wisely, but he was not woodsman enough to draw from the faint indications that survived any inferences on which he could rely.

There was something, however, which offered unmistakable proof that men were living near. They could smell the town as they approached it, the wood smoke and the decaying refuse; only the merest trace stealing on the air, imperceptible to any but nostrils long accustomed to the scent of river and forest. It even seemed that their ears could catch the faint sounds of a community; at any rate, what

Lanu thought he heard worked him up to a fresh pitch of excitement so that he grinned and gesticulated to his father, who stolidly ignored him. This was the path Loa had trodden scores of times; the changes in the forest, eternal yet everchanging, could not prevent Loa from recognizing parts of it. Here, just where he had expected it, began the tangled second growth of the abandoned clearings, and at this point, even to a tyro's eye, it was obvious that the path entered into the tangle. Loa plunged in ahead with the ax.

It was the time when the struggle for existence in the vegetable world in that clearing had reached its climax, when the saplings were stoutly grown and yet not large enough to kill by their shade the undergrowth which had first occupied the cleared space. The saplings grew thick, in desperate rivalry with each other, while all about them the shrubs and creepers competed with each other in a waist-deep tangle. Nor had the felled trees yet been reabsorbed into the forest; there were still trunks and branches sufficiently solid to halt a man, although one lichen-covered trunk onto which Loa climbed crumbled utterly to pieces under his feet — honeycombed to rottenness by white ants, presumably. Sweating with the exertion and the close heat, Loa plunged on; the path could not be called defined in any sense, for there had not been enough coming and going of men or of game to make any impression on the rapid growth of the vegetation. Then he parted the last bush, and gazed out at the town.

It was all so different. There was a street, and there were

houses, and the houses were built, as they always had been, of thick planks split by wedges from tree trunks, and roofed with a thatch of phrynia leaves. But it was not the same street, not the street that had so often appeared to Loa's mental vision in his fits of homesickness. The houses were on different sites, and there were not so many of them. At this end of the town, where Loa had lived, the forest had begun to encroach. Loa's own house, and Musini's house, and the big multiple-house which had sheltered some of his wives, had all disappeared, their places partly taken by a few poor houses and partly by a mass of scrub and creeper which had already established itself on the vacant sites. Not merely was the town smaller, but its center of gravity had apparently shifted towards the other end, towards the marshy brook and Litti's forge. Loa gulped as he gazed out, partly with excitement but mainly in a childlike disappointment that everything was not the same as he remembered it — even though at one time he had been realist enough to remember the conflagration that had started in the town when he was a captive of the slave raiders. But it might as well be a different town, and not his home at all.

Lanu had come up beside him and was staring out at the town too, and the changes that he noticed were having a sobering effect on him, judging by his silence and immobility. There were people walking about the town, and it was upon them that Loa turned his attention after his first sweeping glance. Here was a woman with a hand of bananas on her head. Loa was not sure that he remembered her; maybe it was some daughter of Gooma, the man who was so

[232   ]

expert at cutting the hardwood wedges for plank splitting — Gooma had a string of daughters. Over there a man with a bow in his hand came striding out of a house, and Loa knew him at once. It was Ura, Nessi's husband — it was just as well Nessi was dead then, for living she would have been a tedious complication in any future settlement. Ura must have made his escape when the raiders attacked the town, as must all of these people. A woman emerged from the same house with a little child whom she laid in the shade of the eaves. That was Nadini, and she had been one of Loa's own wives — he remembered her quite distinctly. So she was Ura's wife now. Loa boiled with indignation. He was not sure about how long he had been away, but judging by Musini's condition that child was not his; it must be Ura's. Loa came to some rapid but grim decisions regarding Ura's fate, and Nadini's, and the child's.

At the end of the town there were a good many people visible, and all of them were vaguely familiar to Loa. His memories were all jumbled and distorted now, what with his present stress of emotion and the intensity of his experiences since he had seen them last. There were some girls, laughing and joking as they bore wooden water jars on their heads on their way back from the brook. He could not put names to them.

"Let us go," he said, aloud but to himself.

He took a fresh grip of his little ax and plunged out into the open, and Lanu and Musini followed him. Nadini caught sight of them emerging from the undergrowth; the naked man, lean and scarred, ax in hand; the almost full-grown boy, and the woman far gone in pregnancy. She stared at them with unbelieving eyes. One of the girls saw them and called the others' attention to them; one of them was surprised enough to allow her jar to fall from her head.

"It is Loa!" cried Musini loudly behind him. "Loa, our Lord."

She ran from behind him, clumsy because of her bulky condition, to go before him.

"It is Loa!" she cried again.

She waved her arms at Nadini and the girls, and went down in the proper attitude of respect, knees and elbows on the ground, face close to it, setting the example and then looking round to see if the other women were following it. They did not. Nadini leaned against the doorway of her house, her hand to her heart. The girls nudged each other and giggled in embarrassed fashion. It crossed Loa's mind that he could stop and remonstrate with them, but some consuming instinct within him said "Go on!" and he strode on down the street, forbearing to get involved in some undignified squabble before he should reach whatever vital situation was awaiting him at the far end. Musini scrambled to her feet again and once more ran grotesquely in front of him to herald his approach. On went Loa to the far end of the town, that end where in his day the riff raff, the lowborn, had dwelt with a lack of dignity only relieved by the presence of one or two respectable families such as that of Litti the worker in iron. Loa had always had a faint snobbish contempt for this end of the town.

There was a fair-sized group of people there which

opened up and spread as Musini came up, lumbering and gasping.

"It is Loa!" cried Musini, again, once more going down in the attitude of abasement.

There were some cries of astonishment from the group, and someone started to his feet from where he had been sitting in the center of it. It was Soli, once a leader of the lowclass society who had frequented this end of the town. Loa knew him to be Soli, but the first thing Loa was really conscious of was the fact that the seat Soli had just quitted was a tripod, a distorted stool, very like the one he himself had always sat on to hear the counsels of his advisers and to give judgment in disputed cases. No one save Loa the son of Nasa (whose name no one save Loa could utter) might sit on a tripod stool of that sort. And hanging over Soli's shoulders was a leopardskin cloak — the garment, if not of gods, at least of princes. And in Soli's hand was a battle-ax which Loa instantly recognized as having once been his own — his own ceremonial ax, presumably discovered amid the ruins after the departure of the slavers, and now desecrated by Soli's touch. Loa flamed with uncontrollable rage.

But if Loa was angry, so was Soli. His face was distorted with passion as he watched Loa approach.

"Kill him!" shrieked Soli, with a wave of his arm to the group around him.

"It is our Lord, our Lord Loa," said Musini, raising her face from the ground.

The group stirred but made no decisive movement, save for Ura; out of the tail of his eye Loa was conscious that

[235]

Ura was fumbling with bow and arrow. Loa's instincts came to his help, and he sprang forward with the little ax poised beside his shoulder, ready to strike. Soli could not have retreated before him even if his rage had allowed; that would have been defeat and death. He sprang to meet Loa, whirling the big ax round in a blow that would have cut Loa diagonally in half had it struck him, but Loa managed to wrench his body out of the way. Soli had a substantial covering of fat — as Loa once had had, when his divinity was undisputed — but he was still agile and sure on his feet as he had been when he was renowned as a dancer. He let the swing of the ax carry him round and away, so that he was facing Loa and out of his reach before Loa could spring in. They eyed each other momentarily, prepared to circle round each other. But Loa had at the back of his mind the bow and arrow that Ura was fumbling with; he could neither waste time nor stand clear so that Ura could have a free shot. Instinct still carried him along. He feinted to the right — the natural direction for a right-handed man to take when armed with an ax — and then instantly sprang to the left and struck again, and only Soli's quickness of foot saved him after the feint had deceived his eye. The big ax whistled past Loa's shoulder; the little ax made a deep scratch in the bulging flesh of Soli's right breast — only Soli's supple twist at the hips prevented the blow from being fatal. As it was, the gash it left was six inches long and an inch deep at its deepest. A wordless cry broke from the crowd.

"Yaa-aa-aa," cried the crowd, as the red blood poured in a broad stream down Soli's chest, red in the blinding sunlight, and vivid against the glistening brown of Soli's skin. Soli seemingly did not feel the wound; he brought his ax round backhanded before Loa could recover from his blow, and Loa had to retreat, with the big ax whirling before his eyes so rapidly that, with each swing close upon the swing before it, he had no time for a counterblow, but could only back and sidle away, an inch from death at every swing. He might have exhausted Soli's impetus in time, but the ground was too restricted. Retreating fast, he backed into a spectator who had not time to get out of the way, and bounced forward under the swing of the ax, crashing breast to breast against Soli. Instantly they locked together, their left hands grasping the wrists of the right hands that held the axes; breast against breast, hip against hip, they strained against each other.

"Yaa-aa-aa," cried the crowd.

Loa put his left heel behind Soli's right to trip him up, but Soli bent his body and swung with all his strength, heaving Loa round so that both his feet almost left the ground, but he clung on, dragging Soli with him so that they swung together in an ungainly dance.

Musini, still on her knees, was watching intently; as they circled her she shot out one hand, swift as a striking snake, and caught Soli's ankle for one brief moment. It was only for a moment before Soli's momentum carried him out of her grip, but it was just long enough to put him off his balance. He nearly fell, and his grip on Loa's right wrist was weakened with the effort of keeping his footing. Loa tore his hand free. He had no time to strike with the edge of the ax, but he stabbed upwards and sideways with the head of it, hitting Soli below the left ear.

"Yaa — aa — aa," howled the crowd.

Soli weakened, so that Loa could swing him away from him by his hold on Soli's right wrist, and could then strike with all his strength at Soli's head with the edge. Soli flung up his left arm to protect himself, and the keen little ax bit deep into Soli's forearm just below the elbow, nearly severing it so that the limb dangled uselessly and the blood spouted in a vivid scarlet jet against the sunshine. Yet even then Soli kept his feet. Loa had released his right hand, and Soli braced himself and swung his ax back, the effort spattering Loa with blood from the severed arteries. Loa circled out of harm's way, ready to spring in again, but the drain upon Soli's strength was too great. He looked stupidly down at his dangling forearm, and at the blood which poured from it, and then his body sagged and he stumbled forward on his knees, his leopardskin cloak still over his shoulders. The nape of his neck was a clear target, and Loa struck at it, quick and hard.

"Yaa-aa," murmured the crowd, hushed and subdued.

Loa looked about him, the drops of blood clotting on his chest.

"It is Loa, our Lord," said Musini, on her knees.

"Loa!" said the crowd, and they went down on their knees too, their faces to the dust. Even Ura, with his bow in one hand and his arrow in the other, and with a clear shot at last open to him, went down on his knees along with the rest. Nadini and the water-carrying girls, who had drawn close to see the fight, fell slowly prostrate. Only Loa remained on his feet, and Lanu, who stood grinning in the sunlight, legs straddled wide. Loa's eyes met his, and they smiled at each other in utter accord.

C H A P T E R

X V

LOA TOOK HIS EYES FROM LANU'S and looked about him at
the groveling crowd. He ruled these people again, at least at
the moment. He was tired, and he wiped the streaming
sweat from his face with his forearm, but, tired though he
was, he knew that much was demanded of him on the instant. He might be a god and king again, but he was a god
who had only recently fought for his life under the eyes
of these very people — a god, in other words, who might
soon be thought mortal if he did not act at once in a godlike
manner. There was no logic about the way Loa thought regarding all this; indeed, there was very little thought involved. Most of what he did was done on the spur of the
moment, but it was enough to prove that he had profited
by his experiences.

He stalked over to the tripod stool and sat himself upon
it, the little ax across his knees.

"You may stand," he announced to the cowering multi-
tude, and they slowly got to their feet.

Loa looked round at them. He could not count them, but
his eye told him roughly how much the slavers' raid had
diminished their numbers. More than half of the population
of the town had been captured or killed by them. There

were some new babies, and more, obviously, still to come, so
that the population would soon increase and presumably
build itself up again to its natural figure. The thought of
babies brought his mind back abruptly to Ura and Nadini
— Ura, who had had the inordinate presumption to take
one of Loa's wives, and who had tried to draw an arrow during Loa's fight with Soli. Loa was in no doubt about who
was the intended target for that arrow. He looked round
the crowd again more searchingly, to select men who
would be sure to do his bidding; that was a strange state
of mind for Loa, accustomed to instant and utter obedience
in his town. He had never had any need for an inner court
circle, for a Praetorian Guard, before this. There had never
been any possibility of division; loyalty and devotion to
him had been equal and universal, but that was not the case
now — the proof of that lay at his feet at that very moment. Ura, standing somewhere behind his shoulder, would
certainly object to what Loa had in mind.

"Mali," said Loa. "Famo. Peri."

The three young men whom he addressed anxiously
awaited his commands.

"Come and stand here," said Loa, indicating the space
immediately in front of him.

They came, in some trepidation. A great hush fell on
the waiting crowd. Loa ostentatiously kept it waiting. He
shifted his position on the stool, apparently in search of
greater comfort, but actually so that he could swivel round
towards Ura. He had Ura in sight now, and was able to
watch any move he might make. He repeated the young

men's names without deigning to look round at them; automatically the dignified mode of address, of a great superior to one vastly inferior, came to his tongue — he had hardly employed it for months towards Musini and Lanu. The young men stood tense.

"What I shall tell you to do, do it instantly," said Loa. The crowd sighed nervously, and the young men stood poised.

"Take hold of Ura!" roared Loa, suddenly, flinging out his arm.

There was a flurry in the crowd. Mali, quicker off the mark than the other two, headed the rush into the crowd, but Ura had reacted slowly, taken completely by surprise. No one knows what he might or might not have done, for even before Mali reached him the people on either side of Ura had laid hold of him.

"Bring him out here!" roared Loa, with an imperious gesture, and they led him to the open space, beside Soli's corpse. They held his arms, and Mali took away his bow and his arrows.

"So," said Loa. "This is Ura. This is the man. Lift his face up to the sun so that we can see him better."

Mali put his hand to Ura's chin and forced his head back. Ura blinked with the sun in his eyes, but he made no motion of resistance, paralyzed by the suddenness of all this. Loa stared at him, and then looked round at the crowd. There was no need for haste; a dignified slowness would be more impressive. Over there stood Nadini; she was looking at her new husband with anxiety in her face, and Loa was torn with jealousy. He had never cared specially for Nadini, but it was a dreadful, an unprecedented thing for a man to take a wife of the god's without her being given to him as a great favor and a great condescension, in the most formal manner. Loa had intended to mention all this, but sudden prudence dried up the words in his throat. There was nothing to be gained, and much to be lost, by calling public attention to the fact that Loa might have mortal motives. It would be far more impressive to be incomprehensible, to offer no explanation for what he was going to do. For one speech he substituted another.

"My father, whose name no one may utter save myself, must have a new attendant. Nasa and his fathers await you, Ura."

The crowd sighed again, but Ura said nothing. This was inevitable death, and the lethargy of death was already upon him. Ura might be said to be the first convert to the renewed cult of Loa's divinity. Mali, anxious to be helpful, looked down at the big ceremonial ax which still lay beside the dead hand of Soli, but Loa ignored the hint. He gave his orders for the preparation of the first stake of impalement ever heard of in his town. He remembered well — too well — the methods used by the Arab raiders to strike terror into the hearts of their captives. The town listened in surprise, with a buzz of comment, when Loa finished speaking; and they watched the preparations with deep curiosity. A simple beheading or strangulation was nothing new to them, but this was. The first sound Ura uttered after his arrest was a shriek of agony, but it was not the last, not nearly the last.

Loa stole a glance at Nadini from under his brows; her hands were clasped with the intensity of her emotion as she watched Ura's writhings. Well and good. Then he looked about him with growing distaste. He had never much liked this end of the town.

"There is a curse upon this spot," he announced. "Not even that" — with a glance at Ura dying on the stake — "nor that" — with another glance at Soli's corpse — "can quite take the curse away."

Here Soli had sat in judgment on his tripod stool; it was not policy that was dictating Loa's words as much as bitter prejudice.

"Tomorrow, Famo," went on Loa, "you will put a fence round this spot, from over there, round there, to *there*. No foot will tread on this earth. The bushes and the trees will grow here. And until the fence is made, let no one trespass upon this ground."

He rose from his stool; half a gesture from him was sufficient to make a woman standing near him pick up the stool to carry it after him. The crowd parted to let him through, and tumbled on their faces as he walked past them, Nadini too.

"Come with me, Nadini," said Loa, as he walked by her.

Here was Musini, crouching subserviently, and yet not keeping still. Her shoulders were heaving, and she was writhing as she knelt.

"How is it with you, Musini?" asked Loa.

Musini lifted a face that was apprehensive with pain and wet with sweat.

"Lord," she said. "Lord — I — I — "

Another twinge of pain cut her words off short, for her time had come upon her. Loa stirred the woman next to her with his foot.

"Who are you? Maku? Then, Maku, attend to Musini. Call for any help you may need."

Loa walked on up the street, with Nadini and Lanu and the three young men following close behind him and the rest of the town — save those who lingered to watch Ura's agonies — streaming after them in loose formation, like the nucleus and train of a comet. Nadini's baby still lay in the shade of the eaves of the house here, and Loa, pausing to look round him, looked meaningly at it, amused at the instant reaction of Nadini's clasped hands. Whim, or mercy, or policy, or satiation with blood, led Loa to take no further action, to issue no further order, but to pass on.

"There," he said to Peri, pointing, "there, tomorrow, you will build my house. It is to be long and high and wide."

"Yes, Lord," said Peri.

"Meanwhile in that house there will I sleep tonight. See to it."

Another gesture was sufficient to the woman bearing the stool to put it down outside the doorway, but Loa did not take his seat on it. He was no longer sitting in judgment, he was abandoning for the time his official capacity and retiring into privacy. He squatted in the shade of the eaves of the house.

"You, Nadini, can keep the flies from me. You others

may leave me. No. You — " He glanced up at the woman who had been carrying the stool — "you shall stay too. Whose wife are you?"

The woman shrank back embarrassed; she tried to speak but stuttered.

"Speak!" ordered Loa, but still she hesitated. "Speak, and no harm will come to you. Whose wife are you?"

"I am the wife of no one, Lord. I — I *was* the wife of him whose name I cannot speak. Of him whose arm you cut off, Lord."

There was a horrified moment, for it was the worst of bad luck for a mortal to say the name of, or even to allude to, someone who was dead. But Loa was unembarrassed.

"I cut off more than his arm," he said with a chuckle. "As a widow I shall give you in marriage again. See to it that you speak to me about it later on."

The world was very good. He was home again, he was a god once more. And this woman was well set up and handsome, he reflected, looking her over.

"What is your name?" he demanded.

"Subi, Lord. My father was of the family of Ko."

"That is so," said Loa, meditatively; he ran his eye over Subi again, and then turned to look at Nadini. A distant shriek from Ura came to his ears. It crossed his mind that now he might order Ura to be slain, to put an end to his sufferings, but he decided against it, at least for the moment. Life was good.

But here came an interruption. Several people were hastening towards him, but the urgency of their advance died away as they neared him, and when they were within speaking distance they began to hang back, each trying to leave speech to the others.

"What is it?" asked Loa.

There was further hesitation, but the others shoved Maku forward, the elderly woman whom Loa had ordered to attend upon Musini.

Loa looked at her and waited for her to speak, but she could not bring herself to do it.

"What is it?" asked Loa, much more testily.

In the annoyance in his voice there was an echo, a subtle reminder of the stake of impalement, of the execution ax. Maku gulped and forced herself to announce the bad news. She at least was convinced of the arbitrariness and supreme power of the god Loa, for, innocent herself, she feared the wanton fate of a bearer of ill tidings.

"Musini, Lord."

"Well, what of Musini?"

"Lord, she has given birth. To two children, Lord."

The others wailed in sympathy; Loa heard Nadini behind his shoulder draw in her breath sharply. The birth of twins was the worst of ill omens. People might think, as they always did in similar cases, that while Loa was the father of one of the children some devil was the father of the other. But this superstition was not the root of the matter. The consternation caused by the birth of twins was much more a matter of unreasoning fear. It was an unlucky thing to happen, the unluckiest thing there was, much more unlucky than even such a serious thing as seeing a monkey on the ground to the left, or touching the lintel of a door with one's head. Twin children must always be slain to avert calamity. It was quite deplorable that this should have happened on the day of Loa's return, to Loa's own wife.

Maku screamed when Loa, thinking about all this, forgot to take his eye off her. She was sure that she was destined at the least to the stake of impalement, and she flung herself groveling on the ground before him, her face in the dirt.

"Oh, stand up, stand up!" roared Loa. "Listen to what I have to say."

They rose, whimpering, dust caking on the sweat of their faces and bodies. Loa was having to think with extravagant speed. He felt in his bones that it would be bad policy to admit that Musini's twins portended evil, and with that feeling well established inside him he was able to free himself from thralldom to the superstitions attendant on the event. He had done without so many forms and ceremonies in the last months, and survived their absence, he had had so many beliefs shaken by his past experiences, that once a reasonable argument could be advanced on the other side he was willing to believe even that there was nothing ominous about the birth of twins. But he could not present such a revolutionary theory to his people. If he laughed at one superstition, might they not laugh at another — at the theory, for instance, that Loa was more than mortal? He must do better than that; he must wring some advantage out of this most unfortunate occurrence.

"What are the children?" he asked, more to gain time to think than for any other reason.

"Boys, Lord. Both boys," replied Maku, unable to keep out of her voice some of her surprise that Loa should ask a question so irrelevant to the issue.

"So," said Loa.

His struggle to think logically was reflected in his face, so that the onlookers believed they saw the workings of a spirit within him. He walked through the crowd of onlookers, which parted before him, and sat himself with the dignity the occasion demanded upon his stool.

"This is the Word of Loa," he began, slowly, using the ancient formula which gave his words so much weight that it was the direst blasphemy to debate them. "Musini has given two sons to Loa. Sons they are and sons they will be. Let everyone be thankful for this gift. They will be mighty men, killers of elephants and leopards. As they walk down the street each person will touch another on the elbow and will say 'See, there walk the two sons of Loa.' Musini will give them milk, and if she has not sufficient it will be a fortunate woman who will share her duty. For this is the day of the return of Loa from another world, and all that happens on this day is good."

His audience was staring at him, almost unbelieving. The point had to be made clearer, and Loa was warming to his work.

"I return after these many days," said Loa. "And what do I find? Where I left ten people there are no more than five. Where are the young men and the young women?

Many, many children are needed to replace them. Here are the first two that Loa brings out of his abundance. See you to it, you women, that you do likewise."

The novelty of such a suggestion sent a tremor through his audience.

"Soli, whose name I alone may speak, would have killed these children. But where is Soli? He lies dead. The broad ax of so much power was useless in his hands before this little ax in mine."

Another shriek from Ura in the distance came as Loa paused for breath, and he flung out his hand in the direction of the sound.

"Ura is waiting to bear the message to Nasa. He waits impatiently. Mali!"

At his call Mali came forward, with head low in the presence of Loa speaking the Word of Loa.

"Lord?"

"Go you to Ura. Take with you a club, a club of iron or a club of wood. Say to Ura: 'To Nasa may you now go. Impatiently you wait. Bear with you this message to Nasa. Loa has returned to his town and brought the two boys who later will be men and who will serve Nasa.' Then when Ura has heard the message he is to bear, you will strike him on the head with your club. You will strike him with all the strength you have, so that he will go quickly on his way. Mali, have you heard the Word of Loa?"

"I have heard, Lord."

"Then go. And you others have heard the Word of Loa. Go!"

They went, subdued and impressed, for the Word of Loa still carried weight. Loa heard two more screams from Ura, and then no more. He quitted the stool and went back to the shade of the eaves. He was content; the great heat of the day was over and here in the shade was almost a pleasant coolness.

"Nadini! Subi!" he said. "Bring me food. Food for Lanu and myself."

They glanced at each other, each of them exercising their minds over what they would serve him.

"Hurry!" said Loa.

"Yes, Lord," said Nadini. "What may we bring you?"

"Food, I said!" roared Loa. "Food! Baked plantains in oil — tapioca — give me food and not words."

"Yes, Lord," said Nadini, and she and Subi hastened away.

If Nadini had ever been in any legal way the wife of Ura she was his widow now, from the moment that Mali's club had thumped upon Ura's skull. The child ought certainly to die. And yet? The same argument applied as before, regarding unnecessarily calling the attention of people to any human weaknesses Loa might have. And he had given his Word regarding the necessity of repeopling the town. He could not come to a decision about it at the moment. To save himself the trouble of further thought on the point he turned to Lanu, squatting silently at the side of the house. Lanu had said not a word, he had kept in the background all this time; if he was not awed at the spectacle of his father reassuming his divinity he was at least impressed by it to the point of silence.

"My son," said Loa, "we must find you a wife. You are ready for one."

"Yes, Father — Lord."

"This little ax of so much power was once yours. I made a present of it to you. Do you remember?"

"Yes, Lord."

It was the ax that had shaped bows and arrows for them in the forest, which had cut creepers for them, which had hacked a way for them through thickets. And many an evening Lanu had squatted sharpening it on a smooth stone. Yet despite his familiarity with it Lanu had to admit to himself the likelihood, if not something stronger than likelihood, that it was an ax of great power. And this father of his, whom he had known to howl with terror at the lightning, who was perfectly capable of walking past an obvious mushroom without seeing it, was yet Loa who sat on a tripod stool and gave forth his Word. For that matter, he was the same Loa who had led them back across the whole world, through the unknown forest, back to the town. It was a complex theological problem for a half-grown boy. And there was something else worrying him to which he could not help referring, so that he raised the subject abruptly.

"Do you think all is well with my mother?" asked Lanu.

"Your mother?"

Loa was naturally taken by surprise by the question. He had had so much on his mind that there had simply not been any room for Musini, not even for the Musini who had shown her devotion to him during the hungry pursuit of the slavers' column, the Musini whose capture he had once deplored so bitterly, for whom he had gladly risked his own life. He had forgotten all about Musini even while he had dealt with the problem of Musini's twins.

"I expect all is well with her," said Loa, reassuringly. "When the food comes I will send and find out."

Lanu nodded a little gloomily. He was aware that during the period immediately following the birth of a child a woman was peculiarly susceptible to the attacks of devils and to the poisonings and enchantments of rivals and enemies, so that she not infrequently died. Lanu did not want Musini to die, even though he knew it was unmanly to care a rap about the fate of a mere woman. And Loa eyed him with actually something of apprehension. Lanu was destined to become a god like himself — would, one of these days, after the inconceivable but inevitable moment when Loa went to join Nasa and his other ancestors, actually be the principal god. It was not going to be easy to initiate Lanu into the secrets of being superhuman, at a time when Loa himself had the gravest doubts about his own divinity, and of course stronger doubts still about Lanu's. Loa looked down the street at the busy mortals going hither and yon about their business, and told himself with a twinge of regret that he was of the same flesh that they were. He was aware of a slight inclination to think something quite different, to allow his recent feats to persuade him that he was, really and truly, a being on a higher plane than theirs, but his newfound reaction did not permit it. He had learned

[253]

the truth as a hungry slave, when he had shared a forked stick with Nessi, when he found out that the kurbash hurt him. Loa, when he thought about all this, was a little like a character in fiction of whom he had never heard and never would — Gulliver at the moment of realization that he was of the same species as the Yahoos.

Loa knew, too, that most likely the ideas of those people down the street regarding his divinity would be a little changed at least. Somewhere at the back of their minds must linger the memory that he had once been led off as a slave. They all knew that he had fought hand to hand with Soli. It would be a ticklish business still to claim the moon for his sister, and to maintain that it was his summons that brought her back each month from the embraces of the river. It could be done — only Musini and Lanu knew that he had not troubled to summon her once during all these months — but it might not be easy. The people's blind acceptance of the notion of his divinity must be at an end, along with his own. Instead of going along happily in an unchanging and unquestioning world he would have to evolve a policy which would make a god of him despite the doubters. He had already taken a few steps in this direction when, for instance, he had ordered the impalement of Ura, and when he had given forth his Word on the subject of Musini's twins. There would be a lifetime of it before him, and after that a lifetime of it before Lanu.

The arrival of the women with bowls of food diverted his untrained mind from its colossal struggles with these problems.

[254]

"Baked plantains in oil," said Loa, peering at the contents of a bowl.

Lanu merely smacked his lips, plunged in his hand, and stuffed his mouth. After months of forest food it was good to come back to town food, to the food to which he had been accustomed all his life.

"Go, Nadini, and ask if all is well with Musini," said Loa.

Lanu watched her departing form with anxiety — the arrival of the food had only momentarily diverted his mind from the subject of his mother. Loa filled his own mouth; it was pleasant to feel the good red oil trickling down his chin, to stuff himself full, to know that there was more food than even he could eat to be obtained merely by a shout to Nadini and Subi. But Loa was a man who had once believed himself to be a god, and no man who has gone through that mental change-over can accept unquestioning the thought of the permanence of anything. These plantains and this tapioca tasted excellent, but Loa made himself remember the days when he turned with loathing from bananas and tapioca, when the thought of a continuous diet of bananas and tapioca, however ample, had revolted him. Those days would come again. He shot an exploratory glance at Lanu, who at that moment was engaged in wiping out the residual oil from a nearly empty bowl with his fingers and then sucking them noisily. Nadini's return delayed his opening of the subject he had in mind.

"All is well with Musini, Lord," said Nadini. "She sleeps, and the — the children lie at her side."

Nadini showed momentary difficulty in concealing her

ingrained disgust when she had to mention the revolting subject of twins, but Lanu's face lit up with a broad smile at her news.

"You may go," said Loa to Nadini, and, when she was out of earshot, he turned back to Lanu and to the subject he had in mind.

"Do you remember," he asked, slowly, "those *fish* that we ate on the day that we took the canoe?"

He said the strange word, the word that had disappeared utterly from the vocabulary of the town, with hesitation and difficulty, but Lanu rolled an understanding eye at him.

"Well do I remember them," he said. "There were others that Musini and I ate when we were in the pen in that town. They were good. As good as meat."

"With canoes," went on Loa, "you could get for us more fish perhaps from the river?"

He said "you" advisedly and with slight stress, and the form of address he used was chosen with all the nicety of which he was capable — not the form used by a god to a mortal, nor that used by a parent to a child, but that of a superior person to one hardly his inferior. He wanted Lanu to assume certain grave responsibilities because, vague though the plans were which were forming in Loa's mind, they were plans he did not believe himself capable of putting into execution himself.

"I do not know how to catch fish or how to kill them," said Lanu, but he was not being merely obstructive. Loa could see that he was receptive enough to the new idea.

"You do not," Loa agreed. "But there are men in towns

beside the river who do. Twice we have seen men catching fish in the river."

"That is so," said Lanu. He was willing to be helpful, but he could not grasp yet what Loa had in mind.

Loa was not sure himself, for that matter. Neither his mind nor the vocabulary in which he thought were adapted for logical thinking. The actual formulation of plans was a difficult step beyond the vague aspirations which a whole series of experiences and emotional disturbances had stirred up within him. Theoretical thinking was something that was almost beyond him, especially when he was thinking about something quite foreign to his ordinary life. What Loa really had at the back of his mind was to divert his people's minds from domestic politics by a series of wars of aggression, but the vocabulary at his disposal did not allow him to phrase it as briefly as that, nor in twenty times that number of words. He could only feel the need and grope his way towards expressing it, both to himself and to Lanu. Besides, he was moved by pure ambition as well, and in addition to that by a whole series of other motives, most of them simple enough in themselves, but adding up to a complexity that utterly entangled him. He wanted revenge in general upon a world which had treated him so ill; he wanted revenge in particular on certain individuals and communities; and he wanted, too, to exercise himself, and provide himself with outlets for his activity, now that he was back in a world which could be utterly tranquil at a time when his recent experiences had stirred him up so that the prospect of tranquility was quite distasteful to him.

Misdoubting his own executive ability, he desired to assert himself through the medium of Lanu.

"When we killed those men," he said, laboriously, "when we took their canoe to cross the little river, you wanted to keep the boat. Do you remember?"

"Yes. I remember."

"You thought you might go down the river in it."

"Yes, Lord."

"And I said that when we reached home you might have a boat of your own."

"Indeed yes, Lord. I remember that."

"There are towns here, towns like ours, except that they are close to the river and their people use boats and eat fish."

"Musini and I were captured by such people," said Lanu. "You got us out of their cage, Lord."

"That is right. We could find such a town again. We have only to go seek along the riverbank. You could go with the men from here, and at night, when the town is asleep, you could go into it with the men. With spears and with axes, you could kill those people who tried to fight against you. The others you could fasten in forked sticks, if you wished to. Some of the women we could have as wives, to raise up more children for us who would fight for us when they grew up. And the men — they would know about boats. They would know how to make boats. They would know well how to make boats go upon the water. They would know how to catch fish. You could make them show you how to do these things. You could make them do these things for you."

"Lord," said Lanu, "all this might well be done."

He said it with amazement, a new revelation opening up before him. No physical miracle that Loa might have performed could have impressed Lanu as much as this speech. Lanu would not have been as excited if Loa had stood the little ax on end and made it dance of its own volition. Lanu lived in a world where one did not inquire into the causes of things very deeply; an ax might dance, a tree might talk, just as branches moved in the wind or a river chuckled and gurgled. What Loa was proposing to do was something startlingly different. It was as if he had pulled aside a series of veils which had hitherto enclosed Lanu, revealing amazing new landscapes, all well within reach. The pang of pleasure which Loa experienced when he saw Lanu's admiring reaction to his suggestion was deeper than anything Loa had felt before. He was thoroughly aroused now.

"The men would make many boats for us," he said. "Not one boat, but many. Not little boats, like the one in which we crossed the river, but big boats."

"Like the one which captured Musini and me," said Lanu. "Boats with many men."

"Yes," went on Loa. "Many large boats, so that many many men could go in them. All the men in this town. In boats they could go far."

"Indeed they could," said Lanu. "I would lead them far."

"So you would. There would be no town that could stand against us."

"We would come by the river," said Lanu. "We would step on shore in the darkness close to the town. No one would know we were near. We would kill them. We would take all they had. We would drive them to the boats and bring them back here."

Lanu slapped his thigh in his excitement, as the new prospects revealed themselves in growing detail. Neither Lanu nor Loa was at all aware of how much they were indebted for these ideas to the Arab slave raiders. Every new conception — revolutionary, all of them — had its origin in their recent experiences. The fundamental one, of attacking people who had done them no harm, was due to the example of the Arabs. The plan of the night surprise, even the idea of slavery, were from the same source. There was something, perhaps, of originality in Loa's idea of sea power, of building up a naval strength on the river as a ready means of dominating other people, but even that really found its beginnings in what Loa had seen on the beach at the Arab slave depot. Intense experiences, working on simple minds that had long stagnated, were producing violent reactions.

"You can go out soon," said Loa. "You can take with you one or two men, and you can seek along the river for a town. You can look at it well and secretly. Then you can come back and all the other men will be ready to go with you."

"And the spears and the axes?" asked Lanu.

Loa paused to consider the question of munitions of war. There used to be some spearheads of iron in the town which probably still existed. There must be many axes; the whole culture of the town depended on the steel-edged ax which could fell trees and clear the forest for the planting of bananas and manioc. If Litti the worker in iron had not survived the raid — and Loa could not remember seeing him today — some of his family and trade must still be alive. They could make spearheads and axes; Loa scowled a little as he thought that under pressure they could make them much faster than they had done in the old happy-go-lucky days. Most men could make bows, and the women could be put to work braiding bowstrings. Somebody would have to be detailed to make a fresh supply of arrow poison. Loa turned back to Lanu to debate another new conception, that of the mobilization of the nation for war.

It was a deeply interesting discussion; the father and son went on with it while darkness fell, and they hardly noticed the passage of time. Only a sharp shower of rain eventually broke into their deliberations, and made them seek shelter in the house Loa had appropriated to himself. It was here that Maku addressed them, herself wet and glistening after running up the street in the rain.

"Musini sends a message to her Lord," she announced, at the threshold.

"What is it?"

"Musini says" — the message did not come easily from Maku's lips — "that now she lies awake. She lies with her children beside her, hoping that perhaps Loa her Lord would come and visit her."

Loa could not think on the spur of the moment how to reply to such a remarkable request, so he temporized.

"Go back to Musini," he ordered, "and say that Loa will consider the matter."

With Maku gone, Loa turned the notion over in his mind. It was quite inconceivable that a god should walk the length of the street merely to visit a wife in childbed. He might look in upon her tomorrow if, as was to be expected, business regarding the reorganization of the town led him that way. Musini would be up and about in a couple of days at most. Meanwhile she was of no use whatever as a wife, incapable even of laying a plantain on a grid. But on the other hand the rain had stopped, and there were a few minutes left before complete darkness began. He could step outside to stretch his legs after so much squatting. A breath of air at least — Loa had not been under a roof for a year, and it felt strange to him. Lanu followed him when he rose and stretched and walked outside. Loa breathed with pleasure the sudden coolness resulting from the rain and the disappearance of the sun. The mud was soothing under his bare toes.

"My mother is here," said Lanu suddenly, beside him.

Inside the house it was quite dark, as was to be expected, but Musini had heard their approach.

"That is you, Lord," she said gladly. "I hoped you would come."

A thin wail arose from the dark interior, to be instantly matched by another.

"See, Lord," went on Musini's voice. "Your children greet you. They are fine boys, worthy of their father. Lord, it was good of you to let them live. I — I did not want them to die. Lord — no devil was the father of either of them. There has been no thought in my mind but for you all this time. You knew that, Lord, and so you spared them, the children of my old age. Lord, I am grateful."

Musini's hand, reaching out in the darkness, found Loa's knee. She stroked his calf and pressed his ankle eagerly.

"It is nothing," said Loa, but Musini continued feverishly.

"Lord, you have led us home. You have killed Soli. The people put their faces to the ground before you again. You will always eat your fill, and many women will attend to your wants. But none of them were with you in the forest, to find you white ants when you were hungry. None of them pillowed your head when the rain fell and the lightning flashed, or listened for the tread of the little people with you when all the forest was full of enemies. I have shared all this with you. Perhaps you will never pay attention again to an old woman like me, but I have had what no woman ever had before me or will ever have again, and that will be mine for always. Never again shall I be able to speak to you like this, Lord, but I have said what I wanted to say. I am grateful, Lord."

It was a tactless speech to address to a god. Loa resented, uncomfortably, being reminded of being hungry and of being frightened by the lightning. Whatever Musini might say, it was Loa who owed a debt of gratitude to Musini, and that was not a pleasant thing to think about. Besides, it was unconventional, to say the least, for a woman to speak her mind to any man, let alone to him. Loa could remember the days before the raiders came when Musini evinced a shrewish sharpness that had not conduced to his dignity —

that in fact had nearly sent her to serve his ancestors — and the fanatical possessiveness underlying her recent speech warned him that the same thing might happen again, easily, if similar circumstances ever arose. He must make sure that they did not, that Musini's position as senior wife should be so defined in future as to give her no such opportunity.

All this his brain or his instincts, his infinite experience of wives, told him. He shied away from his love for Musini as a wild animal shies away from a trap, and yet he was moved inexpressibly by that urgent whisper, by the feverish touch of the woman's hand upon him. He inclined more and more towards melting, towards making a host of rash promises. He had to summon up all his resolution to tear himself away, to free himself from the magic hold this old woman, his earliest wife, had upon him. He withdrew himself from her reach, yet even then did not have all the moral strength necessary to end their relationship once and for all. Instead he temporized again.

"Sleep well, Musini," he said, with a kindly note that he could not keep out of his voice. "Feed your children well, and rest in peace."

Walking back from the house he was perturbed, a little sore and resentful. But there was one easy way in which at least he could forget Musini, there was one specific opiate which could at least temporarily negative the sting of his feelings.

"Nadini!" he called as he approached his house.

"Lord, I come," said Nadini.

CHAPTER

XVI

FOR A THOUSAND YEARS at least, perhaps for many thousand years, the forest and its people had lain in torpor and peace. There had been food for all who could survive disease and cannibalism; there had been room enough for all, there had been materials enough to satisfy every simple need, and there had been no urge, either economic or temperamental, to wander or to expand. There prevailed an equilibrium which was long enduring even though it bore within itself the potentialities of instability, and it was the Arab invasions, pushing southwards from the fringes of the Sahara, westwards from the valley of the Nile and from the coast opposite Zanzibar, which first destroyed the equilibrium of the life in the deep central recesses of the forest. On the Atlantic coast, where the great rivers met the sea, the disturbance began somewhat earlier as a result of the activities of Europeans. Hawkins on the Guinea Coast first bought from local chieftains the victims who otherwise would have gone to serve the chieftain's ancestors, and sold them at a vast profit on the other side of the Atlantic. More and more white men arrived, seeking gold and ivory and slaves, and willing to pay for them with commodities of inestimable desirability like spirits and brass and gunpowder; and the demand raised a turmoil far inland, for where local supplies were exhausted the local chiefs soon learned to make expeditions into the interior in search of more. Soon there was no more gold; the supply of ivory died away to the annual production when the accumulated reserves of ages were dissipated; but the forest still bred slaves, and slaves were sought at the cost of the ruin and the depopulation of the coastal belt.

But no effect was evident in the deep interior of the forest. The cataracts on all the rivers, where they fall from the central plateau, the vast extent of the forest, and, above all, the desolation of the intermediate zone, hindered for a long time the penetration of the deep interior either by the native chiefs of the coastal fringe or their white accomplices. The Napoleonic wars delayed the inevitable penetration, and when they ended the diminution and eventual suppression of the slave trade delayed it yet again. Towards the coast the strains and stresses of the slave-raiding wars had brought about the formation of powerful kingdoms — especially in the areas whither Mohammedan influence had penetrated from the Sahara — which subsequently had to be destroyed by the Europeans to gain for themselves free passage beyond them. The Hausa empire, Dahomey, Ashanti, and innumerable other native states, rose and later fell, built upon a foundation of barbarism cemented by European and Moslem influences. In the same way the intrusion of the Arabs from the east set the central part of the forest in a turmoil, so that war raged and no man's life was safe in his own town; and these developments occurred at the moment when Arab influence ebbed away as a result of events elsewhere, leaving the central forest disturbed and yet not further disturbed; as if the highest wave had swept the beach and none of its successors ever reached as high.

And so Loa was able to build up his little empire undisturbed. Those moments of vision — blurred though the vision might be — of his first conversation with Lanu were never succeeded by anything comparable, and yet they proved to be all that was necessary. There can have been few statesmen in the world who have ever carried out so completely a scheme conceived at the beginning of their careers. As time went on, Loa saw every step of his vague plan carried through. He saw Lanu develop from a lively thoughtful boy to a bloody-minded warrior. The raiding parties that Lanu led rarely if ever came back empty-handed. There was the first notable occasion when, having set out on foot, he returned by water, with his men in three big canoes paddled by prisoners. He landed on the river-bank, naturally, at the practicable beach below the site of the vanished town which Nasa, thirty years before, with less vision than Loa, had utterly destroyed. Equally naturally there grew up on the site in time a new little town, the port of Loa's capital, populated largely by the captives taken in the various raids; for Loa, partly from necessary policy, and partly from something resembling good nature, did not send all his prisoners to serve his ancestors.

Sometimes he was ferocious and terrible. There were days when the ceremonial ax was hard at work, when his own people and not merely the slaves spoke with hushed voices in fear lest upon them should fall Loa's choice, when from the grove which sprang up in the accursed spot at the far end of the town there came the shrieks of men and women in agony. But this happened only when Loa's instincts told him it was time to assert his majesty afresh, for often prisoners were too valuable to be sacrificed when they could be incorporated into his own population, as wives for his men or as skilled workmen for his enterprises; and the children could soon be trained into devoted soldiers and subjects. Skilled slave labor built for him the canoe fleet that swept the whole long reach of the river between the rapids; captives taught his men how to handle paddles; and captives, in addition, actually manned the paddles in great part — it did not take long to convert, by plunder and victory, the slave of yesterday into the enthusiastic warrior of today. Lanu, having led armies from boyhood, soon became a skilled and then a famous warrior, and as the years went by his much younger twin brothers began to make a name for themselves as soldiers too, but the ultimate power was wielded by Loa, who never went out on a raid, but who lived in mysterious state in his own town, sometimes weaving plans, but always, according to the frightened reports of both his friends and his enemies, weaving spells that brought him inevitable victory. In twenty years Loa had spread his rule over a wide circle of the forest, so that his boundaries came into touch on the one side with the waning Arab dominion extending from the Great Lakes, and on the other with the new power from Europe which was slowly extending from the sea.

The battle for the mastery of Central Africa had already been fought, and the Arabs had been defeated by the Europeans, before the European tide began to flow finally towards Loa's kingdom. Loa knew of the European victory; he knew of the advancing European tide. He knew about the rifles, and about the devil-driven canoes, ten times the size of the biggest war canoe, which could make their way up the river by reason of the fire in their bellies. He had no superstitious fear of these things. He had been a god himself, and he was a god of a different kind now. The rifles were merely an improvement on the firearms he had seen in Arab hands — in his own hands, for that matter, for one or two of his campaigns had resulted in the capture of smooth bore muskets whose locks had ceased to function even before their ammunition had been spoiled. Similarly the devil-driven canoes were merely an unexplained improvement on the dugout. Loa had no superstitious fear of them, but he feared them, all the same. He thought the invaders from down the rivers would conquer him when the clash came. But Loa was a very old man now, well into his fifties, and loath to accommodate himself to changed circumstances. By yielding to the advancing power he might be able to make terms; he knew vaguely of other chiefs who (some of them out of fear of him) had submitted to the new power, and who had been allowed to continue to live, as tax gatherers and chief executioners, but Loa did not want to live on those terms even if they should be granted him. He did not want to live on those terms.

CHAPTER

XVII

CAPTAIN VICTOR AUGUSTUS TALBOT of the Army of the Independent State of the Congo sat sweltering outside his tent beside the river. Today the weather seemed hotter and steamier than he had ever known it, and fever had brought him down to a state of the lowest depression of mind. Feverish images came unsummoned into existence in his mind's eye. He thought of iced claret cup, deliciously cold, with sections of lemons and oranges floating in the great silver bowl of it, with an attentive mess-steward standing by it ladle in hand eager to dip out any quantity demanded. There would be cold food, too, salmon and cucumber — he would never taste Wye salmon again — and chicken in aspic and lobster with mayonnaise. Talbot found himself smacking his sore lips at the thought of it. Instead of sitting outside a sweltering shelter tent that a big dog could hardly crawl into, he would be in the cool and shady marquee at the edge of the cricket ground. Discreetly in the background there would be the regimental band playing sentimental airs, not loud enough to drown the pleasant sound of ball against bat, and the languidly appreciative cries of "Well hit, sir!" His friends, straw-hatted and striped-blazered and white-flanneled, would lounge through the big marquee with the unhurried elegance of English gentlemen, trained to exhibit no emotion, unobtrusive and yet with shoulders drilled straight in the finest regiment in the English Army, congratulating each other on the fine weather for the cricket festival and perhaps even venturing a mild protest against the July heat — the *heat,* by God! Talbot shifted in the pool of sweat which had accumulated in his camp chair and swore filthily. He thought of the claret cup again, and of the muddy warm river water which was all he had to drink, of the salmon and cucumber in the past and of the few tins of beef — the contents quite liquid when taken out — which alone stood between him and a pure African diet.

He was not a very robust figure, and his face narrowed down from above to a pointed chin under the straggling fair beard. There were the remains of a weak good nature in his features — the good nature which had led him, more sinned against than sinning, into one of the historic scandals of the Victorian Age, resulting in his resignation of his commission in the Green Jackets. His family had turned against him, his allowance had abruptly terminated, and he had been faced, unexpectedly and for the first time in his life, with the necessity of earning money enough to keep himself from actual starvation. So he had accepted a commission in the Army of the Independent State of the Congo. King Leopold of the Belgians was his master, and in the service of King Leopold men of weak good nature either died or changed their natures, and Talbot still lived.

The subtlest and most avaricious of all the public figures of Europe, Leopold, having contrived to obtain a mandate from the civilized world giving him Central Africa as his personal possession, was now proceeding to reap dividends from it. It had been a risky speculation — as any speculation must be which brings in profits of thousands of millions to a single individual — and for a brief while even Leopold, with his vast personal fortune and extensive credit, had been near to bankruptcy. The war with the Arabs, the building up of an army and an administration, had cost enormous sums. But now was the time of harvest. King Leopold's servants were flooding into Central Africa, Europeans with a hard taskmaster urging them on. They armed the native soldiers with European weapons, and gave them some semblance of European discipline, so that opposition to their advance was hopeless. Each new district conquered provided from the accumulation of ages an immediate supply of ivory and gold, and as soon as the looting was completed the inhabitants could be put to labor. Every district could be assessed to produce a quota of palm oil or rubber or ivory for sale for Leopold's benefit, and if that quota was not forthcoming Leopold was peevish, and wrote peevishly to his representatives, who in turn passed on his censures to their subordinates.

There could be no excuse for not producing the quota, for the men in local control had in their hands an instrument admirably adapted for the production of palm oil and rubber and ivory — an instrument whose usefulness they had learned from the Arabs: the hippopotamus-hide whip, the kurbash; in Belgian-French slang, the *chicotte*. And to facilitate the application of the *chicotte*, and to open up fresh fields for its employment, there was the Army. That portion of the Army commanded by Captain Victor Augustus Talbot was engaged at this moment in a campaign to open up a fresh field. Someone in the Brussels office — perhaps King Leopold himself — had noticed on the map a large area not yet conquered, and had sent the peremptory orders which had put the Army on the march, with Loa's town as the objective.

Sergeant Fleuron, the product of a Brussels slum, came up to report to his captain.

"Well?" asked Talbot.

"Perhaps they believe what they have been telling me," said Fleuron, "I do not."

"You interrogated each prisoner separately?"

"I did," said the sergeant.

In his hand there idly swung the hippopotamus-hide whip which he had employed in his search for truth.

"What did they say?"

"Mostly lies, as usual. Some of the lies we had heard before."

"For example?"

Fleuron shrugged his shoulders before recounting the result of his investigations.

"There is a great king over there," he said. "Some say his name is Loa and some say it is Lanu. Maybe 'Loa' is their word for 'king.' Or maybe Lanu is the king and Loa is the name of his god. Loa lives in a great town near the great river. In the middle of the town he has a sacred grove. Too sacred to speak about without persuasion."

"Crucifixion trees, and skulls nailed to branches," said Talbot, out of his experience of sacred African groves.

"And ivory perhaps. Perhaps even gold," said Fleuron.

"Let's hope so," agreed Talbot. "What else did they say?"

"Loa has a mighty army."

"How many men?"

Fleuron shrugged again.

"These men never know. Fifty or five hundred — it is all the same to them. Sometimes Lanu leads this army, and sometimes — "

"Sometimes — ?"

Fleuron went on with what he was saying with considerable reluctance.

"Sometimes they are led by two great warriors, brothers born at the same time."

"Nonsense!"

"It sounds like nonsense, Captain, but all these fellows say the same thing even after tasting the *chicotte*."

"But they cannot mean twins."

"It's twins that they mean, Captain, without a doubt. They use the very word for twins. It's strange to hear them. It's a surprise when they come out with it without any shame. As much a surprise as if a nun were to use a dirty word."

"And who are these twins?" demanded Talbot.

"They are sons of Loa, or sons of Lanu — who can know

where the truth lies when they say such things? But they are so alike that no one can tell one from the other."

"I never know how these niggers tell each other apart anyway," said Talbot. "They all look alike to me."

Sergeant Fleuron had other views. He had the keen wits of the intelligent slum dweller, and in three years he had learned much about Central Africa, including so many languages that he was able to interpret almost any local dialect. Africans to him were distinct individuals, which made the application of the *chicotte* a much more interesting exercise. But he had far too much sense to contradict his captain, so he went on with his report.

"They seem to worship this Loa in a quite devoted manner," he said. "The tales they tell! It seems that a long time ago — you can never be sure which century they are referring to — Loa went away. To heaven, maybe. When he came back he brought these twins with him, and he started working miracles. Apparently it was then that he conquered the country roundabout. He made men travel on the water — from the way they talk, one would think he had invented canoes."

"We've heard about his canoes before," said Talbot.

"Yes, Captain. He seems to have a navy, a genuine navy. He rules all this length of river, from these cataracts here to the falls above. A hundred miles of it, perhaps, and as far inland on each bank as his armies can reach. Fifty miles deep on each side, perhaps."

"A regular potentate," said Talbot. "I fancy we have enough rifles to deal with him."

"Without a doubt, Captain. And there is much water coming down the river at present."

"You mean?" asked the Captain.

"Now is the time to get the steamboat up the cataract."

"Now if ever," agreed Talbot.

He resented having to rouse himself to action. Getting the steamboat up the cataract would be a laborious and ticklish operation. Yet the approaching campaign would be much facilitated by command of the river; and there had been a good deal of sting in the last batch of orders from the Baron. He would have to act soon — he would have to act immediately. If he found excuses Sergeant Fleuron might make a secret report on him. He groaned as he shifted in his chair.

"Are the prisoners still alive?" he asked.

"Yes, Captain. And they will live. I can put them to work. But I thought — "

"What did you think?"

"I thought we could use their ears. For our next report for the Baron. They would be useful."

"Oh, do as you like about that. Why ask *me*?"

Fighting a war of conquest for a miserly old blackguard in Brussels led to some curious complications. Any ordinary government in wartime never stopped to count the cost, but Leopold never stopped counting it. Every cartridge that was used meant several centimes out of his pocket, and he insisted on proof that as high a proportion of cartridges as possible had been expended to good purpose. He was so determined about it that his subordinates locally had to insist too. The Baron to whom Talbot reported used to ask for ears, and wrote irritating reprimands when the number of right ears sent in was less than half the number of cartridges expended. The prisoners Fleuron had been examining would each provide a right ear without the expenditure of a single cartridge, and even after that would still be available for the labor of collecting rubber.

"I'll attend to it, Captain," said Fleuron.

Talbot groaned again as he hoisted his wasted and disease-racked body out of his camp chair.

"I'll come down and look at that damned cataract," he said.

So the next operation of that portion of the Army of the Independent State of the Congo under Talbot's command was the warping of the stern-wheeler *Lady Stanley* and her subsidiary barges up the cataract. The racing currents there were far too strong for the *Lady Stanley's* feeble engines — her boiler had had to be carried on men's backs through the forest round the lower falls, so that it could not boast much thickness of metal — but ingenuity and patience and the labor of a thousand men took her up in time. There were back eddies against the banks which sometimes gave them as much as a hundred yards of ascent at a time. At other times a cable had to be carried out ashore and attached to a stout tree. Then the *Lady Stanley* would wind herself up towards it — aided by five hundred men at the tow ropes — and drop an anchor to help hold her while another cable was carried up to another tree higher up. It was not an inexpensive operation, for the Army was always stepping into potholes in the river bottom and being swept away, or breaking legs and arms in wrestling with the cables — forty men were drowned when one of the cables parted against a sharp rock — and there was always disease to carry off the weaklings.

A thousand men, Talbot disposed of, of all shades of black and brown; men with teeth filed to needlepoints, men with shields of plaited reed, men with shields of hippopotamus hide, men armed with spears, with clubs, with bows, with axes — and two hundred men armed with Remington rifles for whom the *Lady Stanley* carried two hundred cartridges per man. The Baron would want to see twenty thousand right ears by the time those cartridges were all used up! (He had not yet laid down any anatomical equivalent for the six-pounder shells for the gun which was mounted on the *Lady Stanley's* strengthened bow.) A thousand men were under Talbot's command, with a white sergeant and eight white corporals — his two lieutenants had died of fever — and a couple of drunken white engineers to attend to the boiler of the *Lady Stanley*. One of them was a white-haired old reprobate who — according to his own account — had shipped with Semmes in the *Alabama* and had gone down with her when the *Kearsarge* sank her off Cherbourg. Neither engineer ever paid any particular attention to Talbot's orders. They both knew their own value too well, and the *chicotte* and the hangman's rope which maintained a savage discipline among the colored troops were not for them.

Talbot stood beside the cataract, watching a working

party bringing up the lower warp for attachment to the tree by which he stood. They had to wade in the shallows with their burden, slipping and stumbling, but doing their best to keep their footing, not merely in fear of their lives but in fear of the whip in the hand of the white corporal wading beside them. Talbot could trust nobody beside himself to supervise the actual fastening of the cable to the tree — experience had taught him a good deal to supplement the sketchy knowledge acquired during his instruction in field engineering at Sandhurst. He stood moodily looking on as the working party splashed towards him; there were the two barges to be dragged up the cataract after the *Lady Stanley* had made the ascent, and time was passing and losses were mounting.

From the forest some way lower down on his side of the river came the distant report of a rifle, flattened and distorted in its journey to his ear through the heated air between the trees. Talbot scowled; one of Fleuron's sentries, half asleep, must have pulled the trigger, wasting a cartridge without an ear to show for it. Well, whoever it was had an ear, anyway. But he had hardly thought this all out when there were further reports, a regular fusilade, climaxed by the rapid fire of a revolver. Fleuron was the only person in that direction armed with a revolver. The natives must be attacking there, and fiercely, too, for Fleuron to be personally engaged. Talbot's own guard sprang into attitudes of attention, their fingers on their triggers, chattering to each other and peering into the twilight of the forest towards where their sentries were posted. But Talbot stood fast where he was — Fleuron would have to fight it out or fall unassisted; Talbot had had too much experience of forest warfare to attempt to hurry to his relief in a rash movement through the forest, which might well lead into an ambush. The working party came hastily up with the warp, glad to be under the protection of Talbot's riflemen, and would have joined in the chatter if Talbot's harsh orders to the corporal had not put them to work carrying the cable round the tree while Talbot saw to the knotting of it.

The firing down the river died away with startling suddenness; everything was quiet. Talbot glanced down to the *Lady Stanley* lying to the lower warp and her anchor, the current foaming round her bow as though she was tearing along although she was stationary. Everything was ready for the next move provided the fighting had ceased, so he picked up the white signal flag and stepped to the water's edge and waved it. He saw the French engineer wave a red flag in reply from the *Lady Stanley's* deck. Then down the river a black crowd of men emerged from the trees at the water's edge and split into two, each half taking one of the two man-power ropes and moving up the stream to take the strain on them. A white man directed their movements, and by his helmet and his fragments of uniform Talbot recognized Fleuron, who had evidently survived the attack, whatever it was.

When the man-power ropes were taut and the men braced ready a white flag fluttered beside Fleuron, and Masson answered it with a white flag. Talbot saw him step to the steam capstan. The warp by which Talbot stood began to tighten, rising out of the river in an ever-flattening arc from which the water spouted in fountains, while the coils round the tree groaned and creaked. There was always desperate anxiety in Talbot's mind at this moment in case the warp should part. But the men at the ropes hauled away lustily under the lash of their headmen's whips, and the *Lady Stanley* slowly crawled up against the current. She picked up her anchor as she came up to it, crept on, with Masson at the wheel battling to keep her bows pointing outwards against the tug of the warp. She had made a full hundred yards' gain before she was so nearly up to Talbot's tree that it was useless to haul farther on the warp. Her whistle sounded as Masson pulled the lanyard, and the men at the ropes lay back against the strain as he dropped the anchor, necessarily wasting a few precious yards as he allowed the boat to drift back a trifle so that the anchor could bite and divide the strain with the warp. Then, and only then, did Masson wave his white flag again as a signal for those in charge of the lower warp to cast off and begin to carry it up above the one Talbot stood beside, and for the men who towed to relax their efforts and fall gasping on the bank.

Here came Fleuron with the sentries and guards who had been stationed in the forest farthest downstream; now they were to be sent on ahead to cover the further advance of the warps — the expedition was like a caterpillar or a measuring-worm, bringing up its tail to its head in readiness for a fresh move. Fleuron had with him his detachment of riflemen and his bearers.

"What was that firing, Sergeant?" asked Talbot.

"They tried to rush in upon us," replied Fleuron. He made free use of anatomical and zoölogical expressions to describe his enemies, so that his Belgian-French would have been almost unintelligible to anyone who had not long been associated with him.

"How many of them?"

"A full hundred. Maybe more. It was a well-timed rush — they came at us all at once and from all points in the forest. One sentry got a poisoned arrow — he was dead before I left him. My Hausa headman got a spear in his belly. He's dead too. We'd have all been dead if the sentries had not given plenty of warning. The rifles stopped them when they came out of the trees."

Fleuron waved a hand towards one of his bearers who was carrying a length of creeper. Upon it were strung, like pieces of meat on a skewer, a large number of human ears.

"We killed thirty-four of them," said Fleuron. "I got five of them myself in five shots. Then they turned and ran back, what was left of them. Oh yes, I brought this . . ."

He turned to another of his bearers, who opened the bag he was carrying, crudely made from big leaves, and shook out its contents with a thump on the ground. It was a human head, the eyes glaring and the mouth grinning.

"This was the leader," explained Fleuron: "the man who headed the rush. He got a bullet through the heart, luckily, as soon as he came out from the trees. He was wearing a spiral iron collar and armlets, so I think he was a chief."

"A young man to be a chief," said Talbot, looking at the unwrinkled features.

"Yes. It occurred to me that he might be one of those young twins they all talk about, Captain. All the legends say they are as like as two peas; so I thought I would pickle this head in salt and see if we ever get the duplicate of it."

"As you will," said Talbot. "It will be an interesting anthropological study."

There was bitterness in his tone as he spoke; there was something fantastically odd about Captain Victor Augustus Talbot, late of the Green Jackets and once the darling of London drawing rooms, standing beside a tropical river callously looking over human heads and ears, even black ones.

"Thank you, Captain," said Fleuron.

At his gesture the head was bundled back into the bag again, and his scouts began to push cautiously into the forest to cover the further advance up the river to the point to which the lower warp would then be conveyed. Cautiously indeed they went, their rifles held ready across their breasts, halting long and peering round the trees for fear of the death which might come winging at them through the twilight. Talbot watched them go on ahead. Now the lower warp was being unfastened and carried up the river by a corporal's working party splashing through the shallows. He would accompany it in its further journey to the next suitable tree for its attachment. He was about to give the word to his party when a shadow passed before his eyes and something struck the tree beside him with a sharp rap. He looked, and there, lying at the foot of the tree, was a long arrow, feathered with a couple of leaves. The long slender head of the arrow had broken against the tree and lay in pieces beside the shaft, but Talbot could see the barbs that had edged the head, and in the notches of the barbs the thick greenish-brown poison. The arrow, bearing death with it, had passed within two inches of his face. He wheeled to face the forest, his revolver in his hand, but there was nothing to be seen among the trees, nothing save the backs of his sentries stationed out there with their rifles to guard against attacks of this very sort. A fine watch they were keeping! Talbot's lips wrinkled into a feeble snarl. Whoever it was who had sped the arrow had ignored those sentries, and had crept up and singled him out for a target. The sentries were still ignorant of the danger to which he had been subjected. There was only the inscrutable forest before him.

Talbot's headman saw his captain's gestures, saw the broken arrow lying on the ground, and guessed what had happened. Vociferously he berated the sentries for their negligence, and under his urgings some more of Talbot's escort advanced a little way into the forest in search of the assassin, but in a few moments Talbot himself called them off. It was only a waste of time to seek a single enemy among the trees. Once let him get the *Lady Stanley* and the barges up this infernal cataract and he would be able to deal adequately with these devils. He would make them pay for the misery and danger he was enduring.

CHAPTER

XVIII

THE *Lady Stanley* had completed the ascent of the cataract, and now she lay at anchor in the midst of the wide river. Beside her lay one of the two barges, hauled up the cataract by the aid of the *Lady Stanley's* steam capstan and by the efforts of five hundred men at the ropes. It only remained to haul up the second barge, and Talbot would be master of all the reach of river between the cataract and the upper fall. Five hundred men with their equipment and food could be packed into those barges and transported about the river faster than any man could walk in the open — far faster than any large body could move through the forest — while the six-pounder cannon at the *Lady Stanley's* bows would show her enemies something they knew nothing of as yet. Masson and Carver, the French-speaking and English-speaking engineers, were relaxing after their labors with the aid of some bottles of trade gin on board the *Lady Stanley,* while the sun plunged down into the forest, lighting the broad steamy surface of the river a sullen red. Talbot was on board as well, having had himself paddled out to her in a canoe, but he had not yet begun upon the gin. He was leaving that until after sunset; tonight he would drink himself into a stupor, maybe, but first he would enjoy the amenities of the steamboat. On the wide river here there would be a breath of air, different from the stifling atmosphere of the forest. There would be no ants to creep into his clothes. He could have a properly adjusted mosquito net under which he could lie naked and enjoy a more comfortable night — in fact he might not even avail himself of the gin at all, for Talbot was of that self-centered type to whom alcohol often makes no appeal. A night amid quiet and comfortable surroundings meant more to him than a debauch, and out here in the middle of the river there was no chance of assassination.

He would get the second barge up the cataract tomorrow, and move direct upon this town of Loa's, or Lanu's, or whatever the name of the chief might be. They would stand and fight for their capital and their sacred grove, and he could crush them then — there would be no need to pursue them through the forest trying to bring an elusive enemy to action, losing men all the time through ambushes and booby traps and disease, only to find in the end that shortage of supplies would necessitate a retreat without a victory. Talbot in two years of continuous active service had learned much about forest warfare.

The sun had reached the forest, and black night was close at hand. Talbot walked forward and spoke to the two Coast Negroes who supplied the anchor watch. It was their easy duty to stay awake during the night and keep a lookout in case the *Lady Stanley* should drag her anchor, or in case the current should bring some floating tree down across her cable, or a prowler should come alongside in a canoe determined upon theft. He warned them to keep a good lookout. In the barge alongside, half a dozen men were caterwauling their native songs, as was their habit when not kept busy; Talbot leaned over the side and sharply told them to be quiet — he did not want that howling to keep him awake. The twenty riflemen of his bodyguard were already sleeping by the taffrail, and down below in the stifling cabin Masson and Carver were drinking together; the sweat gleamed on Carver's bald head with its fringe of white hair. At present they were amicable, even demonstratively friendly. Later they might quarrel, but on the other hand they might sleep without disturbing him. He bade them good night civilly and returned on deck to where Kamo his servant had made up his bed. The fool had laid the mattress so that his head would be under the low part of the mosquito net, so he walked aft to where Kamo was asleep on the bare planks beside a bollard and kicked him awake and made him do it over again. Then at last with the ease of long practice he slipped in under the net, which he tucked in under the mattress all round, and laid himself down with a sigh of relief and fatigue, secure from insect plagues. The last thing he did before falling asleep was to unbuckle his pistol belt; he took his revolver from its holster and laid it on the mattress convenient to his hand.

The tropical night is twelve hours long. After Talbot had been asleep a couple of hours the evening thunderstorm broke overhead; the thunder and the lightning and the roar of the rain on the awning above him only slightly disturbed him. He woke no more than to assure himself that his revolver was still at hand, and then he slept again, deeply, reveling in the coolness and the unaccustomed feeling of security. So he was wide awake and fully rested long before dawn, even a little chilled by the small wind that stirred the damp air. Under the awning, lying relaxed and comfortable, he could see nothing of the late rising moon, and could not guess at the time. He thought of all that had to be done during the coming day; to begin with it would not be a bad idea to take the opportunity of seeing if the men on watch were awake. He strapped on his revolver again and with a sigh slipped out from under the mosquito net — his joints ached when he moved and he felt the fleeting feeling of well-being deserting him. It was too good to last. Walking quietly forward he found, as he expected, the anchor watch sound asleep, one man stretched out snoring and the other sitting with his forehead on his knees, equally unconscious. Two well-placed kicks woke them up, and they grabbed for their rifles while Talbot turned away smiling grimly to himself at the thought of how they would pay for their slumbers in the morning. He stood by the rail and breathed the velvet night; the little breeze had wakened small waves on the broad surface of the river, which lapped against the *Lady Stanley's* side in harmony with the gurgle of the current round her bows. Low in the sky the moon in her last quarter shed a faint light on the black water surface.

A long, long way off the water surface was blacker still — a solid nucleus in the velvet darkness. Talbot peered at it idly, and then with growing attention. There was a large black mass over there. Then he started, and gripped the guardrail as he concentrated his attention on what he saw. There had been a faint gleam of reflected light over there, and soon after he saw it repeated at another point — moonlight gleaming, perhaps, on a wet canoe paddle. He saw it again and his suspicions were confirmed. He had his pistol in his hand on the instant, without willing it. There were three — four — many canoes paddling towards the *Lady Stanley*, closing in on her. Talbot fired a shot from his revolver as the quickest way of rousing the ship. He fired again and shouted, stamping on the deck to wake Carver and Masson down below. Yells of defiance reached his ears from across the river; round the canoes the water was churned white by paddles in furious action. From forward came the reports of rifles and stabbing tongues of flame as the lookouts opened fire, and Kamo came running up to him beside the rail; Kamo's rifle went off into the air — pure waste in the excitement, and Kamo was yelling weirdly as he snatched open the breach and reloaded.

More black figures appeared on deck as the crew awoke, and overside the fellows asleep in the barge came to their senses with loud cries. Tense and nervous with excitement, Talbot was still able to think. He put away his revolver, snatched the rifle from Kamo, and leveled it with careful aim at the leading canoe. The shot went home, and he grabbed a cartridge from Kamo, reloaded, and fired again. By now his bodyguard was awake, and, lining the rail, were firing away enthusiastically into the mass of the canoes. Some of the bullets must be hitting the target, enough at least to hinder the rush, and at that moment came a decisive intervention. From behind him came a deafening report, a blinding flash of light; someone, Masson or Carver, had roused himself and reached the six-pounder forward, trained it round, and fired. Talbot saw the shell burst among the canoes, and he heard an outburst of screams, but for several seconds after the flash he could see nothing. The cries and the firing in the barge redoubled; a canoe had run alongside and boarded it in the darkness, and now a death struggle was being fought out hand to hand there. As he looked down into the barge he could see black figures glistening in the light of the rifle-flashes. Again the cannon went off and blinded him, but wild yelling behind him made him swing around. As his eyesight returned he saw, dimly, dark figures swarming over the guardrail on the starboard side — another canoe must have run alongside the steamer there. He felt fear within him, but he was like a cornered animal and could only decide to fight it out to the last. His voice cracked as he tried to shout, and he ran across the deck at these new invaders, reversing his grip on the rifle as he ran. He brought down the butt on a black head with a crash, and around him the crew and his bodyguard rallied and flung themselves on the enemy. Someone was standing on the guardrail about to leap down — Talbot's whirling rifle butt dashed him overside again. There could not have been more than five or six men, a single canoe load, engaged in this attack, and soon they were all dead, and Talbot had a breathing space as he stood beside the rail almost alone. On the other side of the ship a rifle was now firing rhythmically and steadily down into the barge, and the flashes illuminated Carver's bald head — already there was more light than came from the rifle flashes, and dawn was at hand. Talbot walked across and stood by Carver, who was systematically killing every man in the barge, for he did not know which was friend and which was foe, and he was taking no chances. Carver was cursing filthily between each shot; he was wildly agitated about these "wretched niggers" attacking at dawn like any white army, and also about their having the sense and insolence to choose for their objective the *Lady Stanley*. There were indeed frightening implications about all this; if the attack had been successful, if the *Lady Stanley* had been captured by the enemy and wrecked or burned, any further advance would have been delayed for at least a year. And — Talbot thought of this with a tremor — if it had succeeded he would be dead like the inanimate corpses all round him, and his skull would go to decorate the crucifixion tree in Loa's grove — if indeed he were not taken alive, to shriek his life away on that same tree. With the dying-away of his excitement Talbot felt an unhappy cold fit overcoming him. He had come here to Central Africa because otherwise he would have had to beg his bread in a London gutter, and at this moment he regretted his choice. He would live longer in a gutter than he would here; nor would life in a gutter possibly be as hideous as this. A shout from Masson, forward, made him swing round.

"I have them, the assassins!" he shouted.

He was training round the six-pounder gun on its pivot, looking along the sights and bracing himself against the shoulder-piece. There was a gray light over the water now, and streaks of gray mist drifted over its surface. From out of one of the gray streaks emerged a dark shape, distorted in the faint light, but just recognizable as a canoe paddling furiously away from the steamer, and a good half-mile away from it. Talbot went over and stood behind Masson as he sighted the gun. When the gun bellowed out Talbot saw a momentary black pencil-mark against the gray; it was the path of the shell speeding on its low trajectory. Straight to the canoe it went, to burst in smoke and spray, out of which for a second rose one end of the canoe standing vertically out of the water.

"A good shot, eh, Captain?" said Masson, turning so that Talbot was once more aware of how white Masson's teeth gleamed amidst the black of his mustache and beard.

Masson now had a telescope to his eye and was sweeping it round over the river.

"A canoe bottom up there," said Masson. "And another beside it. Ha! No, that one is empty. Not a soul alive in it. Not a damned soul. That was another good shot of mine, Captain, was it not? The first I fired — the shot that struck in the midst of the canoes."

"It was that which stopped them," agreed Talbot. "It would have been hard to keep them out of the steamer if they had all got alongside."

Masson walked to the rail and looked over, Talbot along with him.

"One empty canoe there," said Masson. "Another full of water and corpses."

"There were some which got alongside the barge," said Talbot.

"And not a man left," said Masson. "They have had a lesson, these men of Loa."

The soft lead Remington bullets made severe wounds at point-blank range, but there were yet some men alive who had been struck by them, in the barge and on the deck, and they could be prevailed upon to speak — Talbot sent ashore for Sergeant Fleuron to carry out the interrogation. But Fleuron had hardly to make use of his peculiar talents, for a man torn by a fearful wound would readily answer questions if a bowl of water were withheld from him only a few inches from his dry lips. He would gasp out all he knew, for Fleuron to interpret it to Talbot. . . . Yes, the attack on the *Lady Stanley* had been made by Loa's whole fleet. That did not mean all Loa's fighting men — Lanu was still on shore at the head of a great army. The fleet had been led by one of the twins . . . at that information Fleuron showed annoyance, for if the other twin were dead and at the bottom of the river all his trouble in pickling that head in order to compare likenesses was wasted. . . . Loa's town was up the river here, a long two days' journey by canoe in calm weather. The port stood beside the river, on that bank, and Loa's town was only a short distance away from it. Yes, the speaker knew the port when he saw it — he actually lived there. . . .

The two men who survived their wound and their examination both knew the port; with Talbot's permission Fleuron had their wounds bandaged to keep them alive, and he had them laid on deck, secured to the guardrail, for their guidance might save a good deal of trouble when the final advance should be made. They lay on the deck looking round with frightened eyes at everything about them. They were terrified at being aboard this immense devil-driven canoe. Even the wealth of iron all about them frightened them; so did the strange white men — so did the strange black men. The shriek of the steam whistle, the clank of the capstan as the second barge was slowly wound up the last of the cataract, and the roar and bustle when it was drawn alongside, set their white eyeballs rolling. Talbot spared them a glance. These men, shaking with fright, were probably fair specimens of the men who had attacked them. Their fear only proved the fanaticism that must animate them. The attack had been boldly made, even against these frightful machines. They had come on in the face of rifle fire and even of shellfire, and the three or four surviving canoes had flung themselves in a forlorn hope against the steamer's sides. Such wild courage could only be the result of a frantic belief in their own cause. And there was still an army of such fanatics awaiting them on the riverbank, under the command of this Lanu. Well, in that case they would stand and fight, and not have to be pursued through the forest. That would mean a quick finish to the campaign.

The barges were both alongside now, both jammed full of chattering black soldiers. Even to them, who had served the white invaders for some time, the prospect of this trip by water was exciting and a little frightening. The deck of the *Lady Stanley* was heaped with wood for fuel, so much that

Talbot could confidently rely on going all the way up against the current to the next fall and back again if necessary without having to risk a working party ashore to cut more. There were great bags of food; not quite enough to make him feel at ease regarding the supply problem, but all that could be swept up from the country behind him despite the protests of the civil authorities. There were cartridges in plenty for the business in hand. So every possible precaution had been taken, and it was time to start. Talbot shouted an order to Sergeant Fleuron, and Fleuron, with many exasperated orders, set about the business of casting off the barges and stationing men at the anchor windlasses. Talbot caught Masson's eye, and Masson nodded, and sent down a bell signal to Carver below to admit steam to the cylinders. Slowly the current took the *Lady Stanley* astern; another note on the bell and she forged ahead, turning to push her nose accurately between the sterns of the two barges. The beat of the stern wheel quickened and the *Lady Stanley* headed upstream at several miles an hour through the water, at nearly two miles an hour over land. The barges wallowed along ahead of her — Talbot, and the Belgians and Frenchmen too, felt they would never grow used to this method of pushing a tow instead of pulling it, but it was necessary with a stern-wheeler, and was no novelty to Carver, who at some time had worked in a Mississippi steamer. Beside Talbot the wounded prisoners clasped each other's hands in terror at the vibration of the monster beneath them.

In due course the *Lady Stanley* and the barges she was pushing arrived in the river opposite the port of Loa's town.

The two wounded prisoners pointed the place out eagerly enough — they seemed to be glad to see their home again — but it was really hardly necessary, for anyone could know it for what it was at a glance. The *Lady Stanley* hung in midriver, her stern wheel just pushing her against the current, while Talbot surveyed the place through his telescope. It was like a number of other Central African towns, perched upon a rocky bluff overlooking the river; the houses a little strange to Talbot's eyes in that they were long and rectangular, instead of circular as they usually were lower down the river. Even through his telescope Talbot could make out no sign of life; not a soul was stirring although he had a good view into much of the village street. The path down the bluff was clearly visible, and on the beach at its foot lay a single canoe, while beyond the village Talbot thought he could just make out signs of the usual banana groves on the outskirts. But there was no movement, not even a wreath of smoke.

"Try a shot at 'em and see if you can wake 'em up," suggested Carver, who had left the engineroom to come up on deck and watch the course of events.

"All right," said Talbot, and Carver walked forward to the six-pounder.

He trained the gun round and sighted it; the gun went off with a loud bark and a shout went up from the massed soldiers in the barges as, amid the smoke and dust, they saw the side of the most prominent house crumple outwards. Carver swung open the breech and inserted another round.

"That will do," said Talbot; he was accountable to the Baron for those six-pounder shells.

There was no point in wasting further time; it was hopeless to think of trying to exhaust the patience of Africa. If the town were going to be defended he must force the defenders to show their hand. A brief colloquy with Carver settled the details of the landing, and Talbot went into the bows to give Sergeant Fleuron his orders. Then he came back to line his riflemen up along the guardrail. The *Lady Stanley* dropped back down the river to give herself room to get up speed, and then came forward again, pushing the barges valiantly ahead of her. She backed her stern wheel momentarily, and the barges were cast off, heading on up the river under their own momentum with Fleuron and a corporal at the tillers taking them diagonally across to the beach. Up onto the beach they ran side by side, with a grinding of the pebbles beneath them, and amid wild yells from the black soldiers. They had captured towns before, and if they could not look forward to loot they could at least expect an orgy of cruelty and rape. Over the bows tumbled the leading men, and it was at that moment that the defenders showed themselves. There was an answering yell, and dark figures showed themselves everywhere on the bluff, some leaping down with brandished weapons, and others standing, feet braced wide apart, drawing their bows to send their arrows down into the crowd on the beach. But there were rifles awaiting them — Talbot himself was kneeling on the deck of the *Lady Stanley* along with his picked shots, the guardrail forming a convenient rest for his rifle. The range was a mere hundred yards, and he could not miss, sending shot after shot home; from the deck of the *Lady Stanley*, from the barges and from the beach, a hail of lead met

[297]

the charging men. Even so, some of them got through, and plunged into a bloody melee on the beach with those men who had landed. But numbers as well as weapons were against them. The whole force which had attacked amounted to less than a couple of hundred men, and there were more than five hundred in the barges. It had been a forlorn hope, a bold attempt to beat back the invaders by assailing them at the most favorable moment — not favorable enough. Fleuron's soldiers poured ashore and club and ax and spear fought out the battle on the beach, while Talbot and his riflemen picked off the archers on the bluff above. On the beach the battle was won, and the invaders began to push forward; but many more of the defenders died on the beach than turned to try to make their escape up the bluff, running the gantlet of the rifle fire from the steamer. The yelling victors swarmed up the bluff after them, mad with victory; Talbot saw them start the ascent, but he could not watch them enter the town, for his attention was distracted.

Fleuron's barge, freed from the weight of the hundreds of men crammed into her, had come adrift from the beach and was rapidly being carried downstream again; moreover, as Fleuron agitatedly shouted to his captain, her bottom had been damaged when she went aground and she was leaking badly. The *Lady Stanley* had to go down the river after her, imperiling herself amid the shallows close inshore, and heave her a line to bring her fussily back and beach her again to save her from sinking. Talbot and Fleuron hastily landed and went up the path to the town, the sweat streaming down them with their hurry as they went past the many dead. In the town five hundred mad men were raging through the houses, finding little enough on which to vent their fury. There had been three old women in the town, and they had been killed by the first arrivals without a thought for the sport they might have afforded to the cooler heads. Otherwise the place was deserted, abandoned. There were a few poor cooking utensils, the usual domestic gear, but no ivory, no treasure house, nothing worth saving for the benefit of His Majesty the King of the Belgians. But as Fleuron remarked, all the reports they had gathered indicated that this was no more than a suburb of Loa's town, which lay somewhere not far inland. It only remained to count the dead and see if among the wounded there were any who could increase their information, and so Fleuron and Talbot, surrounded by their guard, made their way back to the beach.

Halfway down the bluff Fleuron stopped beside a dead man, face downward on the slope. He lay in a pool of blood, his back, below his right shoulder blade, torn wide open by the exit of the soft-nosed .45 bullet which had entered his breast. But on his head there was still a headdress of twisted iron, and about the arms and neck there were spiral iron ornaments, while beside the body lay an ax — Talbot noticed the excellence of the workmanship.

"A chief, I fancy, Captain," said Fleuron.

He poked the body with his foot, and then at his order two of his men turned it over for them to examine it further. It was not the face of a young man, but that of a man of middle age at least. The breast was scarred with tattooing, but the face was hardly disfigured; the closed eyes and relaxed muscles conveyed an impression of peace.

"He must have been killed in the first moments of the attack," said Fleuron, looking round him at the comparative distances from the brow and the beach.

"I expect I killed him myself," supplemented Talbot — he remembered stopping more than one warrior in mid-career on the bluff; he smiled deprecatingly as he said this, for the English gentleman's habit of not calling attention to personal exploits was still strong.

"I expect you did, Captain," said Fleuron.

"I wonder who he is," speculated Talbot.

"That we shall soon know. I intend to find out," answered Fleuron.

The wounded man who was carried up the bluff to the corpse — groaning as his shattered thighbone was jarred by his bearers — enlightened them instantly, the moment he set eyes on the dead face.

"Lanu," he said. "Lanu. Lord."

Even with Lanu dead the awe and respect in his voice were quite unmistakable.

"Oh, it's Lanu, is it?" said Fleuron.

He asked further questions and turned back to Talbot when the wounded man had answered them.

"This," he said — with a wave of his hand to the corpses littering the bluff and the beach — "This was the only army left. It was as I thought; the other twin was killed when they attacked us in canoes. Every man was killed then —

not a single one came back. So Lanu stood to fight here with all the soldiers left and the old men — look at that gray head over there. And Lanu is dead, and you saw how many fighting men escaped from here."

"If the twins are dead, and Lanu is dead, we ought not to have any more trouble," said Talbot.

Fleuron turned back to the wounded man with a further question, and received an almost voluble reply. Twice at least Talbot caught the word "Loa."

"No," said Fleuron at length. "We shall still have to fight. There is this Loa still alive. He is undoubtedly a man, although whether Loa is his name or his title I still cannot say. He is at his town, up there, with his wives and the women of the country."

"And his ivory too, please God," said Talbot.

"Without doubt."

Talbot looked round about him at the dead again.

"Too many men have been killed," he said. "Who will gather rubber? The Baron will not be pleased."

"The Baron?" Fleuron's gesture indicated deep contempt for the Baron's displeasure. "He ought to know, even if he does not, what we have been through here. And there will be the women left. We must restrain these devils when we reach the town. No killing — not too much, at least. From the women we can breed. Thanks to polygamy in twenty years we can have this forest as full of men as a sausage is full of meat."

Twenty years? The suggestion started Talbot on an unfortunate train of thought. Twenty years of discomfort, of loneliness, of misery and of bloodshed — twenty years in the service of King Leopold. Talbot hated the thought of twenty years more of Africa; and yet if he were not to have to endure them it could only be because he was dead, and Talbot did not want to die. During the past two years he had once or twice touched the revolver at his belt, meditatively, and then withdrawn his hand, for Talbot was sufficiently afraid of the unknown to dread hurling himself through the dark portals of another world. He felt suddenly and desperately unhappy. To shake himself out of the mood he occupied himself with his task again.

"We must make ready, then," he said, "for this move on Loa's town."

X I X

THE WAY through the forest from the port to the town was clearly marked; it was something more like a road than anything else Central Africa could show. Clearly there had been a great deal of coming and going between the two places, with armies going out, and armies returning with plunder and slaves, with trading parties and messengers. But that portion of the Army of the Independent State of the Congo under Talbot's command made the advance from one place to the other with considerable caution, extended on a wide front, and scanning carefully every yard of the way ahead. The necessity for care was early borne in upon them, for there were pitfalls everywhere, and poisoned skewers concealed beneath the leafmold, and bent bows hidden in the undergrowth ready to let loose poisoned arrows at a touch on a strand of creeper. The forest had its human defenders, too; not many of them, but a few who flitted from tree to tree ahead of the advancing line and who sought opportunities of launching poisoned arrows from safe cover. The soldiery fired at these people whenever an opportunity presented itself, and often indeed when one did not. Sometimes the whole advancing line would break out into desultory firing, while Talbot raved furiously at this waste of ammunition on shadows that had no ears. Hardly any of the bullets discharged found a billet in a human target; only one or two lucky shots brought down bowmen who had incautiously exposed themselves.

Talbot, with his bodyguard about him, walked along after the skirmish line. He made use of his eyes as he walked, and he saw that his guard did the same; besides traps and pitfalls there was always the chance that one of those bowmen ahead had managed to creep through the line and was lying in ambush, arrow on string, waiting for a white man to shoot at. Although his pace was perforce leisurely, so as not to overtake the firing line, rivers of sweat ran down his skin in the stifling steamy air of the forest. Talbot looked back with regret to his sojourn in the *Lady Stanley*, under the open sky, with the chance of an unimpeded breeze. This gloomy forest, with the tree trunks standing like ghosts in the twilight, oppressed him the more forcibly because so much of the campaign up to now had been waged on the banks of the open river. He hated this forest, with its darkness and silence. Holding his revolver ready in his right hand, he mopped his face and neck continually with the grubby rag which had once been a handkerchief in his left.

Cries echoing back from ahead of him told him of a new development in the situation, and, continuing along the path, he soon discovered the reason for them. They had reached the outskirts of the town. But here there was something a little unusual for Central Africa — a deliberate attempt to fortify the place. The path entered the abandoned clearings that ringed the town, as they did every town in this area, but the well-trodden and well-marked point of entrance was blocked by a stout palisade. The tangle of small growth and creepers, where it existed, was the best of defense against a surprise attack, but the belt round most towns was never continuous. It was always intersected by footpaths, and there were frequent broad gaps where the banana groves and manioc gardens were under cultivation. Always before it had been easy to force a way into a town by one route or another; this was the first time Talbot had ever seen any artificial obstruction to an entrance.

The palisade was lofty and dense; examining it from behind the cover of the nearest tree Talbot could see that there was another one twenty yards in the rear of it — a remarkable precaution against surprise. The uprights were driven into the earth, and clearly extended into the undergrowth on either side of the gap, while the horizontal members were bound stoutly to the uprights by split cane; Talbot could see a kind of wicket gate in the palisade, but the split cane fastenings around it were so dense and numerous that it was obvious that it did not constitute a weak point in the defenses. There was no glimpse to be got of any human defenders of the gate, but one of his Batetela headmen showed Talbot a long arrow with a jagged wooden head — with poison in the barbs as usual — which had come sailing over the palisade from some point in the undergrowth. There could be no doubt that at least a few archers were waiting, hidden, within sight of the palisade, so that any attempt to storm the defenses without preparation would incur severe loss.

Fleuron came up to report; he had been with the advanced guard and on reaching the gate had moved along the defenses to his right in search of a weak point.

"Dense undergrowth — undergrowth of a difficulty quite incredible — as far as I can see, Captain," said Fleuron. "At the only weak point there was a palisade like this one. That was when I turned back. I left half my guard there. This Loa will have palisaded all points, one may be sure. I will try in the other direction if you wish."

"There would be no advantage to be gained by that, I fancy," said Talbot.

He could send a note back to the *Lady Stanley* and have the six-pounder sent up to him. A few rounds from the gun would make short work of those palisades. But the day was already far advanced; to unship the gun and bring it ashore, and mount it on its traveling carriage and drag it along the path, would take hours, days perhaps. Or he could make use of a more primitive method of attack; burning faggots piled against the palisades under a heavy covering fire from rifles would burn the palisades down. But that would take time too; he would have to wait for the embers to cool at first one barrier and then at the other.

"Oh, damn it all to hell," said Talbot in a fit of pettish irritation.

He wanted to end this business quickly. He had enough men — too many of them, for that matter. Why should he trouble to keep them alive? There could not be more than a few old men left to defend the town. He issued his orders harshly and savagely; and Fleuron, noticing the expression

on his face, bit off short the protest he automatically had begun to raise at his first realization of what was in Talbot's
mind. A hundred riflemen, strung among the trees, prepared to cover the attack. Fleuron and Talbot took rifles,
too, but that was not for the same purpose. The Batetela
headman and the twenty men with axes who were selected
for the attempt looked at the rifles in the white men's hands.
Those rifles, if they refused to move, meant certain and immediate death; the poisoned arrows from the defenses meant
death not quite so certain and not quite so immediate. Their
teeth and eyeballs gleamed in the twilight as they chattered
to each other debating the hideous choice. An angry word
and an impatient gesture from Talbot settled their decision.
They gripped their axes and they ran with despairing haste
up the broad path. A shaft of sunlight reached over the tops
of the trees and illuminated the little crowd as they came to
the foot of the menacing palisade. Their axes rang against
the stubborn cane fastenings. They hacked and hewed feverishly, with excited cries.

Here came the arrows, surely enough. Two men backed
away, with feathered shafts hanging from the barbed heads
driven deep into them — the whole group followed their
example and broke back again, but Fleuron stepped forward
and shot one of them mercilessly, and they turned back
again to their task. The rifles helped them; the Remington
bullets went crashing through the undergrowth in search of
the bowmen hidden there who launched those arrows. Fleuron shouted an encouragement — or a warning. It reached
the ears of the axmen and added to their exertions. Fran-

tically they hacked and pulled, treading their dead and wounded underfoot. One man reached up and clutched the upper horizontal bar, flung his weight on it and was joined by two others, and their united exertions tore the thing down. Two uprights were dragged aside so that they leaned drunkenly in opposite directions. There was a passage of some sort through the first palisade, and Fleuron, yelling loudly, recalled the survivors of the axmen. By giving them a chance of life he could expect greater enthusiasm from those that would have to follow them.

The arrangements for the final assault were quickly made. A hundred spearmen on either side of the entrance were to attack straight before them, plunging directly into the undergrowth and struggling through as best they could. They might turn the flank of the defense should it be prolonged. Another body of axmen was collected to deal with the farther palisade. A hundred spearmen were to follow on their heels, and turn to right and left after passing the nearer palisade and seek out the defenders who might be hidden in the undergrowth along the entrance path. Spearmen, newly brought into the ranks of the Army from the forest, were cheaper than the riflemen who had been given training in the use of firearms. Along the path was ranged the main assaulting column, destined to burst through when the way should be cleared for them. They were excited and eager, keyed up at the thought of entering into the legendary mysteries of Loa's town.

Sweating and shouting, Talbot and Fleuron hastened about to get all in order.

"Go!" shouted Fleuron at last, and the attackers hurled themselves forward.

Talbot watched the axmen burst through the first palisade. The spearmen followed them. Throughout the belt of undergrowth came muffled shouts as the assaulting spearmen plunged and struggled in the entangling mass. As he had expected, the entrance path was sown thick with poisoned skewers, but he had sent in enough men to be able to bear losses. He saw one of the axmen climb straight up the second palisade, poise himself for a moment, and then leap down beyond it. Mad with excitement, the man did not delay a moment, but rushed straight ahead, waving his ax, towards the town. It was time.

"Go!" roared Fleuron again, and the waiting column charged yelling up the path.

For a while the whole entrance was jammed as they forced their way through the wreck of the first barrier; then they flowed on to reach the second one just as it began to give way. Talbot saw them pouring forward and nodded to his escort. They closed round him as they had been drilled to do; there was less chance of a poisoned arrow reaching him when he was surrounded by human bodies. They were wild with excitement, chattering and shouting as they hurried forward with Talbot in their midst. They entered the narrow path through the undergrowth, so narrow that the files on each side of him pressed up against him so that his nostrils were filled with the smell of their sweating bodies, and they picked their way through the shattered barrier while the undergrowth round them still echoed with the cries of the attackers plunging about after the last few defenders. They hurried up the path and through the second barrier, emerging into the main street of the town, the sunshine blazing down upon it.

Their point of entrance was about the middle of it; at the ends to the left and right it widened out into something like open squares; street and squares were lined with large substantial houses constructed of split boards thatched with leaves. At the far end to the right Talbot's eye was caught by a large area of greenery, with straggling trees emerging out of it, filling the whole center of the square. That must be the sacred grove, and near it must be the chief's house and the treasury and the important buildings. It was thither that he directed his escort, hurrying down the street while around him he saw and heard the hideous sights and sounds of a town taken by assault. He would have to beat these fiends off their prey, but first he had better secure the treasury and put a guard over it.

But round about the grove there was no sign of any chief's house. This looked like the poorer end of the town, as one might say. Here were the forges with their stone anvils, a small heap of charcoal yet remaining, the boxlike bellows lying beside it, and everywhere inches deep in the dead sparks of a thousand years' of smith's work. The houses contained nothing except poor domestic utensils and moaning women. The sacred grove was not at all impressive on close inspection. It was small; a single short path led to a little clearing in the center, and in the clearing there were a few human bones, but not very many, and no treasure whatever.

The palace of this Loa must be at the other end of the town after all. Talbot cursed and hastened back up the street. Halfway along he met Fleuron, busily engaged in the organization of conquest. His escort stood guard over a herd of frightened women who crouched and huddled together with rolling eyes as they heard the shrieks of those whom Fleuron had not been able to protect.

"Have you seen this Loa, Sergeant?" demanded Talbot.

"No, Captain. Unless he is among those old men, and I am sure he is not."

None of those trembling gray heads could belong to the man who had conquered all this area of Africa and who had inspired the devotion which had caused his army to annihilate itself in his defense. Talbot pushed on up the street towards the farther open space. Of course. He had been a fool not to see the large houses there. That most distant one, with the decorated gable ends, must be Loa's palace. There were herds of frightened women here, too, women with babies in their arms, women standing weeping with little children thrust behind them. The tide of the assailants was only just beginning to lap up as far as here. The sun blazed down into the open space as Talbot strode up it, with his disorganized escort hastening after him.

There was an eddy among the women clustering round the big house. They parted, and two people advanced from among them. Talbot knew Loa when he saw him; there could in fact be no mistaking him. He had been tall, although his height was lessened because his back was a little bent. He walked stiffly but with immense dignity, his head back despite his bent shoulders. He was corpulent without being obese — maybe advancing years had already removed the fat of middle age. Over his shoulders hung a leopardskin cloak, vivid in the sunshine; about his neck and arms were spiral ornaments of iron, and in his right hand glittered an ax, brightly polished to reflect the sunlight. Beside him hobbled a skinny old woman, her thin breasts swinging with the exertion of keeping up with him. As she hastened along at his side she never took her eyes from his face, craning forward and peering up to see it.

Talbot sorted hurriedly through his memory for words.

"Stop!" he shouted, in one of the few dialects in which he had any mastery.

He threw his left hand up, palm forward, in the universal gesture commanding a halt; his right hand held his revolver ready. Loa did not appear to hear him — certainly he did not look at him. He continued to stride forward, his eyes directed at a point over Talbot's head. One of Talbot's escort dropped on one knee beside him, and leveled his rifle.

"Stop!" shouted Talbot again.

This Loa, if he could by any lucky chance be won over, might be useful, seeing the devotion he could inspire. With him as a local under-governor, it would not be nearly so difficult to organize the district for rubber collecting and ivory hunting. But Loa only walked forward, with the pitiless sky overhead looking down at him, the friendly forest far away, beyond the houses. Talbot's revolver was cocked and pointed at his breast, but apparently Loa did not see it, nor the leveled rifle of the kneeling escort. Then at the last moment Loa sprang, whirling back the ax for a last blow.

But the stiffness of his fifty years betrayed him; he could not leap fast enough to catch the white man entirely off his guard. Talbot just managed to leap aside, in a most undignified fashion, without even time enough to pull the trigger. But the rifle of the kneeling escort had followed Loa's movements, and the bullet struck Loa in the side as he poised on one foot with the ax above his head. From side to side the heavy bullet tore through him, from below upwards, expanding as it went. It struck below the ribs on his right side. It pierced his liver, it tore his heart to shreds, and, emerging, it shattered his left arm above the elbow. So Loa died in that very moment, the ax dropping behind him as he fell over with a crash. The rifleman tore open the breech, slid in another cartridge, and slammed the breechblock home. The skinny old woman saw Loa fall, and looked down at his body for one heartbroken moment. She uttered a shrill scream, and then raised her spider arms. It was as if she were going to attack Talbot with her fingernails; perhaps that was in her mind, but there could be no certainty about it, for the rifleman pulled the trigger again, and the skinny old woman fell dying beside the body of her Lord.